THE COV
OF

THE COVETED HUES OF SKYE

A HUES NOVEL
BOOK TWO

J. L. JACKOLA

Tivshe
Publishing

Library of Congress Control Number 2023900195
Paperback ISBN 978-1-954175-89-1
Hardback ISBN 978-1-954175-90-7
Electronic ISBN 978-1-954175-88-4

Distributed by Tivshe Publishing
Printed in the United States of America
Cover design by Dark Queen Designs

Visit www.tivshepublishing.com

ALSO BY J. L. JACKOLA

To my younger self who repressed her naughty thoughts—
it feels so good to finally set them free.

AUTHOR'S NOTE

Dear Reader,

Thank you for continuing to follow Skye and Mark's journey. Their world and their relationship are about to be tested in ways they never expected.

As you discovered in book one, the Hues series consists of characters who are mature and sexually confident. Book two is exceptionally dark so please be aware of possible triggers. This series contains intense and explicit sexual scenes, language, non-consensual sex, abuse, reverse harem situations, violence, and death.

Buckle up and enjoy the ride!

J. L.

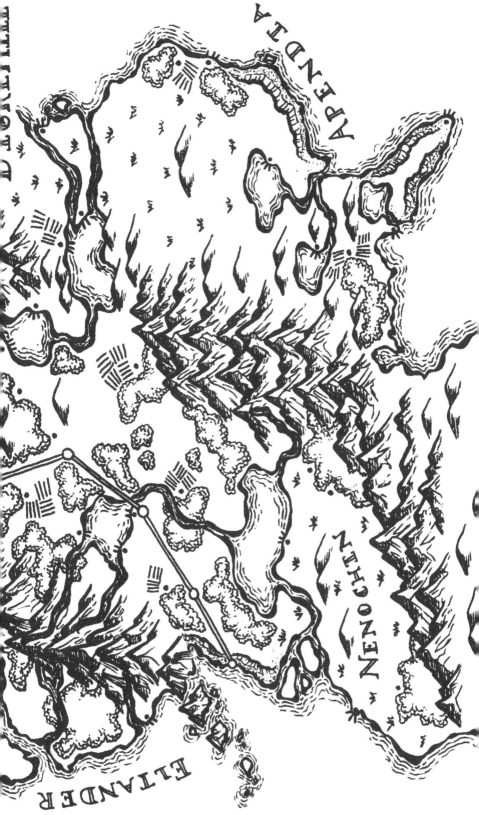

SKYE

As the final words were spoken, the markings around their wrists sparkled, lighting the darkened lines, and leaving an imprint reminiscent of a small tattoo on each of them. Skye stared at the marking on her wrist, then the one on Mark's—the two tied so that they were now bound as lovers, as soulmates, as husband and wife. The ring that now sat upon her finger bore a sapphire gem surrounded by brilliant diamonds, while Mark's finger bore a similar band with tiny sapphires meant to match hers. Both rings symbolized all they'd gone through before this moment.

She looked up and met his hazel eyes, returning the smile they held.

"This would be the part where you kiss," said Noah, nudging Mark from behind.

Mark laughed, and Skye's heart swelled. He weaved his hand through her hair and pulled her close, his mouth meeting hers, sending waves of need through her. His tongue found hers and she wanted more, lost in the moment, just as she was each time they kissed.

"Ahem, not that kind of kiss," Noah said.

They pulled apart, both having forgotten they had an audience, both desperate to move to the end of the wedding so they could see where that kiss led. Skye knew. It would be hours of touching and playing, of ecstasy, repeated with increasing desire, one that never seemed to wane.

Six months had passed since she'd taken the throne. Six months since a legacy and a world unknown to her, one hidden from her for decades, had been revealed. Since she'd discovered the man of her life, whom she'd believed to be off limits, was now hers for the taking.

Life had changed so quickly that there were days she thought perhaps it was a dream, that she'd wake to find Mark was still her cousin, that her life hadn't changed and she'd simply had a very long, intense wet dream. She hoped that would never be the case. Life with Mark was too wonderful, too satisfying, even with all the other mayhem thrown in.

The moment was over before she could savor it, and she was whisked from Mark's arms to be congratulated and forced to socialize with the attendees. Her adoptive mother and father were present, as well as Mark's uncle, Petrian, and Trent. The wizards had attended, now accepted as part of her kingdom. The Fettered Forests were still their home but now they wandered at their free will without fear of retribution; the boundary of magic they'd placed to protect themselves dismantled.

Alex had come with Clover, the girl he still called friend, even though everyone else could see she was more than that. He was attending mage classes at the school Elspeth and Trent had built in the realm, loving every minute of his new life.

Glancing over at Mark, who was in his element surrounded by the Elite and talking shop, Noah by his side, she wondered at their new life. The sight brought a smile to her face. He was finally hers. No longer did she have to silently love the beautiful man with eyes that made her heart soar, who made her weak with just the curve of his smile. He belonged to her and his love for her was endless like hers was for him. With that thought, she snuck away, leaving him to enjoy himself. It had been hours of talking, laughing, eating, and drinking, and she was exhausted. Fingering her new wedding ring, she walked to the small tower she'd had built, Mark on her mind, contentment in her heart.

Mark had questioned her choice to build the small tower, joking of his worry that she'd be locking long haired damsels away for some freakish fetish. She'd laughed, teasing that he was now her only freakish fetish. He'd raised a brow as if to ask what fetishes she'd had prior to him, but she'd changed the subject, leaving his mind to wander.

In all honesty, she'd built the tower as a reminder of where she'd started in her journey as a Mage Warrior. A reminder of the tower where she'd first lived, where Mark had first made love to her, where she'd first discovered the life she could have had.

The space had quickly become a refuge, a solitary to escape to when she needed to be alone.

As she climbed the winding steps, holding the bottom of her long dress so as not to trip, she took in the drawings that lined the walls. They told of a history long before her time, that of the people she'd inherited, the mages of all ranks that now lived freely in the realm where they had once flourished. She'd had the artwork added as a statement of who she was and where she'd come from. The final painting, just before she entered the small room, was of her mother and father fighting an unseen enemy shrouded in darkness. With all she'd discovered, she hadn't wanted Camin depicted as that darkness, so she'd left it unclarified, an invisible being deep in the shadows.

She let her fingers drift across the image, gaining strength in the woman who had come before her and all the Mage Warriors in her line, wishing she were here to talk to and learn from.

Sighing, she continued into her small recluse. There was a soft chair, a small bed she rarely used, only doing so if Mark was needed overnight for something. It was a rare occurrence, but as of late, Theodore had been pushing his troops closer to the border, and the queen to his south, Crimson, had been adding to those troops. There had been no provocation from either side, but there had been intense moments. When she'd taken the throne, taken back the homeland of her ancestors, freed the mages, those who wanted to leave the service of the other kingdoms, Skye had known she would face challenges. But she had magic and had thought that would suffice. It hadn't. Magic didn't help her with the day-to-day obligations of running Kantenda. There were never ending diplomatic dealings with the other kingdoms, people to rule, decisions to make, all things to which she was inexperienced. And the other rulers knew it. Theodore openly mocked her. Crimson did nothing but lust after Mark, and Mechon, the king to her west, sat quiet, an observer to the chaos.

Resting her elbows on the window ledge, she looked out on Kantenda. A kingdom stuck with a queen who knew nothing about ruling it. In her defense, she'd been a financial advisor six months ago, oblivious to her heritage, to this world, to the power she now wielded. A widowed mother trying to make it through each day, trying to avoid the incessant desire she had for the cousin she thought Mark was at the time.

"You know, if I didn't know better, I'd say you were having second thoughts and hiding from me," she heard Mark say behind her.

She turned to see him standing in the doorway, arms crossed, leaning against the doorframe. He looked handsome, his hazel eyes shining, the Elite commander uniform he wore emphasizing the muscle below. They had changed the uniforms to a royal navy with gray binding, the colors of her family. The Elite now served her and the kingdom, the guardians of the royal seat and the sovereign as they'd always been meant to be.

"Well, it's a good thing you know better," she replied with a sly hint in her voice.

He walked over to her, wrapping his arms around her waist. "So why are you up here, all alone on our wedding day?"

Touching her fingers to his face, she traced the strength in his jawline. "Just thinking."

"About?" he asked, raising a brow.

"How much I love you."

"Mmm, as much as I like that answer, I highly doubt that's what you were thinking."

"And what do you think I was thinking?"

"How good I am in bed," he replied, playfully nipping her bottom lip.

She couldn't help but laugh. "Something like that."

He gestured toward the bed. "We haven't broken that in yet. In fact, I think this is the only part of the castle we have yet to break in."

He kissed her, and she melted as she always did.

"Technically, this isn't part of the castle," she said against his mouth as his hands drifted to her arms.

He guided the sleeves of her wedding gown down to expose the swell of her breasts causing a trickle of excitement to drift through her belly.

"Then we have a lot of work to do to get it up to par with the castle."

He reached below the material and gently brushed her nipple, eliciting a long moan as shivers rumbled through her.

"Mmm, I suppose we do."

He drew his lips away and lowered his head before lifting her breast to meet his mouth. His tongue met the hardness of her nipple, dancing upon it until she tilted her head back, the sensation tormenting her. Her body was flush with arousal and she gripped her hand in his hair in an attempt to control the overwhelming sensations.

He moved her skirts around, trying to lift them. "Damn these dresses."

Coaxing his head back up, she pulled him to her lips as she called the hues of the dress with her magic, guiding them to undo the laces that kept her imprisoned within the layers of cloth. She tugged at his shirt as the stays continued to come undone. Helping her pull it over his head, he watched as her dress collapsed to the floor.

"God, I want you," he said, his eyes hungry and fierce.

Grabbing her waist, he brought her closer, groaning when their skin met.

"I'm all yours to take."

His eyes sparkled with lust and as his hand wandered to her backside, they drifted down to push at the silk underwear she'd had specially made for the day. Skye unhooked the buttons to his pants, her fingers fumbling with the urgent need she had to feel him inside her.

She was completely naked now and as his pants fell, his hardness pushed against her, ready and erect, waiting for her. His kiss was demanding as she stroked him. A rumble came, low and feral, from his chest, one that sent a warm tingling through her body. Grabbing her ass, he picked her up and brought her to the bed in one sweep, penetrating her quickly. She lifted her legs, wrapping them around him, pushing him deeper until she quivered at the feel of him. Her body was a surge of currents that sparked with each thrust. His mouth trailed her neck, finding her breast again, and her breath escaped at the electricity that fed those currents. Their lovemaking was always like this, ecstasy that only built with each touch, never fading, no matter how many times they touched each other.

Stretching her arms in contentment, she curved her back, forcing his mouth to take more of her breast. His groan tickled her skin as it echoed through the room. The sound of it called to something deep in her, that unbreakable connection she had to him.

Her hips moved to meet his as her orgasm began its steady rise. Taking the sign, he trailed her stomach, pulling out in a move that elicited a sad pout from her until his fingers found her wetness. A cry clawed from her throat as her body's demand to crumble grew, nearing its breaking point. Mark's tongue hit her sensitive spot causing her toes to curl. With each lick, currents assaulted her until she was so close to climax that it hurt.

Her head fell back, the oncoming wave intensifying, but he didn't satisfy her. Every part of her was on fire, an inferno that was raging to be free, and she tried to push him back to no avail. He chuckled as he rose and climbed atop her again, taking her nipple between his teeth, and nibbling at it as she begged him for release.

"Not without me, Skye," he whispered, his voice hoarse with need.

"You selfish bastard," she growled as he plunged back into her, her readiness granting him easy access.

"God, you're soaked," he moaned.

He pounded into her, her climax rising further with each glide until she clung to him. Unable to do anything more than hold tight, she let herself go to the waves that crashed through her. His own climax crested, and she threw her hips up to meet it, bringing him closer and heightening the sensations that were riveting her. His body shook with the force, her own quaking below him.

He dropped his head to the nook of her neck, breathing hard as he tried to catch his breath, her own ragged and quick. After a few moments, he kissed her neck, then rolled from her, his breathing still deep.

She turned to her side, propping her chin on her hand while tenderly brushing his chest with her fingers, the firmness below, her constant security blanket.

He took her hand and kissed it, turning to face her, and gently brushed her hair from her face.

"That's quite a wedding present," he said with a crooked grin.

"That's just the start," she teased. She heard the seduction in her voice and noted the twinkle in his eye in response.

"Oh, I know. I'm expecting plenty more than that."

She threw her head back and laughed, and he took the moment to run his fingers down her neck, grazing her breasts, stirring her arousal once more. He strayed to her nipple and took one between his fingers, rubbing it until the moan escaped her lips.

"You are insatiable," he breathed, kissing her shoulder.

"Only for you."

"Mmm, good." His fingers moved over her arm, urging her to her stomach. They went on to trace the dip in her back, softly caressing her hips as his lips followed. His touch alone was enough to make her come undone as she felt the rise in her arousal again, the fire he was stoking flaring back to life.

She dropped her head to the pillow, each kiss making her want him more until he moved so that he was atop her back. He gripped her hips, pulling her ass into the air, her cry accompanying the motion. Desire soared through her body as she anticipated his next move. Draping across her body, he turned his attention back to her breasts. She was going to break again, and she welcomed it, the sparks riveting through her. She tried to bring her head up, but he pressed her down, maintaining the control, dominating her. It was a move that brought a shiver to her each time. The force of him, the demand of his actions elevated her desire for him, and she couldn't resist what it did to her.

He'd grown hard again, pressing against her like a needy child, wanting to be granted access once more. And she wanted it, wanted to feel him inside of her again, coaxing her climax to fruition. The warmth of his hands moved to her backside, his fingers sinking into her wetness, his thumb finding her pleasure spot again.

Her body was a mess, the waves of desire, the yearning for him so intense that her legs began to tremble. He knew what he was doing to her, making her fall apart with each touch was exactly what he wanted.

He drew his fingers back and leaned over her. "I want you to come for me, Skye," he whispered against her ear. The low moan she elicited was unstoppable. His mere words sent her over the cliff, her knees buckling with the force that pummeled her. He caught her, holding her by her stomach as her body fell apart against him. Sliding into her, he kept his hands gripped around her hips as she rocked against him, the final sparks of her orgasm still simmering within her. With the feel of him, her body betrayed her again, the simmer growing. She bucked against him, wanting to be driven to the edge and cast into the unending bliss again.

"Jesus," he muttered in a throaty voice, his fingers tightening on her hips.

It was ecstasy and as he plunged harder, release flooded her again, her body spasming with the intensity. He continued to take her, pushing her head down and thrusting harder, the waves of her orgasm cresting again until she came a third time. This time, he joined her, his own orgasm hitting just as she felt him enlarge, ready to succumb.

He held on tight to her, pushing aggressively against her as he climaxed, clinging to her until his grip loosened and he finally leaned forward, kissing her back.

She collapsed, and he dropped next to her, pulling her closer to him and nuzzling her neck. She could feel the pounding of his heart, her own just quieting. Every part of her was tingling still.

"God, that never gets old," he mumbled.

"No, it doesn't," she replied, resting her head on his chest, a slight quiver running through her.

"Some wedding night. You suppose they gave up on trying to find us? I think I may have mentioned to Noah where I was headed, but my mind was on undressing you, so I can't be certain."

She giggled. "I believe I undressed myself."

"That you did. Damn dresses. The only thing they're good for is easy access in a dark corner."

She smiled as the image of the last time they'd found a dark corner came back to her. He was quiet and after a few minutes, she heard the steady sound of his breathing. Relaxing into him, she let her own breathing match his and slowly drifted off, the smile still upon her face.

MARK

Rise and shine and please tell me you're decent!" The sound of Alex's voice woke Mark from his dreams. The feel of Skye's skin against his made the interruption easier. He'd take her over dreams of the training field any day.

"Damn, you're not. I can never unsee that. Why are there so many moments that I can't unsee now?"

"Because you barge in unannounced all the time," Mark grumbled, pulling the blanket up to cover their bodies as Skye stretched next to him.

"He's got a point, Alex. Why are you here? It's usually Noah we're traumatizing," Skye said with a yawn.

She gave Mark a quick good morning kiss. The feel of her breast against him threatened to increase the morning firmness that had woken with him. As if knowing, Skye's hand slipped around it, gripping it firmly and tugging it.

"Skye," he warned.

"Noah was tired of walking in on this, so he volunteered me instead," Alex answered her, hand over his eyes.

Skye slipped her leg over Mark, hiding the motion of her hand, making it difficult to think about anything but the thrill she was giving him.

"Go away, Alex. We'll be down when we're ready. It's our honeymoon. We get at least one day to ourselves," he managed through gritted teeth, biting back the groan.

"No, you don't. There's an envoy from the Apendia Kingdom with a message from the queen."

Skye's hand stopped.

"Crimson? What does she want?"

"Their leader said they have orders to deliver the message to you, Mom. And they brought a wedding gift."

"Huh, that's strangely nice," she said.

"For Mark."

Her hand tightened, and Mark inadvertently jumped at the pressure.

"I'm out of here. You two do what it is you do that I don't want to know about. They're waiting in the throne room."

He bolted, not bothering to say goodbye.

"Good, I can take you now that he's gone."

Mark pushed the covers back, his hands reaching for her waist.

"Not until I'm completely gone!" Alex yelled. "And yuck, that's my mother!"

He had expected Skye to laugh, but she didn't.

"Are you going to relax the death grip you have on my dick?" he asked once he heard the door close.

"Huh? Oh, sorry." Her hand loosened and returned to its prior movement.

"Mmm, that's better. She really gets to you, doesn't she?"

"If she weren't throwing herself at you, it would be easier."

"You have nothing to worry about, I don't have a thing for redheads."

She smiled and moved her body down, her tongue tracing the contour of his muscles until she found his erection, enveloping it.

"Besides, no one has a mouth or a body like yours."

She drew her teeth along his shaft, and he inadvertently quivered.

"She is quite hot, though, don't you think?" she asked, dragging her tongue along him.

It took him a moment to concentrate before he could think about it. He had to agree, if ever there were a rival to Skye, it would have to be Crimson. She had curves in just the right places, breasts that looked like they wanted to be free of the constraints of her clothes, nothing short of round and full like her lips. Her fiery red hair offset her vibrant green eyes.

Skye cleared her throat, looking up at him with her blue eyes.

"What? You asked me, so I was thinking on it."

"A bit too long and happily I might add."

"Are you jealous?"

"No, but if she ever touches you, I will strangle her with that stupid red hair of hers."

He laughed. "Think you may want to finish what you started first?" He gestured to his throbbing erection, the one she was now neglecting.

"I don't know," she said, sitting up and brushing her hands seductively across her breasts. "Will you be thinking of me or her?"

"How about the two of you together?"

Her eyes grew dangerously dark.

"I'm joking! You and only you."

"That's better." She dropped back down, her breasts dragging across his length before she took it back in her mouth. Her moves were forceful this time, and it didn't take long before he was spilling into her mouth, his muscles tensing as his hands pulled her hair. As she did each time, she took it all, licking her tongue along him, claiming the remaining droplets before rising from the bed.

He felt like a puddle of muscles as the effects of the orgasm continued to ripple through him. His eyes trailed her, watching her hands brush her breasts again, this time lingering. She was uninhibited and insatiable in ways he couldn't resist, and he felt the reaction in his softening length. Her eyes met his as she played with her nipples, tweaking and pulling at them. God, she was going to drive him mad. Tipping her head back, she groaned, her left hand slipping between her legs as she leaned against the wall.

Unable to contain his need for her, he rose and went to her. Her nipples were hard enough to cut glass when he brought his mouth to them. Savoring the taste of her skin he let his tongue drift along it. He made his way to her lips, kissing her firmly. She met his intensity, and he pushed her against the wall, dropping his hand to join hers between the warmth of her legs. She was drenched, and the feel sent desire rushing through him. He pushed his fingers deep inside of her, groaning in reaction as her wetness surrounded them. His motion continued until, with an intense moan, she tightened around his fingers, quivers racking her body before he shoved his aching erection into her, knowing he needed release again.

He took her there, bringing her to orgasm again, her climax rising to meet his until their bodies and their breathing quieted.

"Any chance we could skip the royal duties and do this all day?" she asked, breathless, her body still shaking in his arms.

He kissed her, then rested his head against hers. "Not a chance. Clothed or unclothed, Noah will not hesitate to drag us out of here."

"Damn royal duties and titles. Can we go back to our old life? I could be happily married to an ophthalmologist."

He pulled away reluctantly, and she flopped back on the bed.

Laughing, he replied, "I hate to break it to you, but I detested that job."

She brought herself up to her elbows as he dressed. The sight of her breasts was tempting so he picked up her dress and threw it over her. "Get dressed before I take you again."

"I wouldn't be opposed to that."

He groaned, forcing himself to look away.

"You're not going to explain why you detested the job?"

"Because it was boring and tedious, but necessary. The only

reason I became an eye doctor was to care for your eyes. Couldn't have you going to just anybody."

"Was there anything in my life that wasn't a façade?"

"Alex and Sam." Saying Sam's name brought back the jealousy he'd always had of the man.

"But even Sam wasn't completely real. You know that."

"Didn't stop you from loving him and having sex with him enough times to have a kid."

She glared at him, and he immediately regretted the words. "That's not fair, Mark. You know I wanted you."

He skimmed his hand through his hair. "I know, sorry."

"You certainly know how to sour a mood when you want to," she quipped as she pulled her dress on.

He took her in his arms and kissed her. "I know and again, I'm sorry. Now that I have you, the thought of any other man having you turns me green with envy."

"I'm yours, Mark. I will never love anyone the way I love you."

He kissed her neck. "Have you ever fucked someone the way you do me?"

"No." She pursed her lips, her brow raising. "Have you?"

He hesitated, thinking through all the women he'd had. "No, never like this."

"You hesitated," she said as he nibbled her ear.

"Just wanted to make sure."

"Too many to count, right?"

"Something like that," he replied with a wink. He kissed her nose, seeing the flare of jealousy and enjoying it. "Now who's jealous?"

She huffed by him, and he couldn't help but laugh before following her out of the tower.

THEY TOOK time to change from their wedding attire before meeting Crimson's envoy. Mark couldn't resist taking Skye once more before they left the room, an insatiable urge coming over him. He didn't know if it was something in the air here or something else, but he couldn't seem to get enough of her. She made him feel like he was in his twenties again with the stamina of a teenager.

Her body was on his mind when they entered the throne room and he forced it aside, knowing he was on duty.

"My queen," Noah said bowing theatrically.

Mark had to stifle the urge to laugh, it always seemed like an odd thing to see Noah formal, an odder thing to hear Skye referred to as queen.

As Skye took a seat on her throne, one of Crimson's entourage took a step forward. Mark stood at her side, hand on his weapon, his mistrust for Crimson strong.

"Your majesty," the man stated.

Mark checked him out. His clothes were ostentatious, although he'd found everything about Crimson and her court to be ostentatious. He wore pants of a bold mauve with gold embellished braiding down both legs. His shirt was a shade of blue that stood bright against the mauve, the same gold braiding around the cuffs of his sleeves and the neckline that he wore loose.

"Thank you for granting us an audience so hastily," he continued, not hiding the overt sarcasm.

Mark had the urge to punch him but gripped his weapon instead. It wouldn't be good to send the man back to Crimson bloodied and battered.

"Well, as your queen was so gracious to send you unexpectedly on the morning after a ceremony to which she was not invited, you should be happy you're being seen at all," Skye said, her expression never changing.

God, he loved her. He would have given her a high-five if they were back home and thirty years younger.

The man couldn't hide his offended expression, taking a step back as if she'd slapped him. Noah was trying his best to hide his smirk and Mark shot him a look.

"Queen Crimson requests your presence in fifteen days' time for a meeting of the rulers. All kingdoms are required to be present." Mark noted the word *required* rather than *asked*.

"And if we don't heed her request?"

"It will be seen as an act of war against the other kingdoms."

Skye sat forward as Mark narrowed his eyes on the man.

"I could take your head and that would be a less subtle way of starting a war," Mark growled, hand drawing his weapon.

Skye put her hand up, stopping his movement, and stood. She took the stairs from her throne with the grace of someone who had worn the crown for decades rather than months, the train of her dress draping behind her. Each step was a seductive flip of her hips, natural, not forced like some women.

"You would come to my kingdom, into my castle, and threaten me?"

The man didn't flinch. "With all due respect, your highness, it was not a threat but an invitation."

She squinted her eyes, her expression one of sheer annoyance.

"The King of Eltander has already accepted, as has King Theodore."

"I bet Theodore has," she mumbled. The affair between the two royals was no secret to any of them.

"Tell Crimson I accept her invitation, but we will be there on official business only. We will stay for the formalities, then leave. There will be no dinners, no stay, no time for her to covet what is mine."

The man smirked, and Mark had to stifle his own laugh.

"Very well. The queen also sends her congratulations on your nuptials. She has sent a gift." He gestured a boy forward who held a box wrapped in the same rich mauve the man wore.

"Oh, how very thoughtful," Skye said politely, reaching for the gift.

"I'm afraid it is for King Markhem, your highness."

Mark saw the clench of her hand and noted the rise of her

eyebrow. It amazed him she hadn't reached out and strangled the man.

"Very well."

The boy moved to Mark and handed him the package. Mark held it awkwardly, not sure how to react and seriously mulling what Crimson had put inside to aggravate his wife.

"Please tell Crimson we appreciate her thoughtfulness. Noah will see you out," Skye said with a distinct edge to her voice.

Mark remained in place until they were gone, and Noah had returned from instructing the guarding Elite to escort the guests from the castle.

Noah gestured to the package. "Well, are you going to open it?"

"Not sure. I value my body parts too much and Skye might take them if I do."

"Why?" she asked. "I'm not upset. I'm just fine."

Each word came out with greater force, her teeth clenching. She was not fine and the thought of her cutting him off from that detectible body of hers was greater than the need to see the gift.

"Open it," she demanded.

"Skye, I don't—"

"Open it." She had crossed her arms, her breasts pushed up so that they were swelling well above her neckline. All he wanted to do was drop his face to them and let his mouth feel their softness.

"Fine, but don't punish me for whatever it is."

With trepidation, he opened it, knowing whatever gift Crimson had sent him was calculated, intended to elicit a reaction from Skye. Part of him hoped it was a severed body part instead of something certain to be tantalizing.

He untied the ribbon, gave a quick peck to Skye whose lips were pursed, her arms still crossed, then lifted the lid.

"Bring these when you visit, and I'll show you how a real woman uses them." He read the note before Skye snatched it, revealing two curls of rope below—dark red, the same shade as Crimson's hair.

Noah cleared his throat uncomfortably as Skye crumpled the note.

"Is she serious?" she snarled.

"Obviously," he replied, lifting one of the ropes and studying it.

He raised a brow at Skye.

"You're not seriously jealous over this, are you?"

"Are you kidding?" she seethed. "How dare she?"

"She's trying to get to you, Skye. That's all."

"That's not all, Mark. This is clearly intentional."

"And we'll put them to good use," he said with a wink. "Can't say I've ever tried bondage."

"That's my cue to leave," Noah said, backing away.

But Skye didn't laugh or even play along. She threw the crumpled paper at him and stormed away.

"You're not going near that woman, and you're not touching me with those things."

She turned back around, marched over to him, and snatched the box from his hands before exiting with a huff, the door slamming behind her.

Mark looked to Noah. "What was that?"

He shrugged.

"She was like a feral animal."

"I thought you liked that kind of thing."

"In bed maybe but not like this."

Noah laughed. "The Mage Warrior is many things but threaten her mate and she is something completely unpredictable," he said.

"I'm not threatened."

"On the contrary, another woman has her sights on you, and Skye sees that as a threat. Mage Warriors are extremely protective and jealous. In some ways, they covet what is theirs. The same way a dragon might covet its gold in the stories. I think it's something to do with their magic. Her mother was the same way. No one dared even look at Berrett or they suffered her wrath."

"Great. Jealousy is not a trait I find very attractive."

"Eh, with it you get the insatiable appetite she now has." He put air quotes around the word appetite.

"Wait, you mean her magic fuels her sex drive?"

"So, I've been told. Never experienced it myself, but their magic elevates their senses, their desires, their emotions. As tempting as that always sounded, I count myself blessed to have found a nice novice mage to marry. No volatile swings of emotion there. You can keep your multiple sexual trysts. I'll keep my head."

"Funny. Now what do I do?"

"She's your wife, buddy. Me, I'd steer clear of her for a while, but then again, she scares me now."

"Nice. Don't you have troops to train?"

"I could say the same to you, *your highness*."

Mark ran his hand over his face. "Just go. I'll be there soon. I seem to have a dragon to contend with first."

"Good luck with that," Noah said before leaving the room. "Hopefully, you'll return with all of your parts intact!"

Mark stared at the lid to the box before bending down to pick up the fallen ribbon. Only then did he notice the writing on the ribbon.

I will taste every inch of you and drink you dry. You will never again crave your Skye. You will only want me.

"Jesus Christ, she's insane," he muttered. She was a non-caster and stood no chance against Skye. What was she doing?

Playing with fire.

It took some time, but he finally found Skye in her training room. The room was built to suit her powers, a containment of sorts, so she could practice her more dangerous moves. The walls were a rainbow of colors, brighter at the top before growing darker as they neared the floor. The effect reminded Mark of a descent from heaven to hell.

He stood in the doorway as she drew shades of black around her. They played in her hair, turning it a deep shade of ebony, the clothes she wore taking on the same hue. For just a moment, she looked terrifying, deadly, the force of the hues blowing her hair back with an invisible wind.

The darker shades were where her true power lied. She became dark, lethal, and thrilling in ways. All of which made her unique from the mages before her, a link to the shadows where she once resided. When she drew the darker shades, it called to a different part of him, seducing him, giving his own abilities an edge that made him just as lethal.

He was the only one who could approach her when she called the darkest hues, the colors of the Shadow Realm. He didn't know if it was the time he'd spent there or simply his connection to her that made it so.

As he watched her, he took in her beauty, irritated that she would harbor any jealousy about Crimson when there was no one he'd ever wanted but her. She did something to him, and she had claimed his heart and soul long before he'd ever confessed it. Yet the jealousy she had toward Crimson led him to believe she doubted his love for her in some way and that angered him. He'd waited his entire life to have her, longed for her since it was inappropriate to do so, waited patiently, watching as she'd married another man and given him what Mark had dreamed of having. There should have been no doubt about the depths of his love.

He walked through the swirl of color, feeling it as it coated him, attempting to insinuate its way into him, then backing away as if knowing its mistress had already claimed him. She opened her eyes when he wrapped his arms around her waist, the rich blue of them seeing into his soul. Kissing her, he pulled her against him. She fought half-heartedly before her arms relaxed, her hands coming around his neck to play in his hair as she liked to do.

He ended the kiss and dropped his forehead to hers.

"There is, and never has been, anyone else that I've loved, Skye. There is and always will be only you."

The tension fled her muscles, the hues receding, her hair gradually returning to its auburn shade. He picked up a strand and watched as it transformed.

"Better now?" he asked.

"Not really. I don't know what it is about her, but something really bothers me."

"Like her not-so-subtle hints that she wants to make me her plaything?"

"That's not funny, Mark."

"Yes, it is, Skye. There's no way I would ever touch her. She'd have to restrain me and sever my link to your power to even come close to me. And even then, she'd have to force herself on me as I fought with everything I had to kill her."

She laughed. "That's an image. You restrained while a woman tries to seduce you." Her face turned sour. "What if she did that, though? I don't trust her, Mark."

"She's not going to seduce me, and you would take her hands if she ever tried to touch me."

She didn't look convinced.

"Are you really this worried about Crimson? We don't have to go, Skye. We can send a message that states we changed our minds."

"No, we have to go. Things are tense and this meeting can put an end to that, to Theodore's advances. It will look bad if we don't and the last thing we need is for a war to start because I'm jealous of some younger, prettier woman."

He lifted her chin. "You really think she's prettier than you? Have you seen yourself? You outshine her in every way. You're beautiful, Skye, and she is not younger than you. She was a child when Camin's war started, just as I was. In fact, I think she's several years older than I am."

She gave a small smile, and he kissed her nose.

"Better?" he asked.

"I guess," she answered with a sigh. "I still don't trust her, though, or this call for a meeting."

"Well, we'll be visiting Mechon in his kingdom before we go. Let's see what he has to say about the meeting. Perhaps strategize a plan in case it goes badly."

Skye nodded after a moment's contemplation.

"Now, as much as I'd like to ravage you right now, I have an army of Elite waiting for me, and I still need to talk to Alex like we discussed yesterday."

"Oh, I forgot about that."

"Do you still want me to do it? You wouldn't rather?"

"No, I think it means more coming from you."

"Then I'm off to drag him from whatever they do at that mage school."

"Teach magic?"

"I still suspect it's a cult."

She laughed, and he kissed her, stopping the laugh, her smile still on her lips as he nibbled at them.

"You know," she said, her eyes gleaming with suggestion, "we'll both be stuck riding to the Eltander Kingdom for three days with no alone time."

"Hmmm, good point," he replied, kissing her neck. "Then a little ravaging time will be necessary before we leave. We need to keep you satisfied."

"Well, since we leave in the morning, I'm yours all night."

"Maybe afternoon as well?"

She nodded and he let her go, his erection rising at the invitation. "But for now..." he started as her hand playfully danced along it. He grabbed her hand to plant a kiss against it. "That's not nice, Skye."

"No one said I was nice."

He groaned. "We have work to do, then we play."

He gave her a quick kiss on the forehead, knowing he needed to leave before he took her. Reluctantly, he walked away, urging his hardness to relax despite her pout.

"Don't pout, Skye, it's not queenlike."

He ducked as he felt the tingle of her magic, a bolt of fiery red hues hitting the doorframe and blasting the door from its hinges. He peeked back at her, raising a brow.

"That childlike behavior will get you nowhere. Now fix that door."

She stuck her tongue out as she playfully drew another hue. Shaking his head, he made his way out of the castle and through the castle grounds.

The mage school stood just outside the grounds, connecting it by proximity. Skye had wanted it close so that it stood under royal protection, yet separate in spirit, so that there was no royal influence over the education.

Her adoptive mother and father were headmasters who'd taken positions as instructors as well. The whole thing reminded him of those books Alex had read as a teenager. He remembered Skye having read them as well, and the many discussions about how funny it would be if magic existed. He had simply listened and joined them in the movie marathon, knowing the entire time how ironic it was that a woman with power that encompassed that of all those characters, sat wondering what it would be like to have magic.

THE MAGE SCHOOL was about a half-a-mile walk from the castle, but Mark didn't mind. It gave him time to calm his need for Skye and to contemplate the intent behind Crimson's blatant gift. Although he found the attention flattering, he couldn't help but think there was more to it. Sure, she was needling Skye, attempting to invoke a reaction, but why? Part of him was suspicious, just as Skye was, although he would never tell her.

There was more to it than a simple, overt attempt to flirt with him. Crimson was not to be trusted. In fact, he didn't trust either of the rulers to their south. Crimson and Theodore had been rumored to have been bedmates on several occasions. They both still held resentment at having their kingdoms disrupted by Skye's claim on her people. Theodore's ego remained bruised by her actions. Crimson had threatened war, but Theodore had convinced her to change course and free her mages.

Crimson's kingdom, however, had the most mages who chose to remain in their positions, something Skye and Mark knew had been from coercion rather than free will. Those who had left told stories of abuse, of sexual misdeeds. Some had even lost what little magic they had after the mage wars. On many occasions, mages claimed it would return only to fade again as they continued to work in her castle. The novices, whose magic had remained more intact after the mage wars, told stories of their magic waning at various times, sometimes fading completely.

There were suspicions that Crimson was the cause, but no proof of anything but the abuse. There was much they didn't know about her, and too many questions. They had met with her twice since Skye had taken the throne, each time in a neutral location. And Crimson's advances on Mark had not been subtle. In fact, it had been overt and uncomfortable. After the last meeting, Skye had sent Trent, refusing to have Crimson anywhere near Mark. The catfight she'd almost started the last time had been enough for him to agree with that decision. Mark found it humorous, but Skye's jealousy had only grown. She had nothing to worry about. Sure, Crimson was seductive, beautiful, sexy, but she was not Skye. Not that he could convince her otherwise.

Mark let the thought go as he reached the school, looking up at the towering building, tall and majestic in this space just outside the castle walls. Beyond it lied the town of Prenkil. On occasion, he and Noah would sneak out, always under the guise of observing the people, to grab a pint at the local pub and reminisce about the lost conveniences of the human world.

He made his way through the halls, knowing Alex was in his spell class on the second floor. He knocked on the door and slowly opened it.

"Oh my," the professor said, her brown eyes growing wide. "Your highness. To what do we owe this visit?"

She looked visibly frustrated, a slight blush rising in her cheeks as he smiled and greeted her. The girls in the class became suddenly more attentive. Skye always teased him about his effect on women. Crimson being the only one who bothered her, the only one she considered a threat. He chalked it up as the Elite commander's uniform, knowing women had a thing for uniforms. To which she would give him a pat on the hand as if he were a naïve child.

"Good day, Professor Shalare. I was hoping to borrow Alex for the remainder of the day."

"Well, I ..." She grew flustered again.

"Only if it doesn't pose an inconvenience."

"Of course not. Alex, you may go," she said, composing herself. "I still expect your work on my desk in the morning."

"Yes, professor," Alex said, gathering his books and rising to leave with Mark.

Mark noticed his quick glance back at Clover, the girl he'd become close to since they'd brought him to this world. She gave Alex a sweet smile.

"Will you be teaching him physical protection today?" Mark noticed the emphasis on the word physical. Professor Shalare let her fingers rest on her chest, finding the lace that lined her cleavage, having purposely pushed her robe back.

Mark nodded, trying not to shake his head at her move. Maybe Skye was right, but he preferred to think it was the uniform. She was pretty, silver streaks lining her black hair, and if things were still as they'd been in the past, he would have taken her to satisfy his need for Skye. She would have been like every other woman he'd had, a means of satisfying his need for release, a temporary moment of pleasure that acted as a band-aid to his desire for Skye.

"A day in the practice fields is necessary, according to his mother."

"Mmm," she replied dreamily, licking her lips slowly.

"Can we watch?" one of the girls eagerly asked.

"Oh, that is a tempting idea," she answered.

"No, off limits to civilians. Elite only with the exception of my *wife's* son." He grabbed Alex's arm. "Nice seeing you, professor. We'll let you return to your studies."

He ushered Alex out quickly and closed the door.

"What is it with you?" Alex asked. "Seriously. I mean, women threw themselves at you when we were home, but here they're like wild vultures."

"It's the uniform," he said with haste, wanting Alex to drop the subject.

"Not buying that excuse. My professor was about to rip her clothes off and throw herself on you. You're like some sex magnet now."

He let out a laugh. "I've always been a sex magnet, Alex."

"Don't let my mother hear that."

"No, best to keep that quiet. And given her recent jealous streak, I'd leave the behavior of your professor out as well. It'd be a shame if your mother imprisoned her for flirting with me."

"Not for me. That woman is brutal. There's no slipping anything past her. Maybe I should start bringing you to class."

"Funny."

"Why is mom jealous this time?"

This time. Even Alex had noticed the change in her.

"Crimson—"

"Say no more. Mom loathes her. It's like this whole new version of her comes out when that woman's name is mentioned."

"Tell me about it. She's invited us— No, correct that, required us to attend a meeting in her kingdom."

Alex paused his steps and looked sharply at him. "Tell me you're not going."

"Your mother thinks we don't have a choice, and I'm inclined to believe her. We'll still head to Eltander as planned but cut the stay short."

"And ride to Apendia?"

"Yes, straight into the viper's den."

"That should be fun. Does the viper know she's invited a bird of prey?"

Mark couldn't help but laugh. "I'm not certain she does."

They left the building and walked the grounds, the touch of cool air skimming Mark's face, reminding him that winter was on the cusp. He hadn't spent a winter in this world since he was a child and even then, Theodore's kingdom experienced mild winters, far enough to the south to avoid the snowstorms this kingdom suffered.

"So why are you sneaking me out of classes, Uncle...I mean, Mark?"

"I'm not sneaking you out. I'm taking you and you can leave the uncle there if it's easier for you. I told you that."

"Thanks," he muttered, pushing his hair back from his forehead.

Alex was still adjusting since leaving the world he'd always known, his friends, his life. He'd just been starting college when this new life had been thrust upon him. A life with magic he didn't know how to use, and a new school that was no longer school as he knew it, but a mix of ages since many mages had never really trained with their magic because they'd only ever been used for it. The subjects he knew—history, math, science—had been replaced with the ways of magic and the history of it. Then there was his mother, now a queen, with magic that was like something from a movie, who had admitted her love for the man Alex had always called uncle and married him. It was a wonder none of it had pushed him over the edge.

"Your mother and I wanted to give you something."

He stopped walking and turned to Alex.

"We know it's been a lot, especially the change in our relationship. We don't want you to think any of this means you have to give up memories of your father or see him any different. Sam was a good guy, a friend, and your mother loved him."

It hurt Mark to say the words, knowing she had, knowing he'd been the one to push her into Sam's arms to maintain the lie that they were cousins. Watching as she'd taken her vows with him, then spent her wedding night in his arms and not Mark's; it had killed him.

He'd lashed out, taking three women back to his room that night, hoping that they could erase her face and the pain. He'd drunken his way through it as they'd fed his need until he'd taken them so many times they'd left him, too exhausted to give him anymore. It had not, however, satisfied his need. None of the women he'd slept with had. No matter how good they were in bed, or how good they were with their mouths, no one had come close to her.

"Mark?" Alex broke through his thoughts, bringing him back.

"Sorry, lost in memory."

"You don't have to—"

"Yes, I do. Here." He slipped the ring from his pocket.

"Are you proposing to me now, too?" Alex joked.

"Funny. No, your mother and I had this made. You're a prince now. You should have something to show it."

"Prince? It sounds so weird. Plus, I'm not really a prince. I can't ever rule."

His mixed bloodline and full mage status ensured he would never rule. Only a Mage Warrior born of the royal line with an Elite parent could rule Kantenda. It was the decree established long before the land had been ravaged by Theodore's ancestor.

"No, but that doesn't make you any less. You're still a prince." He placed the ring in Alex's hand. "Your mother had a strange habit of carrying your father's wedding ring and college ring around. Don't ask me why—"

"It helped her keep her mind from you," Alex said.

"What?"

"Any time you were with us, she would play with one of them. Didn't you ever notice? It was like her way of reminding her that she couldn't act on her thoughts."

Mark stared at him, realizing he was right. Her habit had

always bothered him before, but seeing it from Alex's perspective made it all right.

"She always loved you, Mark. Everyone knew it." He looked down at the ring. "Even Dad. But he loved her anyway and I know she loved him, just not fully or the same way as she does you."

He put the ring on, the emerald in it sparkling in the sun. "Dad's birthstone. Emerald always seemed girly to me."

"Yeah, same here, but it looks good on you."

"Don't lie. I look like a dork with a big clunky ring that makes me look more of a geek than I already was. Thankfully, in these robes, we all look like nerds."

Mark laughed. "Well, let's get you out of that nerdy robe and into the barracks for a little training."

"Any chance I'll look like you when we're done?"

"Is that what your girlfriend likes, or do you think she prefers the nerd in you?"

"She's not my girlfriend and hey, you just called me a nerd!"

"Just repeating your words and yes, she is your girlfriend. You don't kiss a friend like that."

Alex blushed, Mark teasing him the rest of the way, the two relaxing into the relationship they'd always had before their world had changed forever.

SKYE

The next morning, Skye and Mark started their journey to the Eltander Kingdom. Eltander bordered Kantenda, Skye's kingdom, but she and Mark had yet to visit. Their king, Mechon, had sent an entourage to them bearing gifts in a show of peace when Kantenda had been resettled and reunited with the Fettered Forests. He had invited them to visit, and they'd accepted, planning their stay after the wedding as a honeymoon of sorts.

Eltander had been an ally to Kantenda before its fall, but they had stayed out of disputes, standing aside when Theodore's ancestor had attacked. By closing themselves off behind their walls, they made it clear they were unwilling to aid their allies to the north.

That history made Skye and Mark hesitant, but Mark's uncle, Petrian, had explained that this was in the nature of the Eltander. They weren't fighters and confrontation would have only brought about their demise as well. Their kingdom had also claimed Kantenda when it fell, keeping it safe until Skye took the claim back, Eltander yielding easily to her request for the land. They had been waiting for the heir to the kingdom to return.

It was a three-day journey to Eltander. They camped each

night, and Skye cursed the fact that she and Mark had no privacy. She missed his touch and had grown accustomed to the pleasure it brought. Noah, Alex, Petrian, and several Elite had accompanied them. Alex had begged to see the reclusive Eltander. No one had been invited to the kingdom since Theodore's ancestors had turned on Skye's so she'd acquiesced. Now that their plans had been changed by Crimson's summons, Alex would take Skye and Mark's place, staying to tour the kingdom with Petrian and one other Elite to guard him while Skye, Mark, and the others accompanied Mechon to Apendia.

Skye squinted at the massive wall that had been growing larger in the distance.

"What is that?" she asked wearily. They'd been riding three days and her legs felt like she'd been having rough sex for days on end.

"That is the gates of Eltander," Petrian answered.

"Gates? That's a wall, the highest wall I've ever seen," she said.

"I'd heard tales, but nothing that came close to describing this," Mark said, just as awestruck as she.

"It is an awe-inspiring sight. There is nothing else like it in our world."

"They don't want company, do they?" she asked.

"Not the uninvited kind. They do not have the same level of magic as we do. They are not Mage Warriors, or even full mages."

"But they have magic?" She was curious, knowing Mage Warriors had been granted to Eltander when her kingdom had been taken.

"Yes, it is tied to nature, however, and not to physical objects, as with our people," Petrian answered.

"Oh, that's right, they're like elves," she commented, thinking of Alex's favorite movie, *Lord of the Rings*.

"No, Mom," Alex said, as if reading her mind. "We studied them. They have a plant-based magic, like a spirituality to it, rather than forceful power."

"Huh." She imagined people who grew flowers and tended gardens, thinking it no wonder they'd erected such a massive gate.

They rode on until they drew closer to the entryway. Guards were stationed all along the outside of the gates and above the top of the wall, their bows drawn, aimed and ready to kill the intruders below if necessary.

"Who approaches the Kingdom of Eltander and seeks entry?" one of the guards said, stepping forward.

As surreal as everything in Skye's life had become, this was another of those moments. The guard wore a suit of black armor, as did the others. It wasn't quite metal but a strange leather-like material that appeared to be very thick. His bright green eyes shone below the visor, tips of black hair hanging below his helmet. He wore a cape of rich black that almost blended into the armor.

"We have come to see King Mechon. We are from the Kingdom of Kantenda to your north. Queen Skye and King Mark are expected," Petrian announced as the designated speaker for the group. Mark and Noah stood guard near Skye and Alex in case they were no longer welcome for some unseen reason.

The guard removed his helmet, freeing his lush locks, his eyes studying Skye. He was handsome in a pretty way, not the rugged type Skye preferred, but he was nothing to turn her eyes from. She held his gaze, knowing he was evaluating the new queen they'd surely all heard of by now.

Mark, clearly a little irritated by the long stare, cleared his throat. "May we be granted passage through your gates?"

The man turned his eyes to Mark, observing him in the same intense way. As he turned, Skye noticed the slight point to his ears. She had to resist grabbing Alex and pointing. An elf! A real elf, just like in books. She stared in disbelief, trying to hide her excitement.

"I am Taron, captain of the king's guard. Word of your deeds and your history has spread quickly to these parts. King Mechon is eager to meet you. Come."

He turned and signaled for the gates to be opened. Skye looked over at Alex.

"Elf," he mouthed, a glint in his eyes.

She smiled, then turned back to watch the enormous gates as they creaked open to allow them entry. They followed Taron through. Skye's eyes were wide as she took in the glorious kingdom. A path led along the edge of the wall, lining a vast meadow of flowers with vibrant colors throughout. What looked like white butterflies flitted among them.

As they rounded the field, she spotted the city, but one that looked like nothing she'd seen before. Quaint houses built into vast tree trunks, stood throughout. The trees provided shelter above and within as in the Fettered Forest, their dwellings built within the tree limbs themselves, with wooden paths between. As they left the grove of trees, the houses changed to small shelters made wherever the land would allow. Some within the crest of a hill, some along the shelter of a brook, the material of the houses as if they had been created from clay. And in the center of it all stood a castle, its walls of wood from the trees that seemed to grow into it, and other materials of white that shone brightly in the afternoon sun.

The castle spread upward and out, a small town of its own in its size. She wasn't certain if it was more of a palace than a castle, unsure what the difference was between the two terms, but as they stepped through the doors to the open expanse of the building, she decided that palace was the right word. This was distinctly different from her castle. The great hall was wide and opened out to a view of a lake shimmering in the sunlight, with what looked like lily pads floating in its depths. To the far left, she could see that a short waterfall dropped to it where the land curved up a bit to form a hill. Upon further inspection, she realized it wasn't a lake at all but a river that flowed off to the distance, snaking through open land.

"Wow," she mumbled.

"Breathtaking, isn't it?" Skye heard from behind her.

She turned at the voice, her eyes meeting a piercing blue pair of eyes set upon a soft, friendly face.

"I am King Mechon, and you must be the new queen of Kantenda, Skye. The blue of your eyes distinctly marks you as the ancestor of the Mage King's line."

She couldn't stop staring at the beautiful man before her. His black hair hung shaggy, leaving the short tips of his ears poking through. He had a shade of growth on his face, distinguishing the sharp jawline and the high cheekbones. He was tall like Mark, but where Mark was broad and muscular, this king was thin. She wouldn't have used the word lanky, for the muscles defining his arms led her to believe there were abs lining his thin stomach.

"Her blue eyes are unique," Mark said, with a slight edge to his voice, pulling her from her trance.

"Their color rivals no other," Mechon said. "It has always been said we would recognize the heir to the Kantenda throne by her eyes and I would agree my ancestors were right. You can only be her husband then."

Mark nodded and introduced himself, then the others of their group.

A thin graceful woman with the same coal black hair and striking eyes of golden brown approached them, wrapping her arms through the king's.

"And this is my wife, Revina."

Finally awake from the strange enchantment she'd fallen under, Skye greeted the beautiful woman, trying not to look away from the eyes that seemed to see into her soul.

"You must be tired from your journey. Rest, clean up, and join us for dinner. Then we shall talk. You'll find fresh water in your rooms to clean the ride from you."

He called a servant, who then led them down several halls, all with the same airy, open feel, only light curtains separating them from the outside world.

She and Mark were led to a room at the end of a long hallway. Skye walked into it, drawn to the open balcony, finding they were up on what looked like the second floor, although she remembered no stairs. The view looked out to the river, and she could see down to an open terrace, several long, cushioned chairs upon it.

"This place is like something from a book or a movie," she said, turning to Mark.

He crossed his arms as he eyed her. "Entranced with the king a bit, Skye?"

She laughed and brushed the comment off, spying a luxurious bath with flowers drifting in the water. It was massive and sat in another space that led to the outside.

"Don't tell me you're jealous," she said, pulling her boots off. She caught his eye as she lifted her shirt over her head.

"Damn, that's not fair. First you flirt with the king, then you strip in front of me to take my mind from it."

She finished removing her clothes and sauntered over to him. "I was not flirting."

She began unbuttoning his pants, pulling his shirt from him. Desire flared in his eyes, and he brought her against him, kissing her hungrily.

"Then what was that?" he asked between kisses, his hands bringing her closer to the length that had grown. She pushed his pants down, her fingers running along it playfully, eliciting a grunt from him.

"I'm allowed to look at a handsome man."

"Then I can eye his wife with no qualms."

She drew back to glare at him.

"Mmm, I see how it is. Don't worry, she's not my type—too thin, and not enough meat on her." He squeezed her breast, his fingers grazing her nipple as he said it. "Besides, neither of us could help being attracted to them."

"Why?" she asked, bending her neck back as his lips brushed it before finding her other breast and taking it in his mouth.

"I'll tell you later," he said, nibbling on her, then kissing her. "Now I'm going to take you here and in that inviting tub, before I thoroughly ravage you in that bed."

She shoved his pants down, both of them working to remove them until he was free of them. Once nothing was between them, he moved her close, his fingers grazing between her legs to feel her, and no doubt finding she was ready for him. The groan he let loose confirmed his discovery and it coaxed a flurry of flutters deep within her.

His fingers slid into her, and she tipped her head back with a sigh. They curved, hitting the spot that always sent her climax mounting. She let out a small cry which his mouth quickly covered. His kiss was sensual and sent more warmth flushing through her body. Lifting her, he carried her to a desk-like table in the corner. Whatever had been on it crashed to the floor, but she paid it no heed. She was lost to his touch, the world disappearing from existence as it always did with him. She clung to him, sighing as he penetrated her, and wrapping her legs tighter around him, forced him deeper with each thrust. She'd missed the closeness, the ecstasy of his touch and her need built quickly. The feeling must have been mutual, for there was a desperation to his moves. As she bit back the cry that threatened to explode from her, she felt him grow with his oncoming climax. Laying back, she brought his hands to her breasts, wanting to join him in his release. It had been days since they'd had sex. They'd only been able to sneak in small amounts of play beneath their blankets. The acts had kept them both sated, but she'd missed the feel of him inside her.

He smiled as a delicious laugh left his mouth, the sound only encouraging her arousal.

"Do you want me to play, Skye?" he asked, that smile turning to a devilish grin that made her body buck.

"God, yes."

Pushing her hands away, he pinched and tugged at her nipples, causing a flutter in her belly. Slowing his rhythm, he paced himself before bringing his other hand down to play with her clit, rubbing it gently as he continued to thrust. A deluge of sensation assailed her, her need to break, to fall apart against him growing until he grabbed her hips and came; the shudders bringing her to climax. It flooded through her in currents so that all she could do was let it take her to oblivion.

She lay there, her hair spread behind her and falling in waves from the side of the desk as her breaths slowly calmed. He urged her up, his hands sliding under her hair, fingers weaving through it. There was passion in his eyes, and the overwhelming love he had for her shone clearly. Gently, she traced his face, memorizing it as she did each time, before kissing him again.

As promised, he carried her to the tub where they made love and once they'd washed off the remains of the road, he took her on the bed. There they lay as the sun set, their bodies coiled around each other.

"Let's never leave a single day without having sex," she said. "I think it should be a standing rule, no matter where we are."

"And how do you suppose we manage that on our trip tomorrow?"

She peered up at him and he brushed a hair from her eye.

"Well, we make love in the morning before we leave. Then, while we travel, we sneak off each night and find a patch of trees or maybe a tall stand of grass."

He laughed, kissing her head. "We'll see what we can find. I have no doubt you'll find some way. You can be quite determined when you want something. I will say making you climax below the blankets while the others slept was quite a turn on."

"And my head slipping below said blankets to taste you wasn't?"

"Oh, I never said that."

Her hand brushed his chest, finding his softening manhood and wrapped around it.

"You are insatiable," he said as it responded to her touch.

"We know that, but you don't seem to be complaining."

"Good God, what man would? Is this your way of ensuring I don't look at Mechon's wife again?"

"You can look, but no touching."

"Yeah, right, with your jealous streak, there's not even any looking."

She let go of him and studied him.

"You didn't have to stop."

"I'm not jealous."

He kissed her nose. "Your denial is cute. But I pity the woman who dares try to seduce me."

Her eyes grew darker.

"See, there it is."

"I am not a jealous person. Shit, I put up with you sleeping your way through our youth, Mark. And don't try telling me it wasn't many."

"I never denied that it wasn't. I like sex, Skye, and as much as I would have preferred it with you, you weren't available. There were others who were, but there were never any I loved. You know that."

She calmed. "I know, sorry. I guess I do get a little jealous."

"A little?" he asked with a raise of his brow.

She hated to admit it. She'd never been a jealous person. The women he'd slept with had irked her. She'd been angry that she couldn't be one. The one. And there had been many, but she supposed he'd only been finding an outlet for his desire for her. At least, that's what she told herself. It did stir her ire to even think of him doing the same things to another woman or to think of any of them touching what now belonged to her. But he hadn't belonged to her then.

"Skye? I'm not sure what's going through your mind, but it's getting a bit scary in here."

She focused and looked around. Lost in her thoughts, she'd bled the light hues from everything in the room, turning it as dark as the sky now was. Colors swirled around them.

She closed her eyes, calming her mind and setting the jealousy aside before guiding the colors back gently.

"That's better."

She opened her eyes again.

"Maybe it's best we not talk about the past," he suggested.

"Avoiding it doesn't make it go away."

"But dwelling on it does this. Skye, I love you. I always have, and no one has ever done the things to me and my heart that you do. Your touch is the torch to my soul. I could sleep with a hundred women and none of them could bring me to ecstasy the way you do."

"A hundred? As much as it pains me to say, I guarantee it's been more than that. You were quite the player."

A coy smile formed, one she loved.

"I will neither deny nor confirm for fear of my life."

She laughed and gave him a kiss. "So, tell me why you said we have no control over being attracted to the obscenely pretty couple that rules this kingdom?"

"Because we don't. It's some strange power they hold. They rarely use it, but there's been suspicions that's how they've remained untouched by the other kingdoms. They have an uncanny power of persuasion. The myth says it came from the Death God and that's why they all have black hair."

"What?" she asked, her curiosity piqued. "The Death God didn't have black hair." She distinctly remembered his mortal form and being surprised that his hair had been blonde.

"No, but the gift he gave them darkened their hair with the magic of the shadows."

"Why would he gift them anything? He's the Death God?"

"Legend says when the kingdoms were young, Eltander was seen as weak. Our kingdom had magic, as did Digremile. The others had force, but there's only minimal control over living things. If you ask me, controlling the land seems pretty powerful, a weapon in itself, but they were a peaceful people who would never think to use it as a weapon."

He paused, and she rested her chin on his chest, hearing the rumble of his voice as he started speaking again.

"One of their kings feared they would succumb to the other kingdoms, so he made a deal with the Death God."

"Who would do such a thing?"

"Men in fear or greedy men. There are rumors Crimson's father made a deal with him as well, and then there's Digremile whose demise during the mage wars has always been seen as retribution for breaking a deal with the Death God."

"Why does the Death God have his hand in so many mortal places?"

"I don't know, a lot of it is rumor. No one knows if any of it is more than just storytelling. Although given Crimson's reputation, that rumor might hold truth."

She narrowed her eyes at the mention of the woman she despised.

"Calm down. Anyway, whatever he traded, the Death God gave the king of Eltander and his people this power of persuasion —seduction, some might say. The day it happened, the white of their hair turned ebony."

She looked up at him. "That sounds crazy, right?"

"Crazy is a relative term around here."

"Huh, so either of them could persuade us into their bed?"

"Theoretically, but I've never heard of that happening."

"Strange."

"It is."

"You know they look like elves, right?"

He shook his head and gave her a questionable look.

"They do! Did you see the ears?"

"Really? You're judging them on their ears?"

"Mark, I'm serious. You said there were no elves, and they are elves."

"Quell your excitement, Skye. They're not elves even if they have pointed ears—"

"And a connection to nature?"

"You watch too many fantasy movies. Now it's grown dark, we should get down to dinner. It would be rude to be late."

Sighing, she let it go, deciding she could call them elves if she wanted to. She kissed his chest, then slid her hand back down, and with every intention of tormenting him, grasped him until he turned firm again.

"You are relentless."

"And you respond each time."

"Who would resist?"

She continued to stroke him, reveling in the way he reacted to her touch, the control she had over him. Her own desire rose as he drew her in for a kiss, his hands touching her curves in ways that titillated her. Where she should have been satisfied, her body had come alive again, his touch like a spark that woke her to the depths of her soul.

Her lips brushed his ear and she whispered, "I think we're going to be late."

As his breath quickened, her own need for release rose. His touches were so stimulating that she could barely complete her movements along his length.

"You're a tease, Skye," he said as he slipped his fingers into her wetness. "But I can tease, too."

The moan she emitted caused his length to jerk in her hand. She couldn't move, each swipe of his finger across her clit brought her closer until her body was screaming. There was no explanation for how she came undone with him, nor to how often it happened. She had a constant craving for his touch and each time he provided it, she broke.

He drew away, pushing her hand aside and gripping her wrists. His body pressed against hers, his length settled just against her waiting arousal. The way his eyes looked into hers caused her growing need to surge. They were intense, the hazel ablaze with lust as he smashed his mouth on hers. She met his intensity, the fire he'd stoked in her sat on the cusp of igniting an inferno. He dropped her wrist and grabbed her ass, tilting her pelvis. His kisses never stopped as he plunged into her. Skye's desire peaked until she could take no more and it spilled over her in waves that drowned her. She could do no more than grasp firmly to him as it toppled her. His motion didn't slow as her cry of ecstasy permeated the room along with the hues her magic had drawn. He continued to move inside her, his moves harder and faster until another climax hit her. He joined her, both releasing together in one frenzied movement.

When she could breathe properly again, she met his lips, feeling the smile on them.

"You are amazing," he said.

"I know," she replied.

With a chuckle, he drew back and looked at her, his eyes reflecting something she couldn't place. "What?"

"I love you, Skye. Never forget that, no matter how your jealousy wants to warp your thoughts."

"I'll try not to."

He cocked a brow. "Try?"

"Try," she teased, rising from the bed.

His eyes followed her as she pulled a light dress from her bag. He laid there, hands behind his head, and watched as she cleaned up and dressed.

"Are you going to lie there tempting me with your manhood the rest of the night or get dressed so we can eat?"

"I could come back with a plucky comment about eating, but I'll refrain," he joked, rising. "I'll gladly continue to tempt you with my manhood, as you so primly called it, if that's an option."

He rose and took her in his arms, nuzzling her neck.

"Put your dick away, darling, or I will be having it for dinner instead of what's waiting downstairs. Is that better?"

His laughter filled the room. "That's more like the woman I love."

He kissed her before they dressed, her eyes watching him this time, wondering if it would be better just to stay in the room and make love the rest of the night instead of being forced to socialize with the persuasive couple who ruled this kingdom.

The latter option won out, and they joined the king and his wife, Revina, for dinner. Food was set out in a dining room along the riverside. The marble flooring extended far out from the palace walls to make a patio of sorts.

They ate a feast fit for a king and his royal guests, Skye delighting in delicacies that could only be found in the kingdom. The table was full of lush, vegetable dishes, paired with thin meat that Mechon explained came from a deer-like animal found in the far western region of the kingdom. It was delicious and seemed to melt in her mouth with each bite.

As trays of brightly colored fruit were brought to the table, Mechon leaned back and eyed Skye.

"So, you are braving a meeting with Theodore and Crimson? As I was told by my emissary, the last meeting did not go so well."

"That is an understatement," she responded. She'd stormed out that day, dragging Mark with her, tired of Crimson's not-so-subtle comments and glances at Mark. The last straw came when she feigned losing her balance behind him, draping her breasts across his back, while her hand landed around his waist and directly on his crotch. Skye had been past boiling by that point, and all talk of the kingdoms and negotiations had stopped with the action.

Mark had brushed it off, but Skye knew what it was. Crimson wanted him, and Skye knew her type, the type who would stop at nothing to get what she felt she had every right to take.

Mechon's wife leaned forward, bringing Skye's attention back, her hand seductively positioned under her chin. "Would you say that is due to the company or the company's apparent desire for your husband?" she asked.

From the gurgling sound Mark made, Skye could tell he was having trouble not spitting his drink out. Although Skye tried to ignore the awkward movements of Alex and Petrian, Noah's large grin was hard to avoid.

Leaning her elbows on the table, she replied, "Both, but particularly the latter."

Mechon let out a loud laugh.

"There is a reason we do not attend gatherings with the red-headed seductress," Revina said. "I do not mind sharing my husband, but I refuse to share with her."

Skye wasn't certain what to say.

"Do you share your husband often?" Noah asked, the curiosity in his voice surprising Skye.

"Of course, and he shares me. Do you not?"

Alex looked extremely uncomfortable.

"It's not a norm in our culture but it has been known to be done," Mark said to her relief.

"Ah, you seem as one who has shared," Revina said.

God, how Skye wanted this conversation to end, dreading the answer. Knowing what it was. Wishing she'd spent more time experimenting when she was young, so she'd have more stories to make Mark jealous. She certainly wasn't innocent, but she didn't have his colorful past.

Mark glanced at her as if to ask whether he should answer.

She sighed. "My husband and I had separate lives up until recently, but sharing is definitely not something we do now."

He raised his brow, slyly replying, "But it could be." She elbowed him. "If my wife didn't have a jealous streak that makes doing so extremely dangerous," he quickly added.

"There is so much wrong with this conversation," Alex said. "If you'll excuse me, I believe I'll be turning in."

"As will I," said Petrian with a wink. "Noah you should turn in, as you have an early journey tomorrow."

"As do we," Skye added.

"Please stay, Skye. I did not mean to offend," Revina said as the others rose.

"Noah, we'll follow shortly and see you in the morning," she said reluctantly. "Alex—"

"I know, best behavior."

She smiled and blew him a kiss, nodding to Petrian then, who bid them all in good night.

"Your son is a man, is he not?" Mechon asked after they'd left.

Skye laughed, relaxing some. "I suppose in this world, but where he was raised, he's still like an older child."

"And he acts as if he is," Mark added.

"It seems to me that he's old enough to partake in the ways of flesh," Revina said.

The horror must have shown on Skye's face, for Mechon said, "But of course, not in the ways a true man would."

"I don't think talk of Alex sharing bedmates is something Skye wants to even imagine."

No, it wasn't.

"Then what of you sharing bedmates? You seem too much of a man to find only one woman enough to meet your needs."

Good God. She wanted this conversation to end quickly. How had they returned to it? She was at a loss for words. She felt Mark's eyes on her.

"I think my wife is enough to meet all my needs," he said, taking her hand and squeezing it. "It might be best to change the subject, however."

Revina studied her. "I am sorry for upsetting you. I meant no offense."

Finally finding her voice, Skye replied, "It's fine. I'm a little sensitive about Mark's past."

"Ah, but it is our past experiences that make our present selves so knowledgeable, so prone to bring and receive pleasure."

"That's what I keep telling her." He put his arm around her, pulling her chair a little closer, and she relaxed. "But it's still not something we discuss often. I wouldn't tempt a Mage Warrior's jealous streak. It can be painful."

Revina leaned back and let out a hearty laugh. "Ah, so this meeting with Crimson should be an interesting one."

"You could say that," Skye muttered.

Mechon leaned forward. "We do not trust Crimson. Nor do I trust Theodore, but I particularly do not trust her."

The change in conversation was abrupt, but she was thankful for it.

"She isn't a very trustworthy person, and she does nothing that is not for her benefit," Mark said.

"Precisely. Which makes us curious as to why she has summoned a gathering of the kingdom's royalty."

"Why are you going then?" Skye asked, her own concern growing.

"We do not want to risk war with her. She shares her bed with Theodore on occasion, and that alliance makes her a greater threat."

"It's true. She has Theodore wrapped around her finger."

"Ruled by her seduction," Revina said.

"Which is why Revina will remain behind and we suggest one of you remain as well. Your kingdom is young, you are at risk, unproven—"

"I fought the Death God—"

"You tricked the Death God," Mechon corrected.

"The Elite can handle any enemy," Mark argued.

"Without your queen?"

Mark remained quiet, Mechon's words silencing him.

"Do you think my life is in danger?" she asked, all thoughts of the prior conversation fleeing with the seriousness of Mechon's tone.

"Your life will always be in danger, my dear. You are a queen, you are a Mage Warrior, the most coveted being in this world. You have what Crimson and Theodore crave—what Theodore had, and you stole from him. There is nothing more precious than a Mage Warrior, unless she is a royal Mage Warrior."

MARK

Mark remained quiet as they walked back to their room, Mechon's words repeating through his mind. The other realms coveted Skye. Why hadn't he seen that? She was a Mage Warrior, pure power, and whoever owned her possessed that power. Would there ever be a time she wasn't in danger?

He watched as she walked out onto the balcony; the moonlight shining on her silhouette.

"I won't go without you, Mark," she said as she stared out at the sky.

He came behind her and wrapped his arms around her waist. "I wasn't planning to send you without me."

"Do you think Mechon is right?"

"I wouldn't doubt his words. He may sit in a reclusive kingdom whose walls keep the world out, but he has his spies everywhere. His army is well trained, slipping in and out of the shadows where you'd least expect them."

He dropped his chin against the curve of her neck, smelling the sweet scent of her skin.

"We don't have to go, Skye. I told you that before. We can stay here, as we had planned, and tour the kingdom."

She was quiet, contemplating his offer, part of him hoping she would take it, knowing if she didn't, they would be riding into danger the next morning. Mechon was right, Skye was coveted. She was the last Mage Warrior, a power Crimson or Theodore would pay a hefty price to own, even if it meant war.

Could they take her, though? Neither had magic. She could crush both of them within seconds. Unless they had leverage. Fueled by her power, his connection to her, they were no threat to Mark. Alex was the only vulnerability, and he would be here, hidden safely behind the walls of Eltander.

As if she'd thought the same, she squeezed his hand.

"We go. There's no way either of them can touch me and I will bleed Crimson dry if she dares touch you."

He had no doubt she would, and the fierceness of her threat sparked his desire.

Kissing her neck, he said, "Then it's settled. We leave in the morning with the others."

"Mark," she whispered.

"Mmm-hmm?" he responded, moving her hair back and trailing the back of her neck with kisses.

"Look."

He brought his face up and looked to where her eyes were drawn. "I'll be damned. I guess they weren't lying."

"That's not Revina, neither of them is."

On the terrace where they'd previously had dinner, Mechon had emerged. Two women with long black hair were removing his clothes as he kissed and pawed at their naked bodies. He sat back in his chair as one dropped to her knees and began sucking on him. His head fell back, his hands drawing the other woman closer so that she sat on the side of the chair. Mark watched as Mechon took her breast in his mouth, unable to tear his eyes from the action below.

"Jesus," Mark muttered, his erection prominent against Skye's back.

"Well, you clearly like the view," she said. "Although it's apparently not one you're unfamiliar with."

And there it was, that jealousy she couldn't contain. When would she realize the past was the past? Did knowing he had loved her through every sexual encounter he'd had make it worse for her? Perhaps she felt he should have remained chaste, devoted only to her as she fucked her husband each night. The hypocrisy of it was irritating, but he saw her point about Sam being one man versus the many women he'd taken. She'd had other men before Sam, however, enough to be fantastic in bed. Discovering how far she was from the innocent woman he'd imagined she was, had surprised him. He'd never imagined she knew every way to bend him to her will, to bring him to his knees in bed. He didn't know how many men she'd slept with before Sam, but it still couldn't compare to the number of women he'd had. She was right, he'd had his fill, too many to count.

"What do you want me to say, Skye?" he asked, his hardness diminishing. "That there were several times in my life when I took more than one woman home? That there were even times when there were three?"

"Three?" Her eyes were wide as she looked around at him.

"Dammit, Skye. It doesn't matter."

"But you enjoyed it."

He couldn't help but laugh. "You show me any straight man who wouldn't enjoy having sex with multiple women at one time."

She dropped her head to his shoulder.

"I'm a man, Skye, one with needs that are now met only by you. We both have that past. Sam brought you to climax as many times as I did to the whole of the women I slept with. If it couldn't be you, I found others. But I never loved them."

"I know. I don't know why it bothers me so much now."

"It's your magic—something about it makes you very possessive of your mate. You know, I'm standing here watching a man screw two women, a voyeuristic moment that should really be a huge turn on...and there he goes. He's flipped her. You're killing me, Skye."

She laughed. "Sorry. Look, it's Revina. Oh, and she dropped her robe. Wow and holy cow."

His eyes skimmed Revina's nude body, taking in her pert and small breasts, the confidence in her stride enhancing her attractiveness. She grabbed the hair of the second woman, whose hands had been all over her husband. For a moment, Mark thought she'd punch the woman, but she tipped her head and kissed her instead, rubbing her breasts against hers. Mark's felt his length rising again, the sight too erotic to turn from.

"We should stop watching," said Skye, her voice raspy. "Good God."

Mechon pulled out and came on the woman, a stream of him coating her mouth and breasts.

"I don't think we need to," Mark replied as he moved his hand to Skye's breast, feeling the hardness of her nipple beneath the material of her dress.

She was as aroused by the sight as he was, and the thought was enough to drive him crazy. Bringing his other hand up, he pulled the sleeve of her dress down, exposing her breasts. The catch of her breath as he caressed them made his length jerk in response.

Below them Mechon's wife licked the woman's face and body clean, her tongue dancing with the other woman's before reaching her husband, taking him in her mouth until he was hard again.

A low sigh came from Skye as she leaned back against him. Her hand reached to encompass him, tugging gently above his pants. The action almost broke him, and he couldn't help the groan it caused. There was an ache in him to be wedged deep between her legs, feeling her warmth as she climaxed around him.

"I want you, Skye," he mumbled right before he ripped the bindings of her dress.

Below them Mechon was seated with Revina astride him, her rhythm slow and steady as the one woman kissed and fondled her.

He was licking the other woman's breasts as she smothered him with them. Mark was so hard he thought he might burst from his pants. Skye's fingers undid his buttons, freeing the intense firmness as he squeezed her breasts. He reveled in the hardness of her nipples before he slid his hand down her body and slipped it between her legs. Wetness greeted him, dripping from her arousal. The feel of it accompanied with the view was too much for his body to take, and he shoved her over. Bringing his hand to his mouth, he licked the sweetness of her from his fingers, groaning with the flurry of excitement that shivered through him at the taste. Grabbing her hips, he plunged into her.

Her name fell from his lips as he brought her body against him in rough thrusts. The moan she emitted caused him to grasp her hips tighter. He couldn't slow himself as the scene continued below them. There was no way he could last long, the view was too erotic and Skye's body too welcoming.

Skye's fingers brushed his shaft as she played with herself, driving him further toward the cliff. He tightened his grip as she pushed and pulled her body, bringing him closer, the wetness within her urging him on. She clenched as she brought herself to climax and it took him over the edge. He thrust one more time, powerful and hard as she moaned through the quakes of her orgasm, spilling himself into her, his own grunts joining her cries.

The waves continued, spasms of ecstasy that he didn't want to fade until he finally forced himself to relax his hold on her waist and pull himself from her. He backed away, breathless. Slowly, she straightened and turned to him, her blue eyes dark with desire. She wasn't satisfied yet, and he gave her a sly grin, knowing neither would sleep for the next few hours.

She brought her fingers to her lips and licked them. Mark, entranced with the action, continued to step back until his legs hit the bed. Like a hunter cornering her prey, she pushed him down before climbing atop him and kissing him deeply. There was a hunger behind it as if she were claiming what was hers, but he'd always been hers no matter who he'd been with. It had been her face he'd imagined, her body moving with his. Just as he knew each time Sam had taken her, she'd really been making love to him, seeing his face, imagining his touch and not Sam's.

He weaved his hands through her hair, matching the ferocity of her lust, knowing there was only one woman he would ever need again. What she did to him surpassed anything he'd ever had from his prior encounters with individual women or even multiple women. No one turned him on like Skye did; no one made his body ache like she did; no one brought him to ecstasy like she did, and never as many times as she did. She was and always had been the only one for him.

SKYE

They set out the next morning, saying their goodbyes to Alex and Petrian, then to Revina. Skye had a difficult time looking at Revina without visions of the prior night. She wondered if the activity was a regular occurrence, then wondered if they'd been out there with a purpose, wanting to be seen. There was a glint in Revina's eyes as she bid Skye farewell, as if knowing her evening had inspired an intense night of sex for herself and Mark.

She mounted her horse, and Mark gave her a wink, a mischievous smile on his face. God, how she loved that smile. It was the same smile he'd given her when they'd been kids, only now it sent more than butterflies through her. They set off, Mechon's guards flanking them, two Elite in front and two in the rear, Noah riding in front, all of them at the ready.

The journey would be threefold what it had been to Mechon's kingdom. Crimson's kingdom, Apendia, lying to the far south, bordering only Theodore's kingdom. They rode at a hard pace, stopping each evening to rest themselves and the horses. Skye and Mark snuck away as the others slept each night, finding any bit of privacy they could to get their fill of one another. Her favorite had been as they'd crossed a small mountain range, just outside of Mechon's border They'd found a spot where the moon shone through the forest, reminding her of the Fettered Forests where the wizards lived. Mark had taken her against a boulder, the moonlight spilling across her as he made love to her. They'd laid on the massive boulder afterward, staring at the sky and talking before giving into their need again, ignoring the hard surface below, lost to each other's touch.

They fell asleep there, waking only when Noah's shouts woke them. Hastily, they'd dressed and found him, giggling the entire time before they'd met Noah's disapproving look and received a scolding on how they needed to remember their age and responsibilities instead of acting like children.

The lecture hadn't worked, and they'd snuck away each subsequent night. This time, careful to be back in camp before dawn.

On the seventh day, they reached Crimson's kingdom, traveling over the border with ease. It was then that they stopped sneaking off, more alert to the dangers that awaited them.

Crimson's kingdom was not what Skye had expected, although she wasn't certain what she'd expected. Apendia was the largest of the lands now that Theodore had been stripped of the Fettered Forests—Skye's kingdom being the only one even close to its size with the forests included. Crimson had claimed the fallen Kingdom of Digremile as her own during the war with Camin, ignoring the arguments of Theodore and Mechon. The combined territory eclipsed the other kingdoms, giving her an advantage in trade with Digremile's richness in textiles and fertile land.

Crimson's own land had been unfavorable to her and her father before her, and Skye could see why. The air was heavy and clung to Skye's skin, the sky growing dimmer the further they rode. It was as if they'd ridden under a cloud of shadow when they'd crossed into it. The shadow spanned far to the distance until it broke, and the sun returned over a piece of open land. She couldn't help the chill that settled across her skin.

"The Kingdom of Apendia is said to be a cursed one, a

shadow falling upon every mile of it, the sun never crossing its border," Mark said. "It's been that way since I was a child."

"Since Crimson's birth," Mechon added. "This shadow fell the day she breathed her first breath."

"Well, if that doesn't speak volumes about her," Skye mumbled before asking, "Why is it sunny in the distance?"

"That's where Digremile lies. The shadow only flows to her border."

"Even though she claimed the land?"

"Correct." Mechon nodded. "I like to think it's a sign that the gods don't even recognize her claim."

He spurred his horse forward to ride with Noah, leaving her alone with Mark.

"We can turn back, Skye. There's still time," said Mark.

"No, didn't you say no one but Theodore has been in her realm for decades? I think it's time to see what the fuss is about."

"And what if we don't like what we find?"

"Well, I guess we're screwed, and I'll be forced to flex my powers. I think it's about time Crimson knows who she's dealing with."

"Now that is something I'd like to see," he joked.

She raised her brow.

"Oh, come on, Skye. A cat fight between you and Crimson ripping each other's hair and clothes—" He must have caught her irritated expression, and added, "And of course, watching you smother her with your power."

"Of course," she seethed. "Besides, there wouldn't be time for you to see her ripped bodice or exposed breasts because she'd be down before I even touched her."

"Hey, I never said it was her bodice that was ripped."

She rolled her eyes and focused them back on the shadowed land before her, finding an eerie similarity to the Shadow Realm.

∽

At dusk the next day, they approached Crimson's castle. They'd ridden through town after town where windows were closed, doors shut, as if to keep something away. In the back of her mind, Skye questioned if it was Crimson they feared or whatever lie in the shadows she'd invited into their kingdom.

As they rode through the massive iron gates, the gray castle with its red banners now closer, Skye's hackles raised. This was wrong. She'd made the wrong decision but there was no going back. Her instinct screamed for her to run, but just as with any female in a seventies slasher film, she kept moving toward the threat.

They handed the horses to a few men in uniform while another younger man collected their bags. *Where are the woman?* she wondered as they ascended the last stair and walked through the castle entryway. The further they walked, the greater her urge to flee rose.

Mark took her hand as if feeling the same way.

"This is quaint," Noah commented, taking in the dark décor that reminded Skye of a gothic period. She half expected a vampire to come at them and couldn't help her amusement when Crimson appeared from a separate hallway.

"You're here!" Her red hair billowed around the breasts that overflowed her gown.

"As are your breasts," Skye muttered, hearing Mark's snicker at her remark.

Crimson ignored her and Skye's hatred grew tenfold as she took in Apendia's queen. Crimson seemed to have gained more beauty from the last time she'd seen her. Her thick red hair cascaded down her back in waves, emphasizing her green eyes— the kind they wrote ballads about. She was curvy in all the right places, with hips that swished, and breasts that made Skye's C-cups feel vastly inadequate. Everything about her was vibrant and bold, seductive.

"Mechon." She greeted the king with a kiss, to which he

turned his cheek since she'd been so bold as to try for his lips. "Still denying me the pleasure you give other women?"

"My wife would not be happy."

"She's happy to share you with others, just not me? Afraid I might steal you away?" she teased.

"Unlikely," he replied, and Skye could feel the dislike in his words.

"Markhem," Crimson said before moving toward Mark with hungry eyes.

Skye could feel her hold on her magic slipping and clenched her fists to keep it at bay. Knowing Crimson well enough, Skye stepped in front of Mark, blocking her path.

"Crimson," she said with a tight smile, "looking lovely as always."

She had to force the words out.

"Why, Skye, you get prettier every day. Is it the power, or the man in your bed?" Her eyes went to Mark during her last words, her tongue licking her ruby lips.

"Both," she snarled.

"You really must share him with me."

"I don't like to be shared, and my *wife* doesn't like to share."

"Pity. I play well with others."

"It's been a long trip, Crimson. Are we here to banter about how you crave my husband or to discuss realm business?"

"Oh, you are feisty. I like that about you. I have rooms arranged for all of you—"

"We're not staying."

"Nonsense. You've traveled for days. I've had your bags taken to your rooms and baths drawn. Relax, then join me and Theodore for dinner. We will discuss politics in the morning."

Skye bristled, saying, "No, we won't. This is not a casual visit. Let's discuss business and then we'll contemplate leaving in the morning rather than tonight."

"Are you certain you want to do that?" Crimson asked, and

Skye noted the change in her demeanor, the mischievous way she'd said it.

"Certain."

"Fine. Bemin, show our guests to their rooms. Please make yourselves comfortable and we will discuss business over dinner."

They started to follow the servant when Crimson said, "Oh, Skye."

Skye turned as Crimson gestured her over. Huffing, Skye moved back to her.

"I didn't give you a hug hello."

Skye started to protest when Crimson suddenly grabbed her, pulling her in for a hug.

"I will taste him," she whispered against Skye's ear.

Skye shoved her away, but before she could react, Crimson bounced away, her hips moving seductively with each step.

"Skye," Mark said, pulling her sharp stare from Crimson. The hues of the gray stone had begun to heed her call and she pushed them away, knowing as much as she wanted to strangle Crimson she couldn't.

Mechon eyed her with curiosity, then turned back to the hall and continued following the servant. Mark extended his hand, and she took it, glancing back to catch Crimson's envious glare from a doorway. They followed the servant down what appeared to be another wing of the castle and up a grand staircase with black marble steps. Skye, who knew her coordination skills were lacking when it came to smooth surfaces, gripped Mark's hand tighter.

The others were shown their rooms and Mark and Skye were taken to the end of the wing where their guest quarters lay.

As the door closed, Skye turned to Mark, her hands on her hip. "I thought we weren't staying."

"Be realistic, Skye, we've been on the road for days. Were you seriously planning to talk, then turn around and leave?"

"Yes, that was exactly what I planned."

"We're exhausted—"

"I'd rather sleep on those marble stairs than spend a night in her castle." She began looking through the bags that had been brought from the horses.

"Skye—"

"No, Mark. I am not staying here."

He turned her to him and lifted her face so she couldn't avoid his eyes. "Why do you let her get to you?"

"Because she's so blatant about it!"

"Purposely. She knows it rules you."

"Do you know what she whispered to me when she forced that hug on me?"

He chuckled. "No, but I've never seen a more awkward hug."

"She said she'll taste you. The nerve!"

He laughed harder.

"This is not funny, Mark." She heard the pout in her voice.

"It's hysterical." He brushed a strand of her hair back gently, saying, "Do you hear yourself?"

"Yes, but did you hear what I just said?"

"Yes, and I find it funny. Trust me, Skye, there is no way anyone but you will ever taste me again. I'm all yours."

"That succubus demon—"

He gave her an irritated sigh. "Are we really going there again? Besides, I was drugged and she...it never really tasted me because I never came." He gave her a wink. "I don't know why you let Crimson get to you. She is nothing compared to you."

"Have you seen the curves on her perfect body, and these?" She pushed her hands up under her breasts, gesturing to them.

"It's hard not to, but you outshine her in every way without even trying. That's why she tries so hard and why she taunts you. Have you seen yourself, Skye? You're the most beautiful woman in this world and our old world. You eclipse her and she hates it."

"I don't eclipse her," she said, her anger calming.

"To me you do." He kissed her forehead, then leaned his against hers. "I love you, Skye. Nothing will ever change that, and no one will ever take me from you."

A knock on the door disturbed the moment. A petite servant girl entered, the first female Skye had seen in the castle, followed by several male servants carrying buckets of steamy water.

"The queen thought a bath would be warranted after your long travels," she said with a curtsy. Skye couldn't help but notice the fear in her eyes, the timid aura around her.

"Thank you. A hot bath is just what we need," Mark said.

Skye noticed the tub in the corner of the room. It was a bright white with large black claws at the base of its legs. She took in the rest of the room, only then noticing the gothic theme, and the thick mauve blankets set against the ebony of the large bedframe. The few pieces of furniture in the room were the same ebony wood. The finish didn't appear to be stained, and she wondered where one found black trees.

The door closed, the servants leaving.

Mark pulled her against him. "I think it's time to reinforce how much I desire you and only you."

She relaxed into his kiss and let him undress her. The bath felt better than she'd expected, not only because of the love-making but the heat of the water against her muscles. They stayed in the tub long after the water had grown lukewarm, neither wanting to face what they knew would be an uncomfortable evening.

As Mark dressed, Skye continued to search for her clothes, finally looking in the dark wardrobe. All she found was a long formal dress of ruby red.

"She purposely had them leave my bag," she huffed.

Mark's eyes grazed her naked body. "I wouldn't be opposed to you going like that."

"I bet. And would you be opposed to the others seeing me like this?"

His expression changed. "Definitely. Like you, I don't share."

He'd moved to her, and she couldn't help but trace her fingers over his chest, feeling each muscle.

"Hmmm, we might not make it to dinner."

As if on cue, there was a knock at the door. Noah peeked his head in, and Mark tucked Skye behind him.

"Not decent!" he yelled.

"Still?" Noah asked, lifting his hand over his eyes. "We're starving. Stop fucking your wife and let's eat."

"Don't make me hurt you, Noah," Mark growled.

"That I'd like to see."

Skye was watching the muscles in Mark's back as he tensed, loving that every inch of him was hers. She dragged her eyes away and peeked her head around at Noah.

"I'm having some wardrobe issues, Noah. Go tell Crimson I was having my dessert first and that it tasted too delicious not to have seconds."

Mark let out a hearty laugh.

"There's more to that statement than I want to know. Fine, but hurry up. That woman is too much for any man to bear. My wife would have my head and yours if she knew you left me alone with those wandering hands."

The door closed, and Skye rested her head against Mark's back.

"Looks like red is your color tonight, my dear."

"Red is not my color, it's hers." She stopped, thinking of Crimson's appearance earlier. "Yet she was wearing blue when she greeted us. Blue isn't her color, it's mine. What the hell is she up to?"

He turned and pulled her to him. "Another attempt to annoy you, that's all. Now, as much as I adore your naked body, you need to get dressed."

Sighing, she gave him a long kiss, feeling her arousal grow along with his and knowing if she didn't dress, they'd never leave the room. She drew back and nipped at his lip. "I'm stuck with red, aren't I?"

"Either that or we're not leaving the room."

"My thought exactly," she said, stroking his erection before drawing away to take the dress from the wardrobe.

"That's not right, Skye. How am I supposed to walk now? And what if Crimson thinks it's for her?"

She shot him a look, and he raised his hands, backing away. "Joking, only joking."

"Not funny."

She wrangled the dress on, griping about how no underwear had been provided, to which Mark had no objection, of course.

He sat on the bed, watching her and when she was finally satisfied that she looked presentable, despite the fact that her boobs were about ready to pop from the dress, she turned to him. His eyes said it all. They were large, the hazel of them sparkling in the candlelight of the room. He looked like a man in love, and she knew he was hers. She was the only one he had eyes for; the only one his heart would ever belong to.

"You are gorgeous," he said, standing and extending his hand to her. "If Crimson was trying to make you look any less beautiful, she failed miserably."

She reached up and kissed him, his love for her coming through in the depth of the kiss.

"Let's get this over with," she said with a sigh.

"Then we can get on to me ripping that dress from your body."

She laughed as they exited the room, ready to face whatever game Crimson had in store for them.

MARK

Mark wanted to stay, to skip dinner and make love to Skye again. She was ravishing in that dress. Something about the color deepened the shades of blue in her eyes, the curves of it arousing him even more than her body normally did. He wanted to keep her all to himself.

Sighing, he followed her, watching as her auburn locks bounced along her back. The color of the dress enhanced the sun-kissed strands.

As they reached the dining room, his instinct told him to turn back. His hand touched the hilt of his weapon, his eyes surveying the others. It was too late. Skye had walked in, and all eyes were on her.

"Well, well," Crimson said, taking Skye's hand, "and I thought red was my color. Aren't you delicious? I do hope dessert was yummy, and that you didn't spoil his appetite. I know *I'm* starving." Her eyes locked with Mark's.

"My appetite is well sated, thank you," he replied, trying to grab Skye's hand.

"Uh, uh," she said, pulling Skye along.

Noah and Mechon were seated on one side of a long table and Theodore at the head. Mark nodded to Theodore, who glared at him and Skye, the anger still present from what he saw as a betrayal. The urge to take Skye and drag her from the room struck again.

Crimson led Skye to the seat next to Theodore, leaving the seat empty next to her own at the opposite end. Skye wasn't dumb. He saw the look of annoyance she gave Crimson. She knew exactly what Crimson's intentions were, but Crimson forced her down, then reached for Mark's hand. He snatched it back as he saw Theodore grab Skye's arm to stop her from rising.

"We have things to discuss, Skye. It's better if you are seated next to me."

Mark tensed, and he saw Noah do the same.

"He won't hurt her," Crimson said. "I promise no harm will come to her from anyone in this room. Now sit and let them talk."

She sat in her seat before patting his, awaiting his move.

"I'd rather sit next to you, Crimson," Skye argued. "We have so much to catch up on."

Crimson let out a wicked laugh. "I highly doubt that, dear. Now if you're both done fussing about your seat placement, it's time to eat."

As she said it, servants entered the room with trays and began serving them. Mark looked at Skye, whose blue eyes were the color of a moonless night. She'd managed to free her arm from Theodore's grasp.

"I won't bite," Crimson said. "Well, not hard."

"Dammit," he grumbled, taking the seat, and trying his best to situate it closer to Skye.

They ate dinner as Theodore proceeded to talk business, Mechon and he having a heated debate about trade. All the while, Crimson's hands sought whatever they could reach, touching his leg, his hand, his arm, her foot climbing its way along his leg.

Skye slammed her glass down. "If you don't stop touching my husband, I will bleed you of that red hair and strangle you with the hues!"

"You are much too sensitive, Skye," Theodore said in Crimson's defense. "She's just being Crimson. Trust me, she'll be satisfied by someone other than your husband later."

"As much as I love being tossed around in conversation like this, I think it's time for us to leave," Mark said, rising from his seat.

"Oh no, not before dessert," Crimson cried. "Plus, we do need to talk about territory."

"Territory?" Skye asked.

Mark sat back down as the servants cleared the plates, a new set of servants entering the room behind them.

"Why, yes. Theodore and I want your land."

"Are you insane?" Skye asked.

Mark tuned out the conversation, knowing he shouldn't, given its importance, but his eyes were drawn to the guards who had entered the corner of the room from some unseen door. It unsettled him that they were present, and he couldn't figure out where they'd come from. A dessert plate was set in front of him as Skye continued to argue with Crimson and Theodore.

Mark caught Noah's eyes, seeing the same concern in his. He nodded slightly to Noah, Mechon furrowing his brow as Noah slowly rose from his seat, the others not noticing. Mark was about to gesture to the guards when a dessert plate was set in front of Mechon, his expression changing to one of shock as a blade sliced his neck before Mark could stop it.

Skye screamed as Mechon grabbed at his neck, blood pouring from it. Mark rose and yanked her from her seat. Noah, having drawn his weapon, now fought with the servant and another guard, the servant brandishing a sword, his skills too keen to be a simple servant. The other guards had drawn their swords and were now moving toward Mark.

He felt Skye call her power when Crimson put her hand out and muttered something. Skye froze, and Mark tried pushing her behind him, but the two guards attacked. He parried their blows, his weapon drawn already, cutting them down swiftly, but not before Skye fell to the ground in a heap.

"Skye!" he yelled, running back to her. Something pulled at him, a command he couldn't ignore. It forced him to his knees and no matter how he wanted to rise, he couldn't. Noah was on the ground across from him, struggling as the same force pushed him to the ground. Crimson walked over to stand in front of Mark. A variety of hues encircled her as if she had Mage Warrior magic.

She flexed her hands. "So, it is true. A royal Mage Warrior can control her Elite. Gods, what power."

"What have you done?" he said through gritted teeth.

"My power," Skye cried in a weakened voice.

Crimson ran her hand through Mark's hair, before something forced him to the ground. He turned his head to look over at Skye, watching helplessly as Crimson moved to her and crouched in front of her.

"I told you I would have him—that I would taste him."

Skye struggled, but some unseen force kept her down as it did him.

"Kill their guards, all but that one." She pointed to Noah. "He looks tasty, too. Maybe when I have my fill of this one, I'll take him. Put him in the dungeon."

Theodore stood and walked over to her. Mark could see his feet, hearing him say, "Why waste your time with them? Kill them and we will rule all the lands together."

"You assume I want to always share my bed with you, and that is the wrong assumption. This one is mine."

"Is he worth it?"

"Oh, I do believe he is."

"You play a dangerous game by toying with me, Crimson."

"Yet you return to my body each time, Theodore."

Mark could barely move. Whatever control she had over him was keeping him pinned to the floor.

"And the Mage Warrior? Will you keep her as a pet, too?"

"No, she belongs to someone else. She's off limits to both of us. Now, leave."

"Leave? I thought we—"

"I still have work to do. You have a kingdom to run. You do not want to be here when I call the one who favors her."

There was a long silence, during which Mark's mind tried to comprehend her words. Who was coming for Skye? He heard Theodore tromp from the room.

Mark turned his head to Skye, the effort straining each muscle. She was curled in a fetal position, her eyes meeting his, and she looked as though the very effort was exhausting. A flow of hues sat upon skin like a weight, but they weren't being controlled by her. They were holding her down.

Crimson stooped between them and looked at Mark. Something in him urged him to draw his eyes from Skye to her.

"Fascinating," she said. "I'd always thought it a myth, but it's not. So much power from one source. Daddy's Mage Warriors were nothing compared to this."

She looked at Skye. "You never had any idea of the power you held. To control your Elite and use them as the true weapon they are. Mage Warriors, especially one of your line, are the ultimate control, and Theodore's ancestors erased that from your history."

"What did you do?" Skye asked, her voice shaking.

"Why, I've stolen your magic," she said with a laugh. The red hues from Skye's dress lifted and surrounded her, leaving the material a dull gray.

Mark struggled as the hues crushed her.

"Eh, eh, my pet." That sharp control stopped him again. She was controlling him just as she'd done the hues around Skye.

"Pity I can't just get rid of you, Skye. You're much too pretty to keep around, always drawing attention from me. But I promised."

The red hues flowed back to Skye's dress, her breathing labored as she tried to catch the breath they'd squeezed from her lungs. Crimson stood and Mark followed her with his eyes as she took a knife and sliced it down her palm, letting the blood drip to the ground as she whispered a spell. The ground shook, the room growing dark. Blood rose and spun with the black hues of the room.

"Come, my lover, I have caught you the price as promised."

"No," Mark said as a swirling doorway formed, and the Death God stepped through.

He looked back at Skye. Her eyes were clouded with fear. Even though she couldn't turn her head toward the doorway, she knew. He reached his hand out to her with every bit of strength he had, her hand stretching to meet his.

"You've done well, Crimson. Your talent never ceases to astound me," the Death God said.

"I aim to please. She's all yours as long as I can keep him."

Mark squeezed Skye's hand, struggling to break free from Crimson's hold.

"You really want to keep that pitiful mortal after sharing my bed?"

"Your bed will be taken, I'm sure."

Mark fought harder, forcing his other hand to move.

"Hmmm, so it may be."

"Besides, he's a fighter and I like the fighters. They arouse me so much more than the lame ones do."

He let out a hearty laugh, and Skye was pulled away. Mark pushed himself up against the force and pain that gripped him, his hand reaching for his weapon.

"See what I mean? He looks so tasty."

Skye struggled and as the Death God snapped the hues that held her, she squirmed free.

"Run, Skye!" Mark yelled as Crimson increased her hold on him, his weapon dropping.

She took two steps, then flew back to the Death God, his hand encasing her. He struck her as she scratched at his arm and Mark yelled, pushing against Crimson's hold again.

"Oh, you are going to be fun," she declared.

"Enjoy your treat," the god said as he turned and walked back to the doorway. Skye was screaming, her arms and legs flailing to break free until he turned one last time and threw a wicked grin at Mark. "I know I will."

"Mark!" Skye yelled as he stepped back into the doorway.

"No!" he screamed, breaking free and running to the doorway, which closed before he reached it. He turned and snarled at Crimson. "I will kill you," he said.

"No, you will satisfy me."

He felt a heavy thud on the side of his head and the room faded from view.

MARK

Mark woke. The brightness of the sun coming through the windows.

"Skye," he said, reaching for her. "I had the worst nightmare."

His hand hit the bedsheets, and he turned to find an empty side, the memory becoming reality. Ignoring the pounding in his head, he scrambled from the bed and ran to the door, his bare feet slapping against the stone floor. He tugged at the handle before pounding on the thick wooden door. When no answer came, he ran to the windows, only to notice the heavy iron bars on them.

"Shit!" he yelled, slamming his hand against them. He ran to where his bag had been, searching for his weapon, or the dagger he had stored in it, but it was gone. The room was the same one he and Skye had been in, but nothing of theirs remained.

He shoved his hands through his hair, thinking about how to escape the room and find Skye. He ran to the door again, pulling and pounding it until, finally worn out, he stepped away to sit on the bed.

The Death God had Skye. He'd taken her to the Shadow Realm. What had Crimson traded for her life? Fear threatened to overwhelm him as he questioned Skye's fate. He didn't know if she was still alive or if the Death God was torturing her. The look he'd given Mark before he'd walked through the portal suggested she might still live, but it didn't guarantee she was safe. In fact, it led him to believe the god had other plans. Mark's mind ran through every scenario, each increasing his terror. With every thought, his hands clenched tighter.

Crimson was to blame for this, and he would kill her the first chance he got. He played the events over in his mind, from Mechon's death to Skye's final scream as the portal had closed. No matter which way he looked at it, he couldn't figure out how this had happened. Crimson had no magic, yet Mage Warrior power had been hers. It was like she'd stolen Skye's magic and left her powerless. He couldn't fathom how that was even possible.

As if she knew she'd been on his mind, the door opened, and Crimson walked through. He leapt at her, determined to strangle her, but she raised a hand and he hit a barrier. Some force pushed him back, pinning him on the bed as the door closed behind her. Invisible ropes encased his wrists and ankles, binding them to the bedframe.

"Now, that is how I've always imagined you, Markhem. Tied up and waiting for me."

"Waiting to rip your throat open," he growled.

"Oh, I do like your spirit."

He couldn't move, no matter how he struggled. "What have you done, Crimson?"

She studied her hands. "You know, I never thought it fair that your people get all the magic. As a child, it mesmerized me, but as I matured, I envied it."

She crawled on the bed and straddled him, her robe slipping down her shoulder to expose the swell of her breast. She dragged her fingers across his chest, and he realized he was shirtless.

Dammit.

"So, I found a way to take it, to make it mine. You see, I find that having favor with the Death God, pleasing him the way he likes to be pleased...and oh, how he likes to be pleased...can give one an advantage. When your precious Skye pissed him off, it gave me the perfect opportunity to get everything I wanted."

"So, you sold Skye for magic?"

"Not quite. I did sell her, but it seems I'm not meant to retain magic. Instead, I can syphon it, make it mine for a brief time, rendering the user powerless. I've had that ability for a very long time and when I wield their magic, it's more powerful than it is in them. No conduits needed like those silly full mages need. I find —although it's a fleeting gift—it's a useful one."

"And that's what you did to her?"

"Exactly," she said, her hand dipping dangerously low, tracing the line of his pants.

He bucked to push her away, but it only caused her to laugh and lean closer. Her breast fell over the edge of her robe, full and tempting. "I do like it when they struggle. It's a shame her power has faded, and I had to resort to using a full mage. Her magic was intoxicating, and it would have made what we're going to do even more fun."

"The mages that remained in your kingdom, you forced them to stay," he said, trying to turn the subject and ignore her hand that had moved further down.

"So trusting. Do you really think I'd give up my pets? I depend on them too much. And you see, the Death God has always favored me." Her hand stroked him, and no matter what he did, he couldn't free himself to stop her. "He blessed me long before I returned the favor and gave him my body. How do you think I convinced my Mage Warriors to turn on their brothers and sisters?"

That gave him pause. What did she mean? Had she controlled them like they'd suspected?

"Now, I could use that power of persuasion on you, but I like a little spirit in my men."

"Persuasion? He gave you that ability?"

"Shhh." She drew herself up and pressed her finger to his lips. "Enough talk."

She dropped her robe, exposing her naked body. In any other situation, he would have taken the time to peruse the beauty of it. Instead, he struggled, knowing her intention and fearing his body's reaction to her.

"Get off me, Crimson!" He bucked his body again.

"Not until I'm finished...well, you're finished. You're going to be mine, Markhem, whether you *come* willingly or not."

His mind screamed for escape as she worked his pants off. She climbed back up, wrapping her hand around his length. Slowly she began moving her hand in long, deliberate strokes.

"Gods, you are delectable. I find the Elite to be my favorite." She kissed his stomach, her tongue working down his chest as he fought the rise in his erection. "You know, it always amazes me how a man can deny me, but his body never listens."

"Get the hell off of me, Crimson!"

But it was too late. Her mouth had surrounded him, and his body rebelled against his attempts to control it. No matter how he fought it, her mouth felt too good.

"Jesus, no, Crimson. Stop."

"Not until I taste you. I told her I would and no matter how faithful you are to her, your body will always betray her."

"Dammit!" He moved to fight her, but it only managed to push him deeper into her accepting mouth, causing her to moan wickedly. He gripped his hands against the rush of euphoria, the eventual oncoming wave rising within him as her mouth teased and licked at him. As much as he wanted to deny it, her movements were erotic, and he couldn't stop the climax that was building amidst the trauma of the act. He was a dichotomy of excitement, fear, and anger.

As she took his entire length, an uncontrollable grunt escaped him which only served to encourage her. Her hands massaged his shaft with confidence, increasing his arousal until he could no longer contain it and he came. She didn't stop, swallowing all of it like a hungry dog as her groan pervaded the silence. When the last of his forced pleasure had escaped, she rose and licked her lips, splaying her breasts across his chest.

"You are addictive."

"Fuck you."

"I think I'll take you up on that. I promise you, Markhem, by the time I'm through with you, you will be begging to fuck me."

She wrapped her hand around him again, her eyes watching him intently. His softness firmed against his will as she stroked him back to a full erection. Slowly, she slid her body up his, the feel of her breasts against his skin not helping his attempt to deny the selfish needs of his dick. Her tongue traced the contours of his chest as her hand continued its movement.

"Oh, Markhem. I've dreamed of what you would taste like, and you have not disappointed. I can only imagine what you'll feel like thrust deep inside of me."

The thought caused an unwanted surge of anticipation in him, and he tried to ignore it as her strokes grew firmer.

"I think you need to seriously evaluate your life if that's all your dreams consist of."

She kissed his chest then moved further up, his length jerking against her hand in reaction to the softness of her skin against his.

Damned traitor.

"See, you want me. You always have," she purred as she kissed his neck. He took the opportunity to ram his chin against her.

"Ouch, Markhem, don't be so angry. I'm only here to make you feel good."

"I was feeling just fine before you stole Skye."

She rose and lined him up against her, letting his head linger between her soaked folds. Arousal whipped through him, no matter how much he wanted to deny it the feeling was enticing.

"She is nothing compared to me, Markhem. And I didn't steal her, the Death God did. If she plays nice, he'll treat her as well as I'm treating you."

She lowered another inch, the sensation tantalizing even with his mind on Skye. A knowing glint sparkled in her eye.

"What is he doing to her, Crimson?" he said against the urge to groan.

"If he decided to keep her alive, then he's fucking her. Just as I'm fucking you."

Her body dropped so that she fully enveloped him, and another rush coursed through him. If it hadn't been her, if he hadn't found Skye at last, he would have gladly taken her. She was dripping around him, and it only worsened his rebellious hard on.

He dragged his eyes away from her body, staring at the wall, trying to focus on Skye and praying for his body to listen. But he couldn't keep her image in his mind, nor the worry that should have kept him from the ecstasy that was awash in his body.

Crimson felt too good. Grabbing his face, she turned him back her, his eyes settling on the curves of her body as she moved fluidly on him.

"I want you to watch me come," she said, her eyes coated with desire.

Another wave of yearning washed through him mixed with the hatred he was feeling toward her. Still his eyes watched as she rested her hands behind her and arched her back. The action caused her beasts to curve forward, the nipples firm and protruding. Her breasts were perfectly shaped and called to be touched but he ignored the thought. A moan fell from her mouth, her eyes closing as she brought her hand forward to play with them. They overflowed her small hands, and he inadvertently thought about how they would feel in his. His eyes followed the shape of her body, lingering on the curve of her hips before trailing to the slight patch of red hair that peeked from where it met him. She was built perfectly, built for seduction and for just a moment, he wondered what it would feel like to grasp those hips and urge her motion. To kiss the full lips of red that had fallen open with the stimulation she was giving herself.

Stop it, Mark, he chastised himself, knowing this was exactly what she wanted. That this was her power. He closed his eyes, forcing himself to look away as she sat forward, her rhythm increasing, his erection pulsing. Her body was trembling, her legs quivering as her climax mounted.

He was going to break again. She was too enticing not to. Her breathing increased, her body shaking before her muscles seized around him. Her cry tore from her as her orgasm hit. The moment urged his own release and he climaxed, fighting against it as he spilled into her. She dropped forward, breathing heavy as her hair fell against his chest. As the last waves of his climax diminished, he looked to see that her eyes, now a rich sage, were watching him. A satisfied smile sat on her face, a pink flush to her flawless skin.

"You're even better than I could have imagined."

She lifted herself from him and took him in her mouth, sucking until there was nothing left, the action not unwelcomed by his body, no matter how his mind hated it.

Picking up her robe, she kissed him quickly, and rose before he could headbutt her like he wanted. He glared at her, her laughing eyes merely taking him in.

"You are a keeper. Maybe next time, you'll get me off. I have yet to find a man good enough to pleasure me without my involvement. Maybe you'll be the one."

She licked her lips, letting her hand drift down her body. The attempt to induce a reaction in him didn't go unnoticed, and he purposely kept his eyes locked on hers.

"Don't count on it, bitch," he grumbled.

Not bothering to put her robe back on, she opened the door. The hold on him disappeared and he lunged, the door slamming shut before he could reach it.

SKYE

Skye blinked her eyes open, trying to adjust to the darkness. Her head felt foggy, and she cursed as she tried to stand.

"Thank the gods you're alive," she heard across from her. The voice was familiar, but she couldn't place it until a flicker of light illuminated Camin's face.

"Camin?"

"Yes. Why are you here, Skye? I thought everything was over."

"It was," she said, taking in the bars separating them. "Where are we?" The memories came flooding back to her. "Mark. I need to get out of here and back to him. Where is here?" She pulled at the bars of the small window of her door, then turned quickly, seeing nothing but brick around her.

"You're in the dungeons. I saw them bring you here."

"Who?"

"The demon minions."

"The Death God. He took me," she said, remembering the rest. "God, I'm stuck in hell and Crimson has Mark."

"Crimson?"

"Yes, she's the reason I'm here. She gave me to him, did something to my powers, and now she has Mark."

"I don't know which is worse—being trapped here or trapped

with Crimson. Although he's likely to have a more pleasurable time."

"Really? That's not what I want to hear, Camin!"

"Sorry," he said as she tugged on the bars again, then tried to use her magic to draw the hues from them. She could feel its presence again, remembering how it had disappeared, the feeling crippling her. She called the hues, but they sat just beyond her reach.

"It's no use, there's no way out and the Death God has bound our power. He's too smart to leave either of us down here with magic."

Sighing, she rested her head on the door. "Why are you here? How are you still alive?"

"Trust me, I'd rather have died. They've kept me prisoner all this time, bringing me out when the Death God or his shadow gods want some fun torturing me. They've made me their slave, helping with the Master of the Souls, given me to their demons for various things that I'd prefer not to elaborate on and made my life a living death sentence."

"I'm sorry."

"Don't be. I made my choice."

"Because of me."

"It was necessary. Did you restore our people?"

She smiled. "Yes, the kingdom has been rebuilt, the mages freed. It's beautiful. You would like it."

"I imagine I would, but I'll never see it. You, however, need to find a way out. Nothing good will come from being held by the Death God. Derrant has a vendetta against you for tricking him. I'm surprised he hasn't killed you yet."

"Is there any way out?"

"Not one that I've found. Damn, I wish I knew what he plans to do to you."

She rubbed her arms. "Long, painful torture?"

He didn't answer.

"Camin?"

"I don't think that's why he's keeping you alive. You're

special, with powers that bested even him. He likes to collect unique specimens in case you haven't noticed."

She remembered the demons she'd seen in the realm and in his court, swallowing at the images.

Footsteps echoed through the dungeon.

"They're coming for you. Whatever you do, don't fall under his spell!"

"And how do I avoid that?" she yelled in a hushed whisper.

There was no answer as the steps drew closer and her mind answered her question of what would happen if she fell under the spell of the Death God. Her cell opened to a nasty-looking beast with horns protruding from his shoulders and eyes of fire. It yanked her from the cell. He picked her up and threw her over his shoulder as she punched and kicked to free herself. The horn dug into her side further with each step, but her fear overpowered the pain.

She caught Camin's eye, and he sadly shook his head.

Eventually, she gave up her fight and the demon unceremoniously dropped her on the stairs to the Death God's throne. She picked herself up as the demon walked away. Derrant descended the steps. He was terrifying, his massive stature towering over her, a black haze clinging to him. He was in his god form and terror shivered through her.

"Ah, I frighten you as I should. Death is always to be feared. But this is only a façade." He moved his hand and morphed into the form of a man. Skye couldn't help but be shocked by the transformation. He had eyes of bright blue, hair of gold that shone in the dark surroundings, and a body of solid muscle. His shirt, left open, exposed the definition below, pants resting just above where they bulged abnormally. She'd forgotten how beautiful he truly was.

She averted her eyes from his body and met his hungry stare.

"Not what you were expecting?"

She swallowed. "Not at all."

"I try not to be menacing all the time. It does get dull and tiring."

"Why did you bring me here?"

A wicked grin overtook his features. "For revenge. You made a fool of me, Skye. Now I will make a slave of you."

"A slave? Why not kill me?"

"So eager to die? You are too exquisite to kill."

He moved closer so that he was nearly touching her. She tried to take a step back, but she couldn't. Camin's words came back to her, *Don't fall under his spell.* She could only imagine what kind of spell he would weave, and what it would do to her. The thought of the persuasive power he'd given to the people of Eltander crossed her mind. Fearful of what that would mean for her, she stayed quiet.

His grin grew larger, and she felt the chill rise within her as his hand moved up to touch her hair.

"I've heard Mage Warriors are fierce in every aspect of life, insatiable really."

Her heart hammered in her chest, knowing where he was going with the comment and that he was far too large for her to fight off.

"Don't worry, you won't fight me. You'll come to my bed willingly, as they all do."

"No, I don't think so."

There was a gleam in his eye as he drew his hand back and ran it along her face, his touch changing the chill that she'd previously had to a shiver of pleasure. She relaxed, wondering why she'd been so uptight, so tense. His touch lingered, seeping into her as if to touch her soul. There was no need for hesitation, it was only Derrant. Something in the back of her mind nudged her that this wasn't the man who mattered, that there was another who owned her heart and her body. But it faded, her mind back on Derrant as he pulled her against him and kissed her. It was deep and needy, laced with power that called to her own.

All awareness fell away with the rustle of her dress as it landed at her feet. His hands replaced the material, grasping at her body, his own clothes removed before she'd even taken a breath. Each touch brought a different level of sensation and she hungrily answered with her own touches. She wanted him with a thirst that seemed insatiable. His hands perused her body, lingering to feel the swell of her breasts before he clasped her tight against him. A blanket of gray power engulfed her, and she felt the softness of a bed below her. His body encompassed hers and she lurched back as the girth of him entered her. Pain and pleasure exploded through her body, forcing a cry with each thrust.

Her mind was hazy, her body riveted with arousal, and she clung to him as his tongue danced along her breasts, biting and sucking at her. She was lost to the sensations that enraptured her, the moves of his body. The touch of his skin against hers called to her power, and she set it free, the swirl of black heeding her command and swabbing their bodies. He grunted, his own power slamming into her, knocking the breath from her. Tipping her head back in reaction, she arched her back, clutching to his arms as he drove into her with a frenzy. The world around her was a chaotic storm of power and desire and she didn't want it to end. She wanted more. She found his lips, kissing him with urgency as she felt him climax, his groan echoing through the room.

Derrant rolled from her, catching his breath. She lay still, her mind trying to grasp the thought that she'd not been completely satisfied, that she needed her own release and wanted more of his touch. A memory flitted just out of reach. That of another man, one who never left her unsatisfied. With the thought, her heart ached, but then it was gone, his hand brushing along her face again, her desire for only Derrant remaining.

She climbed atop him, kissing his neck, the warmth of it tingling her lips as she whispered, "I want you to make me come."

"I'm the only one who gets gratification. I can bring a demon for you."

"Shh," she said, stopping his words with her finger. "As you said, I'm a Mage Warrior and I'm very demanding." She brought his hand to her breast. "Now satisfy me and I'll let you join me."

He looked stunned. "I should hurt you for the assumption that you can command me."

She stopped his words with a kiss. Working her hand down to the erection that still stood, she gripped him, trying to comprehend the size of him. For a moment, a thought nudged the back of her mind that she'd had a man with an impressive size before, that this one was unnatural, painful, but she couldn't get her thought to stick.

She stroked and teased him until he flipped her to her stomach, pinning her below him. His hand spread her legs, and he forced himself into her again, pulling her ass into the air. She went to raise her head, but he kept her down. The position sent a thrill that coursed like electric sparks across her skin—it was forceful and dominating, and she welcomed it. His hand reached below to her breast, his magic finding its way to the sensitive nub between her legs as he continued to thrust. The magic stroked her clit, invisible hands fondling her breasts. The sensation of tongues on her nipples slowly increased in pressure until it was so erotic that she was could barely contain the shivers in her body. With each thrust from Derrant, the warmth in her grew until it peaked, her climax hitting her like a tidal wave, a cry of rapture escaping.

He pushed as deep as he could, prolonging her climax, the quivers rippling through her before he continued to slam into her repeatedly, sending a second climax rushing through her. Her body was alive with the residual shivers of her orgasm, every inch of her screaming in exhilaration. She could feel him growing closer and she pushed against him, wanting him to fill her again. But instead of meeting her need, he forced her down and drew from her. Flipping her to her back, he stroked himself, and released on her stomach. She arched her back into the feel of it, the warmth tingling against her skin. Reaching her hand up, she coaxed the remains of him out as a fierce moan rumbled from his chest. When he quieted, she took her finger and wiped her stomach, bringing it to her mouth, and licking it until a mischievous grin overcame him again.

"Yes, I will keep you." He stood and within seconds, was clothed again. "Bathe and I will be back for you to satisfy me again."

A full bathtub appeared, the water steaming. She remained on the bed, staring at the ceiling until a chill came over her, the haze lifting. A room of black décor and candlelight came into view. She sat up, the remnants of him still on her chest, the memories clearing.

"Oh, God. What have I done?" she said, Mark's face coming to her. Her stomach lurched and she pushed herself from the bed, only then noticing the blood between her legs. Bile filled her throat, and she ran to a black vase that sat on a side table, throwing up in it.

She'd cheated on Mark, forgotten about him completely. She'd enjoyed it as if it were the Death God she loved and not Mark.

"No," she told herself. "There was no love there, and it was a spell, Skye."

Slowly, she made her way to the tub, her legs sore, her body aching from him. Lowering herself, she let the warmth ease the ache. She leaned her head back, thinking back on what had happened. He'd placed a spell on her, something that had caused her to forget everything. A persuasion of sorts. Camin had warned her, but how was she to avoid the magic of a god?

There was an ache between her legs where he'd gone deeper than any man should have. Would she suffer it again? Suffer seemed a strange word for it when she'd enjoyed herself to the point that she'd climaxed multiple times. But that had been the spell, not her. She had no way of controlling her body's response if she wasn't herself. Her mind went back to the intensity of the moment. Even if he hadn't spelled her, could she have stopped her body?

What would Mark think?

She lifted her head, thinking of him. Crimson had him, she was sure of it. And she had no question as to what Crimson would do to him. Would Mark be able to stop her advances? Would he want to?

Of course he'll stop her, she scolded herself. There was no way she could touch him. He was too strong. What had he said? She'd have to tie him down to even touch him. But what if she had? What if she'd pleasured herself with him and given him no choice?

She lay her head back. Then they'd both be guilty of succumbing to their body's calls.

Closing her eyes, she shut the thoughts out and focused on finding a way to escape. But how did one escape the Death God?

When she emerged from the tub, Skye found a black dress on the bed. No one had entered the room, yet there it was. With no other option, she put it on. The dress was loose, the material thin and silky with gauzelike straps that made moving around easy. Searching the room, she looked for some way to escape but found nothing. There were no windows, and the door had no knob. Frustrated, she tried using her powers. Her magic had flowed freely when she'd been with Derrant, but now, it was gone again as it had been in the cell.

Laying back on the bed, after pushing aside the black covering that held signs of her escapade with Derrant, she slipped to a fitful sleep, dreaming of Mark, a massive divide between them. The bang of the door woke her, and she jumped up, a groggy feeling over her body.

A demon entered the room, her naked body covered in a green snakelike skin, her beady eyes evaluating Skye. Behind her, a tail flicked dangerously.

"So, you are the one who killed my sister," she hissed.

The succubus who'd held Mark, she surmised. "Your sister had my man."

"And who has him now?" she said, her tail running across her body. "Pity the master ordered me to leave you be or I would have my revenge."

Skye glared at her. "Pity I don't have my power, or I would kill you before you could touch me."

"Isn't it a shame you couldn't stop Crimson with your powers? I've seen what she does to men. You'll never get him back. Even if you do find your way back to him, he'll only want her."

"Why are you here?" Skye snarled, ready to change the conversation, to stop her mind from imagining Crimson with Mark.

"The master has summoned you." She turned and left the door open after walking out.

Skye was loath to follow her, especially after her comments, but she rose and let the demon lead the way, careful to avoid the tail that nipped at her as they walked. The hall was dark, only a pale candlelight lit their way. Upon closer inspection, she realized the flame of the candles held a strange shape. They weren't flames. To her horror, they were in the form of bodies, flames engulfing them. The souls of the damned. The Death God and his shadow gods were indeed cruel.

She stepped back, avoiding the light, too haunted by the sight to look further. From the hall, they emerged to a large open space that looked like it might be an entryway but one which held no doors. They passed a stairway with blood-red carpets, black splotches upon them. She prayed they weren't black carpets soaked with blood, but truly didn't want to know. Finally, the demon led her into a dining room.

A massive chandelier of black iron hung above, lit by the damned souls. A fireplace roared across from the table, a subtle scream of voices echoing from it. She swallowed back her fear as the succubus walked away. At the far end of the table sat the Death God, a goblet of wine in his hand, leaning back comfortably in the chair as his eyes perused her body.

"Come, feast with me before I feast upon you again."

The reflection of the flames played on his blonde hair, highlighting it so that black streaks resided in it. He seemed such a dichotomy in appearance to what he truly was.

She made her way to the chair at the end opposite him, a place setting out for her.

"What do you want from me?" she asked once she was seated.

"To the point, aren't you? I like that about you, Skye." He leaned forward, his open shirt falling aside to expose his defined chest.

A flashback of that chest pressed against her flickered in her mind.

Laughing, he said, "I don't have to spell you if you're ready to please me."

"Never," she said. "Now tell me what you want."

"Aside from your body, you. You are powerful, Skye. No mere mortal. The magic that flows from your veins is almost godlike. I felt it as I took you. It was the most aroused I've been in a very long time."

"So, you want my magic?"

"No, I want you. I covet what others have, and you have domain over the hues of the world and the ones beyond. You will be my queen and share your bounty with me. Together, we will rule like no one before us."

"You're mad."

"I'm a god. One who wants to defeat my brother and take his realm. With you by my side, that's possible."

"You want to use me for my power?"

"And your body," he added, taking a long chug of his wine. He slammed the goblet down and wiped his mouth with the back of his hand.

She stared at him, disgusted by the remark.

"You have no choice, Skye," he continued.

"I have a choice and my choice is to leave." She began to rise, but an unseen force pushed her back down.

"As I said, you have no choice. Your power is already under my control. You get it when I want you to have it."

"I'm already spoken for."

"Not for long. Crimson can be quite persuasive with that body of hers. She can do things that melt even a god. Although I do admit, you are very much her rival."

"She won't seduce Mark."

"Why? Because he loves you? Love means nothing when it comes to our natural needs, and Markhem will crave what Crimson has to offer. She'll give him no choice. Forget about him and rule with me."

"No," she said, but her voice sounded weaker, the emotion of what he'd said affecting her.

"Then you leave me no choice. If you won't come willingly, you'll come anyway. As often as I let you." He laughed as he approached her. "You see what I did there? A play on words?"

She rolled her eyes, then backed away as his hand reached in front of her.

"I don't need to touch you to control you, Skye. I just enjoy touching you. You and your powers are mine."

She felt the haze as it reached for her, coating her mind and her memories, her worries about Mark fading, replaced only by the god before her—beautiful and with eyes only for her.

"Show me how much you need me, Skye." His voice was like soft ribbons against her skin.

She brought herself to her knees and tugged him toward her, undoing his pants to free the hardened length within. Lifting her eyes to meet his, she let her tongue glide along him. His groan rumbled through the room as she circled the tip of him, tasting the pre-cum that had emerged. She closed her eyes and thought of him nestled deep inside of her, warmth surging through her lower body and driving her to continue her movement. Gripping his shaft, she worked her tongue over him, then dropped quickly, filling her mouth with him as much as she could—he was too large for her to take entirely. The idea of that length sent a flutter of hunger through her. She clenched her legs in response and a wicked laugh escaped him as if he knew what just the thought of him did to her.

His hand pushed her down further, lending a discomfort her mind fought to ignore. Grunting, he brought his hips against her, pumping with urgency, the movement arousing her so that she drew closer to her own climax. He moaned and stilled her head with a forceful shove, his body shaking as he came. The bitterness of him slid down her throat until he finally relaxed, and his hand released her.

"You are amazing and for that, I will ensure you are satisfied, something I never do."

He yanked her up and threw her over the table, his hands ripping the dress from her. One hand kneaded her breast, while the other moved lower, plunging into her and moving with a rhythm and force that sent arousal pummeling her. A cry of elation escaped as her body shook against him, squeezing his fingers until he withdrew them, and his firm erection plowed into her, taking her back over the edge within a few thrusts.

Her mind lost all their prior conversation, now only occupied by him and the pleasure he was giving her body.

MARK

Mark lost count of the days. Too many had passed and yet he remained a prisoner. Food was brought to him, slipped through a small door that opened at the bottom of the main door, the trays disappearing as he slept. Crimson came to him irregularly, sometimes every day, sometimes every two. Each time, she held him down for her pleasure; each time his body succumbing to her touch, her mouth, her body as she rode him. It felt too good no matter how he resisted.

He paced the room, his feet slapping against the cold stone floor. It had been three days since she'd last returned, that much he knew, and he suspected she'd pay him another visit soon, if not this day. If only there was a way to break her spell, to free himself while she was there, to force her to free him. She was too strong. Whatever magic she was syphoning for her visits to him, he couldn't break through.

He was weaker without Skye. Her power fueled him just as it did the other Elite. The bond between Mage Warrior and Elite unbreakable unless severed like Crimson had done. His mind drifted to Skye. He didn't know if she was still alive, or if she was hurt, suffering abuse at the hands of the vengeful god. It pained him to think of her that way, and even more to know he couldn't stop it.

He felt the familiar tug at his body as he heard the door. He fought against it, but to no avail, the magic binding him. This time, he was restrained to the large chair that sat near the barred window. Crimson entered, her red robe draped loosely across her shoulder. Her lips were full and colored, layered in gloss.

"Markhem," she purred, the door closing behind her. The sleeve of her robe fell, exposing her breasts. His eyes dipped to them unwittingly, and he quickly drew them away.

"Did you miss me?"

"Can't say I did," he said, fighting against the invisible restraints.

She stood before him, her eyes perusing his body. After her first few visits, she'd had his clothes removed from the room. He'd enjoyed aggravating her with the extra chore of undressing him, but that had been a fleeting amusement.

"You've been gone a while, Crimson. Where do you go when you disappear? Torturing other defenseless men?"

She dropped to her knees, her hand grasping him, her eyes never leaving his as she woke his body. "I have other pets. Your friend is quite tasty—"

"Noah? Jesus, you couldn't leave him be?"

"My main objective in life is pleasure. When I find something I like, I take it."

"Regardless of whether they belong to someone else?"

"I don't think she does the things I do." Her tongue grazed him, and he closed his eyes at the invading waves of desire.

"You're a bitch, Crimson. You take what's not yours, you destroy lives all for your gratification—all without consequence to you."

She rose slowly, her breasts grazing his erection before moving up his chest. Turning her body, she grasped him to align herself before sitting upon him. A grunt escaped him against his will. She knew how to work a man and with every rise and fall of her body he grew harder, his eyes unable to resist watching the motion of her ass as she rode him. The moisture that surrounded him didn't help. She was dripping, and another groan escaped at the thought. He cursed himself as she rocked harder against him.

He gritted his teeth as her movements increased, her body leaning forward so that he went deeper with each penetrating drop she made on him. He was close, and he knew it was only a matter of time before she broke him.

"Everything in this world is mine, Markhem, including you."

"You don't get to take what you want," he forced out.

She stopped moving, and he bit back the need to scream for her to continue. Slowly, she lifted herself from him, his balls throbbing at how near he was to coming, the movement painful. She turned and leaned into him, his length pressing on her stomach, twitching against his control.

"But that's exactly what I'm doing. Why fight it? You know you want me. I can feel it each time you fill me. You're a sexual man, Markhem—better suited with me. And Skye is better suited with Derrant." She slid further up his chest and positioned him again, his tip resting just inside her soaked warmth. She was torturing him and loving every minute. The feel of her, the agonizing ache that was gripping him as she left him lingering there was almost unbearable. As much as he hated what she was forcing upon him, his body wanted it, especially when release sat just out of reach. To his relief, she enveloped him again, and another grunt escaped against his will. She smiled knowingly as she rocked against him.

"I was with her last night."

"What?" He wanted to grab her, but he couldn't move.

"I went to the Shadow Realm for a little fun with Derrant. See, your no fun, Markhem. I must take, take, take, but Derrant, he gives. He fucks me like a real man. It took some getting used to in the beginning; he is exceptionally large, but then again, he is a god. Skye's gotten used to it quickly."

"What the hell are you talking about?"

"Always with these strange terms, Markhem. Hell?"

"Shut up and tell me what you mean."

She ran her hand up his chest and drifted closer to his face. He would have rammed her with his head, but he wanted to know what she meant. All thoughts of where his dick still sat fled.

"Derrant has taken a liking to her. I can see why; she tastes like honey. The two of them together...it's intense. I couldn't help but join it."

"You lie. He's forcing her if you aren't."

"Oh, no. She enjoyed every moment. The way her power spills out when she's in that state and the way she comes for him was enough for me to get off. Derrant has met his match. You won't ever get her back."

He stared at her, too stunned to respond. She was telling the truth. Skye's magic did spill out when she was truly lost in the moment. Power coated them like a velvety touch that always brought him to climax with her. His heart dropped, and the anger hit, the betrayal stinging. As strong as he'd been, fighting against this beautiful woman, Skye had given herself over from the start.

Crimson's lips were dangerously close to his, her green eyes watching him.

"What are you going to do, Markhem?" she whispered. "Deny yourself the pleasure she's getting every night and day?"

"Fuck it," he muttered and brought his lips to hers, tasting the berries she'd stained them with. Aggressively, he kissed her, forcing his tongue in her mouth, letting go to the feel of her as she began to move again. He felt the hold slip, and he was able to move his arms, bringing them around her waist.

Anger fueled his moves as he guided her hips up and down, but it only encouraged a moan from her. He rose, gripping her waist and brought her against the wall, fucking her hard with an intensity she matched. Abandoning all thoughts of Skye, he allowed himself to take every ounce of pleasure he could from Crimson's body. After all the times he'd denied himself the feel of her, he took her with a fervor that was unstoppable. His mouth found her supple breasts, the ones his eyes had lingered on countless times, enjoying the softness of them, the silkiness of her skin. Her heart was pounding as he sucked them, and he could hear her labored breaths. The sound further heightened the fire that was burning through him. She pulled at his hair and brought his mouth to hers again. The anger that had overtaken him fueled his hunger and he grasped her waist firmly as his climax built until it tipped, and release took him.

When he finally calmed, he kissed her again, knowing he wanted more of her. And she was more than willing to satisfy that want. Sliding to the floor, her mouth encompassed him, taking in the erection that hadn't ceased. He closed his eyes and weaved his hands in her hair, leaving his mind blank to everything but the feel of her mouth until again he could no longer contain it. With each lick and suck, his orgasm climbed until he clenched his hands with the flood of ecstasy, his head falling back.

His legs shook with the intensity of his climax.

"I knew you were worth waiting for, Markhem. You are my equal," she said, licking the final drops from him.

He closed his mind to the thoughts that screamed that he wasn't, that Skye was. And as her hand curved around his now waning erection, coaxing it back far too easily, he filled his thoughts with only Crimson again. Giving over to her sensuality and the way it called to a feral part of him, one that didn't want to be controlled. She ran her tongue along his neck, pushing her breasts against his chest.

"Make me come," she whispered. "Please. No man has ever done so, but I know you can."

He lifted his head and raised his brow, bringing his hands to her ass. "You lie."

"Only by my own hands and other women I've shared men with. Skye gave me an amazing climax, one of the best but I know you can do better."

His anger flared, and he shoved her back into the wall in a move that knocked the breath from her. Bringing his hand to her neck, he stared at her. Her words had ignited the ire in him again and part of him wanted to hurt her for it, the other part wanted more of her. Wanted to hear her scream as he broke her.

"The Death God made her come, which he never does. She cried out in ecstasy. Give me what he gave her."

Rage burned within him, pushing thoughts of Skye further away. He occupied the space with Crimson, kissing her roughly again, his hands sliding to her voluptuous breasts, coaxing her nipples out with no effort. Knowing she was the type who preferred it rough, he pinched and tugged at them, bringing his mouth down to taste them. She squirmed with each bite and lick, her movements only further increasing his own arousal. He wanted to take her again, to feel the ferocity she matched with his, the way her body moved in demanding ways against his. But he wanted to hear her scream first, to break the woman who had broken him so many times.

Dropping his hand, he rubbed her clit with his thumb as he continued to torment her breasts. Her head fell back, her body lurching in response. The sigh she elicited was erotic and called to that part of him that wanted to experience more of her. She was so different from Skye that it fed the side of him that drove his more volatile emotions. His fingers brushed along her moisture, sinking deep into it. She was drenched, and he could tell she was reaching her threshold, that she would climax at any moment. A loud moan escaped him at the thought, his erection throbbing uncontrollably.

Her gasp was one that called to his aggressive side, the need to dominate her, to own her and he thrust his fingers into her with a force that caused her body to arch again in response. The move sent her breast further into his mouth and he moaned again, her own cry stimulating every part of him. She was nearing release, and he wanted to feel her fall apart for him. Wanted to see her body shudder from his touch. He removed his fingers and slid his tip into the wetness. In small circles, his fingers brought the moisture to her clit. Her body tensed as he slipped along her warmth. The move was torturous, and his length pulsed with the need to bury itself in her. Her climax built, her pelvis pushing against him until a cry escaped her and he knew she was lost.

He penetrated her as she cried out, feeling her taut muscles clenching around him. Her body convulsed against him as the orgasm ripped through her. He picked her up, his hands grabbing at her ass, and pounded into her as her climax receded. Carrying her to the bed, he drove into her, kissing her fiercely, feeling another orgasm rising in her again.

He slowed his movement, bringing his lips to her breasts, trying to calm the need to succumb to the torrent that was ripping through him. Every part of him felt like it was ablaze. Tipping her pelvis, he increased his rhythm, biting at her breasts as her nails dug into his back. Her body spasmed around his length, and he almost lost it. He hadn't felt this out of control, this overtaken with lust and aggression in years, and it reached a part of him that he rarely touched. Her head dropped back with a cry as her body shook, the wetness increasing around him as she came.

She was dripping now, and it urged him on. He continued to take her, forcing her lips to his, bringing her back to their act. Those lush lips that had been made to be kissed, her mouth delicious and inviting. He'd wanted that mouth, wanted to touch her like he was, to kiss those lips and fuck her like this, but he'd denied himself the satisfaction until Skye's infidelity had given him permission. Now she was his for the taking, and he planned to take as much as she'd let him, maybe more.

Crimson returned his kisses eagerly. There was a sensuality to the way she kissed that matched the way she moved her body, and it was one he couldn't deny. Her arms wrapped around him, and her hands pulled at his hair. Entwining her legs around his body, she forced him deeper until he broke. Waves of pleasure rippled through him. Minutes seemed to pass as he tried to gain control of his body. Finally, he dropped his head to her neck before rolling from her.

He stared at the ceiling, breathless. He hadn't taken a woman so recklessly since before Sam's death—before Skye had been widowed, ready for his taking but never touchable. Before that, he'd been relentless, needing a replacement for her—a release from his pent-up desire. That's what this had been, an unrelenting release of built-up need but fueled by his anger toward her. The multitude of times she'd come to him, building him up, waiting for an opening.

Crimson rose and he could see the quake in her legs as she walked to her robe.

"I knew you were good, Markhem, but you put even the Death God to shame. Now be a good boy and rest until I'm ready for more."

He brought himself to his elbows. She stopped in front of him, climbing atop him again to kiss him.

"You'll do just fine ruling alongside me."

"What?"

"Skye will rule by Derrant's side. That means you can rule by mine."

Anger resurfaced. "She won't rule by his side," he said through gritted teeth.

"She will. The Death God covets her and her power. And you've just shown me you want me, that she's disposable. Let the Death God have her. I can bring you pleasure like you need, the kind you had before her."

She drew her body from his and stood.

"I thought Theodore was set to rule with you."

She laughed. "Theodore is but a plaything. He's old and not nearly as capable as you. I will run him and his kingdom through as I take the other kingdoms. Together, we will rule this world, Markhem."

She blew him a kiss and left the room.

Mark dropped his head back, staring at the ceiling. He didn't want to think about Skye. Instead, he thought of Crimson's body, the curves, the way she'd spilled over him as she came. Had he wanted her that entire time? She was a desirous woman, everything about her screamed sex. No. In the heat of passion, he'd thought he had, but he'd never wanted her before. This was all due to her manipulation, the way she'd built him up, his body wanting for her touch, building that need to climax each time she'd come to him. Making it hers until just the right time when he would willingly take her. And God, how he'd taken her. His length threatened to grow again as he thought on it. He wanted more of her. She was no novice in the bedroom, and if he couldn't have Skye, he'd have her. Just as she'd wanted, just as she'd planned, just as she'd told him from the start.

He ran his hand over his face. Had it been a trick? Had Crimson known his anger would lead him to take her? His jealousy, that need for revenge clinging to the lust she'd built in him all this time?

No, it wasn't a lie. He knew Skye well enough to know how she climaxed. She was having sex with the Death God, giving him all the things she'd given Sam before Mark. Anger grew again until his common sense woke up.

Why?

She loved him, just as he loved her enough to fight Crimson off for as long as he had, and her enough to fight the Death God off. But could one fight a god? He thought of Mechon, poor dead Mechon, his people given the power of persuasion by...

"The Death God," he said, sitting up. "Shit. What have I done?"

Skye wasn't voluntarily sleeping with Derrant. She was under his coercion, likely not even remembering Mark. She wasn't cheating on him, and Crimson had known that, twisting the truth, using it to draw him in.

It had taken so little for him to fall. He'd taken her at the mere thought of Skye's infidelity, never questioning, doubting Skye without hesitation.

He dropped his head to his hands. It was too late to take it back. What was done was done and he would suffer the consequences. Would she ever forgive him? Not only had he taken another woman, but he'd also taken her multiple times, pleasured her, slept with Skye's enemy. He didn't think it could get any worse.

Sure, she'd worn him down, time after time, but it didn't matter. He brought his head up and sighed.

Think, Mark, he told himself.

He couldn't change what had happened, but could he use it to his advantage? Crimson had freed his limbs. If she left him free, he could kill her the next time she came to him. It would be easy, but he'd be dead the minute he left the room. There was no doubt she had guards posted. She was too calculating not to.

Leaning back, he thought through his options. Crimson hadn't questioned his desire to take her, and she'd freed him the moment she believed he would. That was a weakness he could use as his advantage. But it would cost him.

He ran his hand through his hair. His anger had already cost him so at this point, he had nothing to lose. But could he put on the façade that he was still angry at Skye and trick Crimson, gain enough trust that he could escape? Skye was still locked away in the Shadow Realm and he had no way to rescue her. Even if she left him for this, he would still rescue her. He loved her too much not to. But how did he get to her?

Crimson. She traveled back and forth. He would need to manipulate her enough to coerce her into taking him there. It would require a lot. Was there a downside to it? He'd have to continue sleeping with her, which in itself wasn't a bad thing.

"Idiot," he chastised himself for the thought.

No matter how he spun it, he'd still be willingly sleeping with her. But sex was the only way to Crimson's trust. He rubbed his hands over his face, cursing his stupidity. Rising, he put aside the predicament of Skye, the betrayal he'd accomplished in one easy move, the idea that he may have just lost the one thing he'd wanted his entire life. Instead, he strategized, planning his next move. It was time to turn Crimson's own game around on her, to destroy her as she'd just destroyed him.

SKYE

Skye woke, the bedsheets soft and wrinkled around her. Derrant had left. He was never there when she woke, and she wondered if he even slept at all. Did gods sleep? She stretched, her mind slipping back to his touch, craving it as she did any time he wasn't near. Last night had been long. They'd taken each other multiple times, something she wondered if she'd ever done. There was a familiarity to doing so, something in the haze of her mind that told her she had, but it slipped away as her mind wandered to the night prior to the last one.

There had been another woman, her hair red and thick. Skye had argued against it, a flicker in her mind telling her she should remember this woman. Another part of her was jealous that his attention wasn't only on her. They had laughed, a strange reaction, an odd knowing to it, as if there had been more to the laugh than she'd understood. A joke of sorts.

Then she'd been pulled in by Derrant, his touch ecstasy as the woman had joined. She'd been lost in a tide of touches and kisses, her body brought to the edge of desire more times than she could remember. She'd done things she knew with certainty she'd never done. A thought flitting through her mind that questioned if this was what he'd experienced. But she didn't know who the he was or why the thought was there. The thought had fled as she'd climaxed again, Derrant pulling her back to the present. As the woman had gone to leave, she'd whispered, "I'll be sure to tell him you're enjoying yourself as he's touching me."

Now her mind wondered at that comment, just as it had the morning after. Who had she meant? It certainly wasn't Derrant, for he had been touching both of them. What was it she wasn't remembering? Was there someone else?

She rose and picked through the numerous dresses that had been brought to her, picking a black one, her fingers lingering on a lush red one that hung toward the back of the wardrobe. Something about it always drew her to it, but she could never bring herself to wear it.

After dressing, she wandered the halls, something Derrant permitted her to do now. There were certain areas she was barred from, and she was not permitted to leave the castle. The demons she passed eyed her menacingly, but none ever touched her. She was Derrant's, claimed by the Death God who ruled over the Shadow Realm, the shadow gods bowing to his command. No one would dare touch her.

She walked past the hall of souls where she knew he judged those cursed to his realm, handing down sentences for whatever sins they'd committed in life. It was a place she was forbidden and one she wanted to avoid, the screams carried far down the hall, often echoing through the castle. As she passed through the throne room, she glanced up at the thrones of bones high above the stairs where Derrant and the others would sit. A memory brushed her consciousness, seeing Derrant descend those stairs toward her. There was someone with her, but she couldn't make him out or determine why she felt he was important. A doorway opened, pulling her from her thoughts and Derrant stepped through as it closed, locking away the darkness of the Shadow Realm.

"Ah, Skye," he said, morphing from his terrifying stare to the glorious god he was. Angry one night, he'd ravaged her in that state. The experience had been terrifying yet erotic, the shadows enveloping her, her magic calling to them, the fear in her fleeing with his touch.

He wiped the blood from his naked chest, and she furrowed her brow.

"It is necessary to keep even my minions in check, my dear."

She worked her fingers along his abs. "And did that involve fucking one first?"

"It may have," he said with a glint in his eye. "I fucked her over the body of her dead mate and the mortal they'd stolen from the living realm, then I tore her head off. No one steals more than their quota, and no one sneaks it by me."

A shiver went through her, and he pulled her against him, groping her breast as he kissed her. Her pulse raced. He tasted of sex and death, power that emanated from every pore of his body. He stopped his kiss and walked away, leaving her craving more.

"I have something for you now that you've proven yourself to be mine. Come." He gestured for her, and she moved quickly to his side. In his hand he held a black crown of iron, etchings of haunted souls adorned the top; it was haunting, and another shiver passed through her as he placed it on her head.

"You will rule the Shadow Realm by my side, forever my slave and my queen."

She touched the crown that felt heavy on her head, a strange thought that she was someone else's queen passing through her mind.

"I was planning to kill you, Skye. To tear you to pieces for your deceit, but you are by far too special to destroy."

She felt her power return. He only granted her use of power when they had sex. She expected him to take her, preparing herself for the intensity of it, but instead he said, "It is now time for you to claim the full potential of the magic in you. To rule by my side, you must be powerful enough to stand on your own."

He stood behind her, pressing against her to take her arms. She leaned her head back against him as a wave of need passed through her. He chuckled, draping his tongue along her neck. His need for her pressing into her back. "Not yet insatiable one."

"Why not?" she asked breathlessly, as his hand moved to caress her breast.

"You are my equal in so many ways, Skye. You were born to be my queen." He gripped her hip, forcing her against his erection. "Now is not the time."

His hands drifted back to her arms. "Close your eyes and listen to the flow of your magic as it courses through your body."

"I'm too turned on to think on anything but you."

"Use that desire and focus it on your power. Your magic is sensual. That's why you are so incomparable in the bedroom. The two are intertwined. Let your desire mingle with the magic."

She closed her eyes, feeling her arousal, then reached for the magic, calling it to meet her desire. The two connected like an ignited spark within her. They danced through her body, but what she saw visually now was something she had never experienced. Not only did she see the hues, but the myriad of colors that lay below them, dancing like ribbons before her. Even in this colorless world, a rainbow of hues greeted her, rich and new, undercurrents of color.

She moved her arms from his and walked toward the colors, calling them to her, letting them drift along her skin, warm and comforting. She felt them like a warm breeze, her hair lifting in response as the breeze built. It grew in strength as she tried to grasp them again, losing control of them quickly. They pounded against her, each vying to be used.

"Skye," she heard Derrant, but couldn't free herself from the storm that now surrounded her. "Skye, you must rein the hues in."

"How?" she asked, worry attacking her as the colors began to sting her.

She couldn't see anything, the world a deluge of color.

"Grasp control and send them back before you bleed my throne room," he commanded.

"I don't know how. They're too strong."

"Concentrate and find that connection again."

Easy for you to say, she thought.

Her arousal was gone with the overwhelming flood of color. She reached back in, thinking of his touch, her hunger for him, and the whirlwind settled some, but not enough. A different touch slipped by her grasp, bringing with it a deeper need, a feeling that set her heart ablaze and the wind died down.

She closed her eyes, feeling the hues upon her skin, intermingled with that touch, her need for it cresting, and slowly the hues fell away, returning to their homes. Derrant's lips were on hers and that feeling escaped. She tried to catch it, to remember who the touch had belonged to, wanting it back, but it was gone. It disintegrated like the hues had, Derrant's touch erasing it as he pushed the sleeves of her dress down, letting it fall to the floor.

"More practice is needed, but you will make a formidable queen. Together, we will bring my brother to his knees and make every realm of this world ours," he whispered, his sudden nakedness against her. She cried out as he entered her, the pleasure washing over her in waves. Her thoughts slipped for a moment to the fact that he'd just returned from having sex with some dead demon, but it fled as he took her to his throne, sitting so that she was astride him and in control.

She lost herself to him as she set her powers free again, forgetting all thoughts of the other touch that had fueled it only moments before, forgetting everything but her god.

MARK

Mark groaned with his release. Crimson's legs were wrapped tight around him, pressing him into her. With a final grunt, he rolled from her, letting her snuggle against him as he calmed his breathing, her fingers tracing the contours of his chest. He wasn't sure how long it had been, his days and nights were now caught up in Crimson's relentless sexual needs. He'd thought Skye was insatiable, but Crimson was on an entirely different level.

When he'd first decided to continue having sex with her, to manipulate her into trusting him, he'd pictured Skye each time. But the two were different, too different, and he couldn't help but drop the image, taking Crimson as she was. If Skye weren't in his life, he would have considered Crimson as a choice. She was strong willed, beautiful, with a killer body, and moves that melted any resolve of faithfulness. It was no wonder men both desired and feared her.

If he was correct, it had been a few weeks since the day he'd taken the misstep and found himself down the rabbit hole from which he could never emerge. He was in too deep now, and he knew Skye would never forgive him. Not only for his intentional infidelity, but for the intentional one. It didn't matter that he was doing it for her. It was the entire idea of it that would kill her. Having sex with Crimson wasn't painful, it was pleasurable. Regardless of his end goal, he was enjoying it. What sane man wouldn't?

Crimson kissed his chest. "I saw Theodore yesterday."

So that's why she'd been away the prior night.

"I stole mage power to travel to him."

"And?" He wondered why she was telling him this. Was she expecting jealousy? Most likely. He didn't care, as much as he enjoyed screwing her, it was only a part of his goal. He had no feelings for her.

"I fucked him."

She *was* expecting jealousy. *Damn. Time to play the part, Mark.*

He turned to her, then twisted so that she was beneath him. He saw the flash in her eyes, the excitement as he feigned the jealousy.

"Am I not enough for you?" He grabbed her arms roughly, kissing her until she was breathless. "You have me and now I don't satisfy you?"

"Oh, you satisfy me enough for ten men, Markhem. I needed information."

"And you had to sleep with him for it?"

"Oh, you beautiful, foolish man. Of course, I did. My body is a weapon. I use it to get what I want and that's what I did."

"Your body is mine." He inwardly cringed as he said it.

Her eyes lit up. "Yes, it is. All of me is yours." She kissed him deeply, and part of him felt regret at what he was doing. The kiss was one of someone who thought she loved him. He recognized it, had broken off more relationships than he cared to count over such a kiss, knowing he could never love another.

He couldn't love Crimson back but couldn't walk away from this. Freeing Skye depended on it. His regret slid away as he remembered Crimson was the reason for being in this mess to begin with.

He took the kiss, feeling her body respond as she melted below him. Let her believe he felt the same as she urged his manhood to life again. Good gods, he was going to have to make love to her, crossing the line once again.

Her usually forceful moves were tender, vulnerable, as he gave her what she wanted, making love to her. This time he had to imagine Skye, picturing her below him, moving to a rhythm with him. As Crimson drew her breath with the peak of her climax, it was Skye he heard as he let himself rise with her. He thought of her magic against his skin and the clench of her muscles around him as she crested. His own orgasm joined hers, their bodies intertwined in one massive release that left them both quivering. Skye and only Skye remained on his mind, her name almost slipping from his mouth as he rested his head in the crook of Crimson's neck.

"Only for you," she whispered, as the last spasms of his climax slowed.

As he lay there, holding her, moonlight drifting through the windows, he felt no remorse about leading her on. She'd stolen Skye from him, handing her to the Death God, and used Mark for her own selfish needs. She'd commanded her Mage Warriors to murder the others in the war, killing his parents and Skye's father, along with countless others, Skye's mother lost among them. She deserved what was coming. Although there was a part of him that wondered if she'd ever truly been loved by a man. She used them, taking pleasure and giving pleasure, but had she ever loved, been loved?

He glanced over at her. Still snuggled against him, she seemed vulnerable in that moment. As her soft green eyes met his, he felt sorry for her. She'd turned herself into the villain but below lie a fragile, beautiful woman, who likely deserved to be loved as deeply as he loved Skye. It wouldn't be him, but she deserved someone who saw her as he was seeing her in that moment.

"What?" she asked.

He smiled. "Nothing, just thinking how beautiful you are," he answered honestly.

Her eyes brightened, and he kissed her head.

"What did Theodore tell you?" he asked, hoping his question didn't raise suspicion.

"The Elite are rising. They've convinced Revina to attack me. They don't know Mechon is dead. They're coming to rescue him, and you and Skye."

Skye's name on Crimson's tongue angered him, but he kept it at bay.

"The Elite are weak without her power. It's been severed from me, so I know they have no connection to it."

She peeked up at him as if waiting for him to betray her. "And what will you do?"

"Lead your army to victory."

She relaxed. "Really?"

"You are my queen now. I will die protecting you."

She pulled herself up, so that she was atop him, her red hair falling around her face.

"You won't die. They won't make it this far. There are advantages to bedding Theodore. His army will stop them before they reach my borders."

"So, you trade sex for protection. Is that what you're doing with me?"

"No," she said, dragging her fingers up his chest. "I'm giving you everything."

He wanted to run from her honesty, knowing she was doing something she never did, lowering her walls, trusting the wrong man. But instead, he pulled her down to kiss her, entangling his hand in her hair.

"No more sleeping with Theodore," he said, forcing his tone to sound possessive.

She pulled away, pouting.

"If you want me by your side, at your throne, you get on one else." He was praying this worked and didn't backfire on him. It was a risk if she said yes. Then he'd be stuck.

"Not even the Death God and his shadow gods?"

"Gods? You mean you screw them all?"

"Sometimes, but Derrant is the best."

"No more."

She bit her lip. "I'm supposed to see him tomorrow night, to visit and play. I can't avoid him...he owns me."

"Owns you?"

"It's a long story. Daddy made a trade, and I was traded. Derrant will kill me if I don't go."

Mark's mind tried to wrap his head around that piece of news, but he didn't have time to dwell on it. Now was his chance.

"Then I go with you."

She eyed him, her brows furrowing, distrust crossing them.

"Why?" she asked, backing away.

He grabbed her roughly and flipped her, hovering over her.

"Because I don't want you fucking the Death God."

She relaxed a bit. "And how will you stop him?"

"He has her. He doesn't need you."

"And what will you do? Join in? Help him fuck Skye? Will you make her come while he thrusts inside of her?"

She was needling him, watching for a response, waiting for a slip. He bit down the anger, the urge to slap her. Instead, he brought his head down and took her nipple in his mouth, working it until he felt her arousal. She moaned before her hand reached down to grasp him, working him until his firmness grew with her strokes.

Licking his way to her mouth, he kissed her passionately, her words fueling him.

"No," he said, drawing back and pushing her hands away. He held her wrists above her head and spread her legs open with his thigh, penetrating her with a force that sent her head tilting.

"I'll wish them luck, bid her farewell, and take you right there while they both watch. I'll make you come so hard that your screams will fill the room and she'll know she's no longer mine. She made her choice and now I've made mine."

"I like that, but those are just words." He thrust harder to prove his point.

"That's not a word," she said with a grunt. "Show me with more than just your body. I've manipulated enough men to be leery. Show me I'm your only one. That you're mine and only mine."

Her hand freed from his grasp and made its way down his arm while he tried to figure out what she meant. As her fingers touched his wedding ring, he knew.

"Take it off, remove the last piece of her, and prove yourself to me."

He paused, his heart hammering. It was only a ring, but to him and Skye, it meant so much more. It meant fifty years of longing and living a lie. The ring meant they'd finally been free to love each other as they always had.

"Markhem."

She was waiting, and if he fumbled, all of this would have been for nothing. He sat back, yanked the band from his finger, and threw it across the room, where it landed with a rolling clink.

Her smile lit the room, and that vulnerable innocence that had appeared earlier returned.

"Yes, you are mine and we will travel to the Shadow Realm together, then we will join and rule this world as one while Skye rules the Shadow Realm with Derrant. Let them have their shadows while we take the light."

He kissed her fiercely, and she grabbed at him as if she never wanted to let go, pushing her hips forward until he was deep within her. He continued to take her, all the while strategizing how to bring his plan to fruition and steal his wife back from the Death God, then win her forgiveness.

SKYE

Days passed in a blur of endless night, the realm of shadows giving Skye no glimmer of the change of days. She sat upon the stairs to the throne awaiting Derrant's return, fingering the crown that now adorned her head, heavy and distinct. She was queen of the Shadow Realm in essence. Derrant would officially give her the title in one day's time, marrying her before the shadow gods and the demons of the court. Closing her eyes at the thought of his touch, she brought her hands back down, her fingers brushing the ring she wore. It was a lovely ring, a splash of color in this drab, dark world. White diamonds lined the navy gemstone, enhancing its brightness. She often wondered at its significance, knowing it meant something that sat on the cusp of her memories but never quite knowing. Derrant had tried to take it from her, but she'd pleaded to keep it, pleasuring him until his mind had moved from it. He hadn't forgotten it, and she knew she'd have to relinquish it to him upon her vows to him. The thought saddened her, but the reason for the emotion remained aloof, hidden in the haze.

Derrant entered the throne room, a mischievous grin on his face.

"Skye, looking ravishing as always. I do believe I'll enjoy ripping that dress from your body this evening."

He came to her, greedily kissing her, pushing her back against the hard steps. She reached for him, a desperation driving her but he stopped her, pulling away.

"We have company coming, so save that need."

"Company?" she asked, not rising as he loped back down the stairs.

"You'll be sharing our bed this eve."

A flare of jealousy besieged her. The emotion was the same anytime she discovered he'd frolicked with one of his demons. Uncontrollable, a hot white current that hit her, calling her power.

"Quell your magic," he said, turning back to her, "before I take it from you again. You've shared with her before. In fact, you enjoyed it as much as I." He licked his lips. "I do so look forward to watching the two of you play again."

She saw the rise in his pants in reaction to his statement and desire swept through her, replacing the jealousy.

Before she could reply, a portal appeared, the magic splaying outward from it. Derrant turned to it, rubbing his hands together in anticipation. The woman she remembered with the lush red hair stepped through. A man followed beside her. As the doorway closed, Derrant erupted.

"You dare bring him here?"

"He is mine," the woman said, clinging to the man in a way that spoke of their familiarity. Derrant hit her with his power, and she was pulled from the man's arms. Recovering, she argued back, the two quarreling.

Skye's eyes were drawn to the man as he ran to her, the others not noticing.

"Skye!" he said, dropping in front of her. "Skye, it's me."

She stared blankly at him, not knowing why he was talking to her, but something nudged at her that she should know.

"Skye, wake up. It's me, Mark." He glanced over his shoulders at the fight. "We don't have much time."

He reached for her hand, but she pulled it back. There was a familiarity to him, but she couldn't place him. He dropped down in front of her. "Dammit, I was right. You're under a spell, Skye. Wake up!"

The room quaked with Derrant's fury.

"He's tricked you, you whore!"

"No, he hasn't. Markhem, tell him. Markhem?" There was a sadness to her voice that pained Skye. What had this man done to the woman?

"I don't know you."

"Markhem?" the woman called, but he continued to stare at Skye.

"You have been betrayed and now you will pay," Derrant roared.

While his attention focused back on the woman, the man before her grabbed Skye and kissed her. She tried to pull away, then stopped as a tingling sensation swept through her. The haze lifting.

"Mark," she murmured.

He rose and grabbed her hand, pulling her behind him as she met Crimson's eyes, a destroyed look on her face as Derrant opened the ground below her, yelling, "Your soul is mine! I'll deal with your ignorance later."

A scream resonated as she disappeared through the hole, the ground closing over her and cutting it off.

That look pained Skye's heart, and she stopped, drawing back as Derrant turned on them. Mark tried grabbing her wrist again, but she avoided his reach.

"Skye, we need to —"

"Do we?" she asked, feeling Derrant's power rise.

"No, you don't," Derrant said. "You will die for your boldness, Markhem. And she will still be mine."

She felt his magic, the familiarity of it, then turned to Derrant before he could send it toward Mark. "No, don't. I need to know something first."

Something about the hurt in her voice must have spoken to him, for he called back his magic.

Looking back to Mark, she met his eyes.

"Skye, what are you doing?"

"Did you sleep with her?"

She saw the guilt before he could hide it, her heart breaking.

"Willingly?" she asked in a whisper.

The flicker in his eyes in that moment was all she needed.

"I did what I had to do, Skye."

She remembered the look in Crimson's eyes. She knew the look. She'd fallen in love with him. Her heart cracked further, but she didn't have time to deal with the pain. She hardened herself and turned from him, walking over to Derrant.

"Skye? What are you doing?"

"Don't spell me," she told Derrant. "I've made my choice."

She pulled his head down and kissed him. The emotions flooding her were tearing her heart in two—pain, betrayal, fear, each stabbing her like a sharpened knife.

"Skye, no! You can't." Mark's voice broke.

She drew from Derrant and turned to Mark. "I can, just as you did."

She numbed herself to her pain and walked away, saying, "Banish him to the shadows, let the demons feast on him."

Derrant laughed, a sound that echoed through the throne room.

"Skye, don't do this. Please, I did what needed to be done to find you."

A doorway opened.

"Wait," she said. Derrant glared at her, but she ignored him, walking back to Mark. The pain in his eyes was laced with hope. Hope she would crush as he'd crushed her. "You did what felt good. You should have found another way. You're resourceful, Mark. Now find a way to survive the shadows." She used her magic, drawing color from her wedding ring until the silver of its band created a small weapon. The ache in her heart threatened to break her but she forced it away, too angry and hurt to acknowledge it.

"Here, I wouldn't want you to die too quickly." She pulled her wedding ring off and placed it in his hand atop the knife. His face dropped. "You don't deserve me, Mark. In a days' time, I'll have a new husband and my heart will heal. I hope she was worth it."

She shoved him, and he fell through the doorway.

"Skye, no!" he yelled, his shocked eyes never leaving hers as the doorway closed. Heartache like she'd never experienced tore through her yet she didn't break the façade.

"Well, well," Derrant said. "That was unexpected."

She turned away from the now-empty space and walked to him, dropping her dress from her shoulders. She saw the reaction as she drew closer.

"No more spells," she said, pulling him to her and kissing him.

"No more spells," he repeated, his hands exploring her body. He grabbed her ass and pressed his hardness against her.

She pushed all thoughts of Mark from her mind, freeing Derrant from his pants before ripping his shirt from him. She wanted him, wanted to experience him without the spell. Wanted him to erase the heartache that was cleaving through her body and replace it with pleasure. His hand tangled in her hair, a feral groan echoing through the hall as she wrapped her hand around his enormous erection.

He pushed her against the closest column; the force causing her to catch her breath. Her back arched with the impact, numbing her further from the ache she was trying to bury. His mouth savagely pulled her breast, sucking and playing with her nipple as his hand pinched the other. A mixture of pleasure and pain assailed her. He drew away, lowering himself and pulling her hips forward.

"You've been a loyal girl. For that, you will receive reward," he muttered before sinking his mouth into her.

A cry fell from her when his tongue hit her sensitive spot with a ferocity that sent her clinging to his shoulders. She pulled at his hair as he plunged into her, tilting her hips. Each lick led her further from the pain and closer to the rapture she needed in this moment. Derrant continued to torment her with his mouth and as his hand rose to twist her nipple, she was overcome with arousal. Her climax spilled through her, a welcome ecstasy that erased all other feeling.

He didn't give her time to settle the quakes, rising and thrusting himself into her convulsing body. He took her as the waves receded, and she accepted him, her own need fueled by the emotion she'd pushed aside. Her magic escaped to dance with his, the room a kaleidoscope of hues until he came, continuing to pound her body through it. His hands gripped her waist painfully, his erection never ceasing as another orgasm rocked her body.

"You are a queen. One who will satisfy me like no other," he said against her neck.

Moving her to the floor, he took her again before bringing her to the bedroom where he urged her mouth downward. She took him as deep as she could, blocking her mind with each move of her mouth, each grunt he emitted until he filled her once more.

Satisfied, he drifted off to sleep but Skye lay there, content but exhausted. Sex with him was always exhausting. She realized that now, never having been fully aware before. She'd grown accustomed to his size with time, except on those occasions where he'd taken her in his god form. The memories of those times were terrifying and painful enough. She didn't want to be fully awake the next time he took her that way.

She stared at the ceiling, letting her mind wander back to Mark, then stopped, knowing it would hurt too much. Instead, she listened to Derrant's steady breaths until sleep finally stole her.

MARK

D ammit!" Mark yelled, pulling himself from the tangle of vines he'd crashed into. "Goddammit!"

She'd cast him out, pushed him away. Never had he imagined she'd do that through even the worst scenarios he'd pictured. Never had he thought she'd choose the Death God over him.

She'd known. Read his guilt, the guilt he'd carried since willingly taking Crimson that first time, then all the other times as he'd fucked his way to finding her. He ran his hand over his face, looking down at the small knife in his hand, her wedding ring sitting atop it. She'd bled the colors from it so that it was now a dull gray, no shine to the stones even, a comment on her feelings at his infidelity.

He picked the ring up and clenched his hand around it, an ache pounding in his chest. Did it matter if the color was gone? She'd chosen and judged him for his decision. She'd never wear it again. Ignoring the temptation to throw it, he put it in his pocket, unwilling to give it up yet. His wedding band rested there as well. Crimson had forgotten its presence on the stone floor, and he'd rescued it, hiding it from her. There been no certainty at the time the Skye would take him back and let him wear his ring again, but he'd taken it nonetheless.

He tucked the knife into his belt, wondering if he should just call the beasts of the shadows forth to kill him or trudge back to the castle to let the Death God kill him.

A rustling pulled him from his thoughts, and he looked up to see the two demons who'd served Camin shimmying toward him. At least he hoped they were the same ones and not two who would eat him without hesitation.

"What do we have here? Look what we've found. A lost pup and Camin no longer protecting him," the one said, her long tongue licking over her lips. So much for thinking they'd hesitate.

She drew her fingers along her sister's breasts, his eyes drawn to the movement. He'd forgotten how seductive they were—in a horrifying way.

One morphed to Skye's image, naked and beautiful. He shook his head, backing up.

"No! Get her off your shape now!"

She shifted back to her demon form. "Oh, that's right. We heard the Death God has tamed the Mage Warrior. Their wedding is planned for tomorrow. Isn't that a shame?"

"Wedding?" Jesus, he was marrying her? Why? Why bother when he already had her? The Death God covets her power, he remembered Crimson saying.

"What does that do to her if they marry?"

"Why it makes her completely his, queen of the realm."

"No, there must be something more," he said as the one ran her hands down his arms, reaching for his crotch. He snatched her hand. "What does it do to her?"

She snarled, and her sister took a defensive position.

"It makes her power his."

"Why would he need more power? He's a god."

"Banished to rule a land of shadows. Her power grants him rule over color, a link to the other realms, greater than the small one we have."

She snatched her hand away.

"He'd have the ability to traverse the realms," he said.

"Yes, and take back his place in the Upper Realm."

"Overthrowing his brother. He's using her."

"Would you expect anything else? I've heard she's lucky to have lived."

"And to experience the touch of Derrant every night," the one closest to him said.

He shot her a dirty look.

"Oh, but someone is jealous. Derrant's touch is to be envied."

"No, it isn't."

"Enough talk. Since the Death God has Camin locked away in his dungeons, you have no protection. It's been a long time since we've feasted on living flesh."

"Camin is in the castle?"

Their excitement fell. "Stolen from us by you and the Mage Warrior, brought back by the Death God, only to suffer punishment in place of the Mage Warrior. Enslaved and used. Even we would not dare to see him."

"Shit."

"Now, it's time for us to play."

They slithered closer, and he tried to find an escape route, memories of what they'd done to their last living soul playing through his mind. They both morphed, changing into women, extremely attractive, well-endowed women.

"Come play," the one said, her long brown hair touching just to her nipples, lips thick and puckered as she dropped them to her sister's oversized breast. He tried to draw his eyes away, but it was hard to, and he realized that was part of their power. Seduction. His arousal grew as they kissed and the brown-haired one weaved her hands roughly into the blonde one's hair. Their hands were touching each other in all the places that turned him on further. They turned his direction, their hips moving in a spellbinding way.

Leaves crunched from behind them, their expressions changing to fear, both turning suddenly and backing up toward him. With their change in intention, the spell lifted. A heavy thud echoed through the silence, then a low growl.

"What is that?" he asked, forgetting their naked bodies and his bulging pants, thankful to be out from under their spell. He grabbed the small knife Skye had given him.

"A hunter," the one said next to him.

"What does it hunt?"

"Living and demon."

"Dammit, get behind me," he said, not knowing why he was protecting two demons who had planned to eat him moments before. He should have pushed them toward the beast and run, but that wasn't the kind of man he was. He held the knife secure as the beast emerged. Its paws were massive enough to squish all three of them easily. It stood at least six feet tall, its fangs hanging well past its drooling lips, razor sharp just as the horns that protruded from its head. How the hell was he supposed to kill that thing with such a tiny blade?

"You two run," he commanded.

"No, running only entices them to attack faster."

"Great."

The beast roared, slobber flying through the air, the trees around them shaking with the force. Mark stepped forward, curving his knife through the air like he would his Elite weapon. In that moment, he felt a tingle, the blade stretching and curving before lengthening through the other end. The stone, which now sat in the middle of the weapon, glowed with magic.

Skye's magic.

He stared at the stone, feeling the call to his blood, the rise in his strength. She'd cast him out purposely. Had she been acting just as he had? Had it all been a rouse?

The beast took another step, the ground quaking, bringing Mark's attention back to it. Smiling wickedly, he twisted the weapon in his hand and ran, sliding under the attacking jaws. Slobber rained down on him as he hopped on the paw, then threw himself toward the beast's belly, hooking his weapon in and letting it drag. The beast rose on its back paws, further accelerating the speed at which the weapon sliced it open.

Dropping, he avoided the swinging tail and rolled aside, the howl from the beast splitting his ears as it fell with a heavy thud atop its innards.

Mark relaxed his grip, and the weapon returned to its original size. Wiping the slobber from his face, he looked up at the two demons.

"Do you know where Camin is being held?"

They turned to each other, whispering and gesturing. He didn't have time for this. He needed to get back to Skye.

They stopped, and the one said, "Yes. You saved us. Why?"

He sidestepped the beast, avoiding the sea of blood that was spreading.

"That's what I do. I protect."

"But we were going to eat you."

"Yeah, not a good moment for you two. Now I need to get back to my wife and Camin might just be the one to help with that. How do I find him?"

"We will take you, if you keep us safe, as payment for our lives. But we must move; the blood will call others."

He heard a strange howl in the distance. "Good thought." As they trotted away, he asked, "Why do they call it a hunter?"

"Because that's what they do. They are hunters for the Death God."

For the Death God. Had Derrant sent the hunter to ensure his death? Not entirely satisfied with Skye's sentence? She'd banished him instead of having him killed, then given him a weapon to survive. She still loved him and if she was tricking the Death God again, she would die, no matter how he desired her in his bed.

Mark picked up his pace, pushing the demons to move faster. He had no idea how far they were from the castle, but he did know he had only one day before Skye became the Death God's true queen and brought about the fall of the Upper God.

SKYE

"Today is the day," Derrant said, rising from the bed. Skye watched how his muscles rippled with each step he took. Her eyes took him in as he dressed, remembering the demanding way he'd taken her steadily throughout the prior day, as if holding her prisoner, testing her loyalty to him, testing her choice.

She sat up, and the sheet fell to expose her breasts. They were sore from his constant attention, and there was an ache between her legs from the repeated times he'd taken her. His eyes hungrily sought hers, and he came to her, grabbing her breast and kissing her greedily.

"There are few who can tolerate my stamina. Crimson was one. Pity she is no longer an option, but you make up for what she's taken from me."

Curious about the fate of the woman who'd stolen her happiness, Skye asked, "What happened to her?"

The memory of Mark's guilt, the cries of Crimson's broken heart, came back to her. Had he fallen for her? The thought threatened to break her. Had he brought Crimson to ecstasy like he had her? She bit back the anger and the pain as Derrant responded.

"I have yet to decide her fate. For now, she suffers with the harrowed souls."

He squeezed her breast painfully before turning to leave.

"I sent a hunter after Markhem. You can set your anger aside now. He's certain to have met his end by now."

He glanced back for her reaction.

"Shame, I thought he'd suffer at least a few days before something ate him," she forced herself to say.

Laughing, he left the room.

She repressed her emotions, the urge to scream in anguish clawing for escape. She'd wanted Mark alive, had gone to great risk to ensure he survived, praying he would find his way home. She didn't want to think about what he'd done with Crimson—the betrayal—but she didn't want him dead. She still loved him.

Burying the pain, she composed herself and waited, knowing Derrant was meeting with his shadow gods in preparation for today's ceremony. It made no difference to him that she was already married. Although if he was right, then it didn't matter. She was a widow, once again.

She held her stomach and bit back the cry that begged for escape. Rising, she soaked her body in the warm tub he'd left for her, trying to keep her mind from Mark. She let the water ease the ache between her legs, the affliction in her body and in her heart.

When she left the tub, she searched through the clothes Derrant had given her for anything comfortable. Finally settling on a black dress with ties that crisscrossed along the back, leaving her neckline plunging with a low dip like he liked it, she made her way from the room.

Slowly, she walked down the halls, just as she would have any other day. Her speed hampered today by the uncomfortable bruising between her legs. Derrant had always been rough with her body, adding a level of tantalizing desire to him, but on this last day, he'd been extra rough. At one point, he'd morphed into his terrifying god form, all pleasure stripped from her with the transformation. Her horror overtaking it along with the pain of him. He'd apologized for the loss of control, taking her slowly the next time, the softness of his touches bringing her to places she'd only gone with Mark. Then the force had returned.

It was as if he suddenly owned her, pulling at her powers, forcing them loose, even climaxing to their touch.

She shook the thought away and walked on, past her usual routes, sure to keep her eyes averted if she passed a demon. At last, she made it past the usual halls and headed to the lower levels, sure to stay cautious no matter that the Death God had no need for guards. Even the possibility of disturbing the residents in these levels posed a threat to her mission.

She kept to the shadows, passing cell after cell of miserable creatures in torturous positions. Derrant had told her they kept their toys here, souls who were there for entertainment. Whatever sin they had committed warranted degrading punishments.

She averted her eyes, the moans, and cries enough to color her imagination. Eventually, she made it to the deeper dungeons, recognizing the cell doors from her brief stay. She needed to hurry. Derrant would discover her absence soon and when he did, he would bring his wrath upon her.

"Screw it," she muttered before calling, "Camin!" in a hushed whisper. "Camin, where are you?"

"Skye?" she heard from the end, followed by a chorus of voices from the other cells. She ran and peeked through the small bars, standing on her tiptoes.

"Camin?"

"What are you doing? Go back before he discovers you!"

"No, I can't. We need to escape."

She drew the black from a shadow quickly and unlocked the cell door, aware that Derrant would know the minute she used her magic.

She barged in as his roar shook the foundation.

"Skye, he'll kill us both!"

"We're already dead. Now stand back."

"Do you have a plan?"

"No, I'm winging this completely," she said as she pulled the brown from the door and the shades from the bricks, blasting through them. She prayed they could make it out alive and into the Shadow Realm before Derrant found her.

Another roar grew closer as the bricks fell away to reveal Mark standing on the other side.

"Skye?" Mark said, his face shocked.

She stared at him in disbelief, wanting to run to him but then remembering the look of guilt.

Derrant roared her name, his voice closer.

"Reunions later," Camin said, running toward Mark and dragging her with him.

Derrant appeared in the cell, the wall caving around him with the force.

"Shit, shit, shit," she said.

"If you have a plan, now's the time, Skye!" Camin yelled.

She gathered the hues she could find in the darkness, reaching in as Derrant had taught her, down to her desire, then aimed it, a portal forming. All three jumped as Derrant crumbled the ground below them, the grasp of his power grazing her arm as she fell, the doorway closing behind them.

MARK

The demons had kept their word, surprisingly, and led Mark to the castle. No guards lined the exterior so he had no trouble approaching it. Why guard a place no one would ever voluntarily venture to?

"He is here," the one said. She'd been sniffing the air as they'd moved closer.

"Where?"

She pointed directly in front of them to the castle wall. "Straight through there."

"So, if I get to that part of the wall, I'll find him behind it?"

She squinted at him. "Do not doubt my capabilities. I can find a living soul easily." She moved closer, licking her lips and touching his chest with her sharp claws. "You all smell delicious."

He brushed her claws away. "How do you know it's him?"

"Living souls don't last long in our realm. There are only two in the Death God's castle, one male, one distinctly female."

Skye. Mark's heart raced at the thought of her, a mix of anticipation and fear.

"The rest of the journey is yours. We will go no closer. No one risks the wrath of the Death God. We have paid our debt to you."

"But I fended off more than one beast out there," he argued.

"But there was only one we could not defeat. We just like watching you fight. Are you sure you don't want to participate in some wicked fucking before you go to your death? We won't kill you, I promise," the other said, morphing again before pressing her nakedness against him.

He pushed her away, trying to ignore the rise her invitation had caused. "Blondes aren't my type."

"She won't take you back, you know," she said, taking his hand and placing it on her breast before he could stop her. Her nipple rose at his touch.

"She has tasted the Death God. No woman would give that up." She moved closer, her now brown eyes lustful. "And you have tasted another. I can smell her on you. Was she worth it?"

He shoved her away. "Go, crawl back to your forests and find someone else to seduce."

A sly smile crossed her lips. "She was." She let out a laugh, then scampered away with her sister to find their next victim.

He shook his head, trying to clear the thoughts of his actions with Crimson from it. He stared across at the castle wall. There was a chance they were right. Skye might not take him back. She might choose to stay in the Shadow Realm and turn him away for his transgressions. He wavered for a split second. Maybe he should leave her here, let her keep the Death God.

No, he told himself. He needed to free her. Derrant was using her and regardless of her feelings about what had occurred, she needed saving. Her life and the balance of the world depended upon it.

There may not have been guards, but the land surrounding the castle was treacherous. Thorns cut him, mud tried to pull him under, snakes barred their fangs at him. All the while, he kept his focus on the wall where Camin was imprisoned.

Finally, he reached it, but he hadn't thought his plan through. Staring at what looked to be solid brick, he brought his weapon out. He eyed the weapon, then the wall. There was no way it would penetrate the stone.

"Fuck," he muttered. Backing up, he glanced around, wondering if there was a way in. The castle was enormous. It went on for what looked like at least a mile. Even if he made it in, how would he ever find Camin? Sighing, he contemplated his next move until the stone moved slightly. He readied his weapon and stepped back, worried that Derrant had discovered his presence.

The wall exploded, and as the debris settled, he met Skye's eyes.

"Skye?"

Derrant's voice boomed Skye's name. Camin was beside her rambling beside her about plans.

Mark stood there too stunned to move as she called her magic. He couldn't believe she was there, standing so close. Yet there was distance. He could feel it in the way she'd looked at him, see it in the dull blue of her eyes. Her hues formed a doorway as Derrant appeared behind them, his presence waking Mark from his trance. Skye grabbed him and yanked him through the portal. A blast of magic skimmed his back as he fell to the ground, rolling to a defensive position as the portal closed.

All around them the world was a cluster of fire and lava, the heat intense.

"Where are we?" Skye asked, avoiding his eyes. Given the circumstance, she looked beautiful. She wore a loose black gown that cut in a plunging V-neck, the back tied with lace that zigzagged across her open back.

He wanted to gather her in his arms and pull the dress from her body, but now was not the time, nor did he think she'd invite such a thing. As happy as he was to see her, she seemed hell bent to ignore him.

Hell.

He looked around, dragging his eyes from her.

"We're in hell." As he said it, cries of torment echoed through the air.

"Hell?" Camin asked.

"It's the other world's version of the Shadow Realm, but with heat and fire instead of shadows and demons. Skye, can you get us out of here?"

"I don't know. I'm not even sure how we got here. I haven't had much practice with forming portals other than the few I made when I first tricked Derrant." She glanced at him, then back at her hands.

The air began to shimmer, magic touching his skin.

"Brother!" a rough voice called. "How dare you enter my realm uninvited."

"Shit. Derrant's brother. I'd forgotten the gods are all related, ours and those of the other worlds," Mark said. "We need to get out of here."

A portal of black and shadows appeared across from them.

"Now, Skye!"

She created another with the red and black hues of hell, and they jumped through just as Derrant stepped through his portal. The devil roared, flames growing, scorching Mark's pants as he leapt.

They fell through another space, hitting a cold stone floor.

"Ouch," Skye said.

Terror slipped over him as he met the eyes of a man across the room, his brilliant blue eyes morphing to an endless black.

"What the Fates?" the man cried.

"Skye, get us out of here!"

He felt her magic as he saw a silver-haired woman conjure her magic, the silver-haired man next to her doing the same.

Camin grabbed Mark, and they fell again. This time, they tumbled into a crowd of people. Seeing their reactions, knowing this wasn't the right place, he took Skye's arm and ushered them down a quiet side street.

"Holy shit! What are you doing, Skye?"

"I don't know, Mark!"

"Where are we?" Camin asked, looking around with wide eyes.

Mark ran to the end of the street, taking in the shorts and the castle in the distance, the heat of the summer sun. He knew exactly where they were, but based on the clothing styles, they weren't in the present day. They were back in the eighties.

"Definitely not a period I want to return to," he mumbled, running back to Skye and Camin.

"Of all the places you send us to a Florida theme park in the summer? And how are you doing this, Skye? We're not even in the same time period!"

"What?" Her eyes finally met his.

"We're in the eighties. At least you got us somewhere we know. Who were those other people? Did you feel their power?"

"It was the power of the gods," Camin said. "The gods rule many parts of the universe and beyond. All are related, all have their own worlds, all leave each other alone. Unless they share a world. Skye, you need to get us home, now."

"I'm trying," she said. He could hear her frustration, knowing the emotion and her anxiety were contributing to the out-of-control dimension hopping they were currently doing.

"Think of home," he said to her, trying to keep his voice calm.

"I don't know if I can anymore," she replied in a whisper, her words shredding his heart.

"You need to."

She closed her eyes, and he saw the hues gather again; the portal forming. This time when they jumped, he landed softer, feeling carpeting below him.

A shriek assaulted his ears, followed by something heavy dropping. Mark looked up to see Jane, Skye's neighbor, staring in horror at them. She had taken them home. Home to the past, where none of this had happened, before their lives had changed, before he had cheated on her.

SKYE

S kye's nerves were on fire. She didn't think she could create another portal. As Mark told her to take them home, his demands raising her anxiety, she thought of the only safe place away from all of this—from the reality of Mark's indiscretion, from her own time with the Death God and her behavior once she'd turned her back on Mark, from a world she no longer wanted to be part of. She thought of home. Seeing Jane's horrified face as they crashed through the portal had not been what she'd expected.

"Really, Skye?" Mark asked, not hiding his irritation. "You take us back here? When? Are we back in our past? So, you can run away from things?"

"Shut up, Mark," she snapped.

"I thought you were dead," Jane said in a shaky voice.

They both turned to look at her.

"Dead?" Skye asked.

"Yes, well, you. You all disappeared so long ago and the place... it was a mess, broken windows and doors, furniture in disarray. The police...well they suspected foul play."

"Foul play?" Mark asked. "By whom?"

"You."

"Holy shit. They think I killed Skye?"

"And Alex...I need to sit. Where did you come from and why are you dressed like that? Who is that crazy-looking man?" She sat on the couch, staring at them.

"Crazy?" Camin asked.

"Well, you are in a bit of shambles, Camin," Mark said.

"So, I didn't take us back to the past." Skye shot Mark a look.

He scowled at her, then ran his hand through his hair. "All right, let's think about this."

"Jane, why are you in my house?"

"They're planning to auction it off. It's been over six months. Your estate is selling it since they couldn't find family. I came to pack up some of your personal stuff."

"Jesus, I need a drink," Mark said, heading to the basement.

"Yeah, that'll help," Skye snarked.

"Really, Skye?"

"Why are you two fighting so much?" Camin asked.

"Ask Mark."

"I could say the same to you."

Skye turned, her eyes lethal. "Could you? Could you really? It was a spell, Mark. Some of us had no control!"

That guilty look crossed his face again, reinforcing her suspicions.

"You wouldn't know that from the awkward walk you have, Skye. The one you gained after the spell was lifted."

He slipped into the basement before she could find something to throw. She stared at the space he'd been, seething over the comment and the look of confirmation that he had indeed cheated on her with Crimson. Heartache threatened to overwhelm her but she knew this wasn't the time for it. Sighing, she finally turned from the basement doorway and looked at Camin, who seemed baffled.

"It's a long story. Are we safe here?"

"I think so, for now. The gods don't like other gods in their worlds, hence the reaction from the fiery place."

"Hell. That was the devil's angry voice. The one I'll have nightmares about once this nightmare is over."

"Interesting."

"The devil? What are you talking about?" Jane asked.

"Another long story," Mark said as he emerged from the cellar with a bottle of wine. "Since we have time, Camin, you need a shower. How long has it been since you bathed?"

"Shadow gods don't care about hygiene," he said. "What's a shower?"

"Follow me."

Mark took him up the stairs, Skye's eyes tracking them until he glanced back at her. She looked away in that moment. The anger in his eyes was gone, replaced by sadness. She lowered her eyes, staring at her hands, until Jane finally asked, "Skye, what is going on?"

"A lot more than I can explain. Why don't you head home?"

"No, I think it best if I stay. Where's Alex, Skye?"

"Alex is fine and alive. He's...how do I explain this?"

"At school," Mark said from the top of the stairs. "Skye, can I see you in the kitchen?"

He walked past her, and she followed slowly. The kitchen lent a familiar feeling of comfort. The door to the deck had been repaired. Her fingers brushed the counter where she and Mark had made out—the memory no longer a comforting one.

"I don't want to talk about this, Mark," she said, backing away.

"We need to—"

"Do we? I know what you did. And nothing will take that away. I just, I can't even look at you without it hurting."

A wounded look crossed his eyes, and she turned away, joining Jane in the front room.

She didn't want to talk to Mark. The wound was too fresh. He didn't have to tell her he'd slept with Crimson, that he'd done it willingly, that he'd taken another woman, a woman she despised while Skye had been locked away with the Death God. How many times had he slept with her? The thought of him in the throes of passion with Crimson threatened to gut her. Her mind filled in the blanks she didn't want completed. Images abounded of him in Crimson's arms, calling her name like he did Skye's, and bringing her to orgasm while his own climax joined hers.

"Skye?" Jane dragged her from her thoughts. "I think something's wrong with you."

Skye relaxed, the hues she'd inadvertently summoned collapsing back. They sat in silence, Mark thankfully staying in the kitchen. In time, Camin came stumbling down the stairs, struggling with a pair of jeans Mark must have given him, a T-shirt hanging from his arm. He looked too thin, but he did look better.

"How do you seal these blasted things?" he asked, struggling with the zipper.

"Here," Jane said. She rose and helped him with the zipper. Skye watched a faint blush color her cheeks. Jane was an awkward woman, her brown hair touched with wisps of gray, her green eyes kind. She'd never married, inheriting her house next door to Skye when her father had died. She'd cared for him until that day. There was no man in her life, no one to know what a sweet, albeit awkward, woman she was.

"Thank you," Camin said as she helped him with the t-shirt. "The clothing here is very odd."

Jane came back to where Skye sat. "He cleans up well," she said shyly.

"Yes, he does," she replied with a smile.

"Now what?" Camin asked.

"Now, we find our way back to our world," Mark said, downing a glass of wine.

"I don't know if I can."

"You have no choice. The Elite are rallying Revina to march with them on Crimson's kingdom. They want to rescue us. Theodore is planning to stop them before they can pass his kingdom."

"Do I want to know how you know all this?" she asked.

"Because Crimson fucked Theodore for the information and the support."

"And then she shared it with you?" she said with a raise of her brow.

"Yes," was the only answer she received.

"If that's the case, it's imperative we get back immediately," said Camin. "Otherwise, we'll have a war on our hands."

"Crimson's kingdom no longer has a queen," Skye tersely added.

Camin's eyes widened in surprise. "Another part of that long story?"

"Yes," they both snapped.

A quiver went through the air, then the feel of magic brushed her skin, the air in the room growing thinner.

"Break time's over," Mark said. "Time to do your thing, Skye."

"Camin, can't you?"

"No, the Death God took my magic. Even if I had it, I can't travel any further than the Shadow Realm and back. No one but you can transcend the veils between realms."

Fear plunged through her. She had to get this right this time.

"What's going on?" Jane asked.

"Looks like you're going on a trip," she replied, calling the hues to her, grabbing the navy and grays she never realized she'd decorated her house in.

She thought about her castle, pushed past the present, and thought of the happy moments with Mark. The wedding, the night after, all the nights before, holding onto that sensual feeling Derrant had taught her to use—all from which created the portal. They stepped through; the room exploding behind them, Derrant's roar echoing around them as they fell hard on the castle floor.

She stood quickly, looking around, relief filling her as the familiar settings of the great hall met her glance. Jane was babbling in fear as one of the younger Elite came running to them.

"Thank the gods!" the Elite said.

"Brickard, have the other Elite left?" Mark asked, his voice deep and official, sending arousal through Skye as it always did when he was in commander mode.

She cursed her weakness and brushed the feeling aside.

"They left many days ago to Eltander. The last message we received was two days ago. They had gathered forces and started toward Apendia."

"Two days. That would put them midway to Theodore's kingdom," she said.

"We need to stop them."

"We thought Crimson had kidnapped you, or worse, killed you. None of us could get answers."

"Yes, it was something like that," Mark said, the anger gone from his voice.

A sting of jealousy drifted through her. She didn't know what had really happened, but whatever it was, it had involved Mark sleeping with Crimson. She turned away, not wanting to dwell on it.

"Where are my parents and Trent? Where's Alex?"

"Gone—all the full mages traveled with the Elite."

"Skye, can you portal us there?" Mark asked, avoiding her eyes.

"No, it's too risky. I'm not strong enough with the skill and I'm drained right now. We could end up anywhere."

"Then we ride. Camin, stay with Jane. Try to explain everything to her when she wakes."

Skye noticed Jane had fainted, and Camin had her in his arms. Mark grabbed Skye's wrist and rushed toward the main doors. She snatched it back and after a hurt glance, he ran out the doors to the stables. She followed, rubbing her wrist as if it would rub away the stain of his infidelity.

They stood in silence while the stable hands readied two

horses, Skye spying some pants and a tunic, along with a small pair of riding boots that looked like they would fit. She stashed them in her saddlebag. Mark gave her a look but said nothing as the stable hand brought them canteens of water and some food for the journey.

The ride was quiet. Skye had nothing to say to him, and he gave her the space. Every step the horse took ached against her sore thighs, and she knew he'd seen her grimace as she'd climbed the horse. His look failed to hide the anger reflected in his eyes. Did he think she'd enjoyed it? Done what he had and willingly slept with Derrant? Her mind wandered to the orgasm she'd had in the throne room, Derrant's tongue plunging into her with a force that had weakened her knees. Her body responded to the thought, and she gripped the reins tighter, focusing instead on the soreness between her legs from when he'd taken her over and over that prior day.

Had she enjoyed it? Let thoughts of Mark go with her, thoughts of his betrayal, given over to the urge to have someone else take his place for a moment, just long enough to take the pain away? She knew the answer, but she didn't want to admit that perhaps she had. Perhaps it hadn't been an act.

She stopped her mind from dwelling on it, staring blankly ahead as the land passed them by.

They settled for the night to rest their bodies and the horses. Skye lit a fire with her magic while Mark hunted for food. She contemplated changing into the clothes she'd found, the dress she still wore was not the most comfortable of outfits to ride in, her bare feet making it worse. But Mark returned, and she set the idea aside, not wanting to take her clothes off with him there, knowing that no matter how angry she was, she still craved his touch.

They ate in an uncomfortable and awkward silence. Staring into the fire afterward, neither knowing what to say until Mark spoke.

"We need to talk, Skye."

"Do we?" she snapped. "Do I really need to hear how you fucked Crimson?"

"It wasn't like that—"

"No? So, you didn't willingly sleep with her?"

He remained silent, and she stood, walking away.

"Once."

"Only once?"

"Dammit, Skye," he said, rising, "you don't understand."

"Then help me understand!"

"She wore me down. Tied me up and forced herself on me every day. Jesus, I had no choice—"

"But you did...maybe not every time, but at some point, you did," she said sadly, believing what he'd told her.

He looked down at his hands. "Just the one night, but you have to understand, I was angry. I thought you'd betrayed me."

"You assumed I'd do that to you?" Knowing he'd not had faith in her hurt her to her core.

"She wore me down, then twisted the truth. She manipulated me."

"And you fell for it. It doesn't matter what the excuse was, Mark, you willingly had sex with her." She wanted to run from the conversation but there was nowhere to go, so she faced it head on. "How many times, Mark?"

"Just the once."

"I know what your once means. How many times?"

His expression was pained, and she wondered how long he'd carried the guilt.

"Twice that night and..."

"And?" She put her hands on her hips.

"And she went down on me."

"Well, isn't that just a kicker? So, you got off willingly three times. How many times unwillingly?"

"Seriously? I didn't have a choice."

"You weren't under a spell. She had no magic."

"She had magic, which she used to bind me, to tie me down.

There was no place to go. And don't lecture me on what I did without consent."

"Did you make her come?"

He didn't have to answer the question, his look said it all.

"In your anger, you had sex with another woman twice, let her give you a blowjob, and gave her an orgasm. That's quite a temper, Mark. How many times did you make her come when you weren't angry?"

His eyes hardened. "I did what I had to do after that moment of weakness. The rest was to find you."

"And you didn't enjoy fucking her?"

"Did you enjoy fucking the Death God? I hear you had quite a time with him and Crimson. For someone so uptight about my threesomes, you didn't hold back!"

She felt like he'd slapped her. "I wasn't in control!"

"No?" he said, grabbing her arms. "And how about last night? I noticed you're not walking too comfortable." He pointed to the slight bruising on her arm where Derrant had squeezed her as he'd climaxed. "Didn't get this during that night of passion? Did he make you come, Skye?"

She yanked her arm back. "Shut up, Mark."

"Why? It's okay to yell at me but when the table is turned."

"I didn't willingly take him." But she heard the doubt in her voice. "You slept with Crimson. A woman I despise. All our lives I've had to watch you sleep around, countless women in your bed, all while you claim to have loved me. Did you bring them all to climax?"

"How many times did you sleep with Sam?" he growled. "How many times did he make *you* come?"

She slapped him, her anger boiling over.

He brought his hand to his cheek, and looked back at her, a lethal glare in his eyes. There was a moment where they simply stared at each other before he grabbed her roughly and pulled her to him, kissing her. She fought back, not ready for it, her own anger too high, but he didn't let go and as his hands ripped the ties of her dress, she felt her body react, warmth spreading. A longing for his touch swept through her. As much as she hated what he'd done, she still loved him, and she'd missed his touch. She craved him and her desire rebelled. She relaxed, kissing him back, opening her mouth to let his tongue explore. He gripped her ass as she pulled at his shirt, slipping it over his head, the moment's separation giving her pause until his lips found hers again and need took over. Her hands found the muscles of his chest, lingering over each one. Her chest, her muscles, her man. She needed to reclaim him, just as he wanted her to.

The sleeve of her dress slipped, and she dropped her arms to let him guide it from her, reveling in his touch. With each rough caress, each kiss, each lick, she let it wash away the stain of Derrant upon her skin and Crimson from her mind.

He lifted her, pushing her back against a tree, the bark scraping along her back. As he thrust into her, all else but the feel of him disappeared. Their moves were rough, demanding, the need too great for anything more, the emotion too high. She felt his orgasm peak and wound her legs further around him as he spilled into her, moaning her name with the action.

The exhilaration of hearing her name was dampened by the thought that it hadn't been her name escaping his mouth when he'd been with Crimson. It gave Skye pause to wonder if he'd even thought of her during any of the times he'd slept with her. No, she knew he hadn't, at least not the time he'd willingly had her. He'd been too angry with something Skye hadn't done. Angry enough to push her aside. But she'd been angry, too. She questioned if she'd done the same thing the day she'd cast him to the shadows. If she'd let her rage guide her moves, jumping straight into Derrant's willing body, letting him have her for just that moment.

Mark lifted his head and looked at her, his erection still full and resting inside her. His eyes held hurt, just as she knew hers did. Why did fate always feel the need to part them? He dropped his head against hers.

"Did you let him have you after you pushed me from the throne room?" he asked, his tone soft.

She swallowed, loosening her legs, but he lowered his hands to catch them and forced them in place.

"Then you're just as guilty as I am, Skye. Your anger at me drove your moves just as mine did."

"But I knew you were guilty."

"Does it matter?"

She nodded, the tears she'd been hiding pushing against her eyes.

"There's no one else that I love, Skye, but you. There never has been, nor will there ever be. There's only ever been you."

His lips grazed her neck and as much as she wanted to reply that he had a good way of showing it, she wanted him to continue. They met her mouth again, and she responded. He held her securely and walked them to a patch of ground where he gently lowered her. His mouth found her breasts, licking them until waves of pleasure cascaded through her. He kissed her skin, working his way along her stomach, then her legs, pausing for just a moment at the bruising on her inner thighs before kissing them. He moved all the way to her feet, as if he were reclaiming her as his. And perhaps that's what they were both doing.

An attempt at healing, even if it seemed too soon. She couldn't be without him, knew it in the depths of her soul and no matter what he'd done she would come to forgive him. There was no other for her, Mark was it, the other half of her soul. Turning her back on him had been hard enough before they'd been united, now it was impossible.

He worked his way up her other leg, letting his tongue trace the curve around her clit, and teasing it until her back arched with her need for him. He kissed his way back to her lips, where she returned his kisses as he entered her. Every nerve in her body was pulsing with her need for him, but she knew she wanted to do what he had done and take back what was hers, to erase the traces of another woman from him.

She pushed at him until she'd forced him to roll, then she picked herself up and looked at him. There was a flinch to his eyes, a quick flash of memory and she knew this was how it had started with Crimson.

Figures.

She leaned down and kissed him, his hand weaving through her hair and forcing the kiss deeper as if he too wanted her to wash away the touch, the memories. Just as he had done, she let her mouth reclaim him, ripping the traces of Crimson from him as if lifting a scar from them both. Her tongue traced the muscles of his chest and as she worked her way from his legs she took his length, blocking out the thought of Crimson taking it. He groaned deeply, a sound she knew was only for her. She didn't stop as he had, needing to take it all back, needing her mouth to be the only one in his memory.

As he released, she let his essence flow down her throat, reveling in the thickness of it, the warmth of him, until there was nothing left. She made her way back up and kissed his neck, her hand threading through his hair.

"You are mine, Mark. No one does the things I do like I do to you," she whispered in his ear.

"Jesus, no they don't. No one comes close."

"Not even Crimson."

"Well, maybe a little." There was a twinkle in his eye, but she wasn't certain she was ready for it.

"Then let's fix that."

She dropped her hand, wrapping it around his softening length, coaxing it back, something that took little effort. All the while her eyes never left his, the intensity of their gaze flaming the fire within her.

She leaned over him, whispering against his lips, "Whose touch do you crave?"

"Yours and only yours."

She searched his eyes for any doubt, any sign that Crimson had taken that from her. Finding none, she kissed him, and he returned her kiss with an urgency that sent flames rushing through her. His hand slid along her body, brushing the side of her breast, lowering to the curve of her hip until he removed her hand from his firmness. His fingers rubbed along her wetness, and she shivered as he said, "And whose touch do you crave, Skye?"

She tried to speak but he lowered his mouth, taking her nipple and sucking on it gently. A thousand currents flittered through her.

"Whose?"

She couldn't deny it was his; he was the only one she'd ever craved.

She shuttered as his fingers plunged into her and he pushed her down onto them. Her moan was uncontrollable, the feeling setting her body in a blaze of fire that rushed through her. As she moved against him, they pushed deeper into her, his thumb brushing her clit until she could take no more. She climaxed, her body squeezing his fingers as his other hand forced her convulsions in place.

"Yours." The words came out as a hoarse cry. "Only yours."

He removed his fingers while the waves continued crashing over her and flipped her to her back, thrusting deep into her, the climax rising again before it had even stopped, before sending her hurtling to oblivion. Mark held her close as he continued to move within her, slowing down until her body calmed, his moves becoming gentler. He made love to her, slow and soft, until they both climaxed as one, clasping to each other as if letting go would rip them apart once again.

MARK

Mark rose early the next morning. He'd lain with Skye in his arms, feeling the rise and fall of her breaths. As he'd watched her sleep, he'd taken in the beauty of her and the softness of her skin against his. He'd missed her painfully. He knew the previous night hadn't erased the infidelity, that would take more time, if it was even possible.

Skye's words had angered him—and in his anger he'd kissed her, forcing away the distance that had stood between them. She'd felt so good. It didn't matter to Mark how many times Crimson had forced herself on him or how many times he'd lain with her after his first slip-up—she was no match for Skye. The experience had been different with Crimson, and he'd enjoyed himself. She was sensual, demanding, and experienced, but it was still Skye who he wanted.

Mark readied the horses, letting Skye sleep while he gathered some breakfast of berries and grains for them. He stooped next to her. The air was warm enough in this region for them to sleep unclothed, and he perused her body, as he always did, only this time noting the bruises that lined her thighs. He hadn't realized the extent of them in the dark. Slight patches of purple and a dim brown marred her perfect flesh. He traced his finger over the bruised imprint of Derrant's fingers on her arms. He'd been rough to her and judging from her thighs, he had a stamina that rivaled Mark's, but in a hard, uncaring way. He clenched his fists in response, but then he remembered Skye had let Derrant take her and the wound reopened in Mark's heart. He didn't know if they'd ever reach the point when their wounds would heal.

Skye rolled over, her body stretching long and seductively. He wanted her again. A need for her called to him, and he felt the rise in his pants. Now was not the time to indulge his fantasies, however. They'd rested too long and had one more full day before they would reach the suspected path of the Elite. There would be time when they camped for the night, and he'd take her then if she let him.

She gave him a small smile and brought her hand to his cheek. Sadness clouded her eyes as she dropped her hand. "I don't know how long it will take me to forgive you, Mark. I'm not sure I'll ever forget about it, but...I love you too much not to have you in my life. I need you too much. And the possibility of you not being in it hurts worse than what you did."

Mark nodded, his heart too torn between hurt and excitement to respond to her words.

Instead, he said, "You should get changed. We've a long way to ride, and I may have destroyed your dress."

"May have?" she asked with a raised brow.

"'Certainly did' would be the better term."

He helped her up and couldn't resist bringing her in against him to hold her. Her skin was soft and as she kissed him, his body reacted. Noticing, she gave him a sexy smile and her hand found its way down to his pants.

"No, Skye," he said as she wrapped her fingers around him and stroked him. "We need to ride."

"Yes, we do. I need you again, Mark. To wash it all clean again. I need you in me."

"God, Skye, you just finished telling me you can't forgive me yet you—" A groan slipped out as she undid his buttons and her skin met his. "You're killing me. We need to go. We'll miss them if we don't."

She pulled her hand away and stopped kissing him, a look of hurt on her face. Mark grabbed her and drew her back in. "I want you, Skye, desperately. I promise each time we stop to rest the horses, I will fuck you so hard you won't have any memory of the past few weeks. And I will let you ride me all night if that's what it takes for you to know that there are no memories but those of you in my head."

"You really know how to woo a woman, don't you?" she replied coyly.

"So I've been told."

She proceeded to dress, and Mark watched her, which did nothing to help his pounding erection. The pants she'd taken from the stables were slightly big, so he cut a ribbon from the back of the destroyed dress for her to use as a belt. She tied the long-sleeved tunic in a knot at her stomach just above her pants, leaving a slight flash of skin. Gathering her hair in a messy bun, she wrapped another smaller piece of ribbon he'd cut for her around it.

"Ready?" she asked. "What? Why are you looking at me like that?"

Shaking his head, he walked to the horses.

"Mark?"

He offered a hand to her so she could mount the horse and looked up at her. "You look like one of those sexy fantasy show girls. It's a hot look on you. We may end up stopping for an early break." He gave her a wink and got onto his horse, ignoring the bulge that was pressing against his pants.

THEY RODE STEADILY, taking breaks throughout the day, and just as he'd promised, he made sure to pleasure her at each stop.

They both still needed to wipe away the memories, the stains that lingered from the last few weeks.

As the sun began to set, Mark started scouting for a place to camp. Skye had remained silent since their last stop save for a few comments here and there.

They'd been in the open for what felt like hours since they'd passed through the last town, and he noted a patch of trees ahead of them. He was calculating the distance when Skye asked something completely unexpected.

"What was she like?"

Mark tried to hide his surprise, unsure how to answer her. His heart thudded as nerves assailed him. "What do you mean?"

"Was she good? Memorable?"

"Skye, I don't think—"

"I want to know. Something drove you to climax each time she seduced you."

"I'm a man, Skye. My dick has a mind of its own; it doesn't know loyalty or love. I have no control over it."

"But it must have been good for you to give in and consent."

He sighed. "My anger—"

"Your anger didn't touch her and kiss her. Your anger didn't make her come."

"Yes, it did." He stopped his horse, trying to fight the image of Crimson's body that Skye's words had caused in his mind. Angry that she wouldn't let it go. "Do you really want to talk about this now?"

"Yes. I want to know."

"Fine. Yes, it was good. She's experienced, demanding, and fierce in bed. Are you satisfied?"

"Not to mention that killer body."

"Yes, she's voluptuous, in all the right places. Was the Death God good? If you want to know, then I want to know. What was he like?"

Skye thought for a moment. "Very well endowed," she replied and urged her horse forward, leaving Mark to consider her words.

"Was that an insult?" he asked, catching up to her.

"By no means. He's unnaturally large. It took a while to get used to it."

"But you did," he quipped, irritated by her observation.

She gave him a side glance. "You're well above average, Mark. He's a god. I would expect everything about him to be larger than life. Did you like her curves?" she asked, changing the subject.

"I...not particularly. I prefer your curves."

"Her breasts are huge, though. Didn't you like that?"

What was she doing? Her questions had him flustered so he turned it on her. "Did you? You had sex with her as well."

She looked taken aback.

"I must say, all the guilt you gave me about past threesomes and you turn around and have one with them?"

"I was under a spell."

"Did you enjoy it?" He felt a rise as he pictured her naked with Crimson.

"I don't know. I wasn't myself."

"Would you try it again?"

She narrowed her eyes. "I don't share."

"You shared Derrant."

"I don't love Derrant, and I won't share you."

That response satisfied him, although the image was still there.

They reached the trees and found a place near a river for shelter. While they removed the saddles, he asked, "Why did you ask about Crimson?"

She put the saddle down, then blew a strand of hair away from her face. "I guess I'm looking for a reason. Something to justify the deed."

She turned and walked toward the river, removing her clothes as she walked. Mark watched as she waded in, dipping her head back. The setting sun reflected on her skin, lighting strands of gold in her rich brown hair.

She wanted a reason, something to validate his indiscretion, and he had none.

Mark stripped and joined her, bringing her body to him.

"I don't have a reason, Skye, other than blind rage and stupidity. She got to me. She wore me down by having sex with me every day until she used the thing I feared the most against me."

"Every day?"

"Just about. I was bound, Skye. She had my arms and legs tied with magic. Then she took advantage of my unruly, rebellious sex drive."

Her hand grasped him, and he responded to her touch. "So, you're blaming it on your dick?"

"Completely."

She laughed. "What was the one thing you feared the most?"

"Losing you to another man again."

Her eyes softened.

"Listen to me, Skye. I love you. There is no one else like you. Crimson is beautiful, sexy and yes, she's good in bed." Skye cocked her brow, about to reply, but Mark stopped her with his finger. "But she is not you. It's your body that I want, your kisses, your touches, your moans—only yours. What I did was entirely unfair, and I can't take it back, but there was never a moment when she replaced you in my heart."

She moved closer, her hand still stroking him, then brought her lips to his. "I want to forget it all, Mark. I want to be back on our wedding night before all of this happened when we weren't scarred by the touch of others."

"We were already scarred, Skye," he said in between kisses. He moved her hand, picked her up and made love to her there with the river water slowly gliding around them. As her climax heightened, even the hues in the stars dimmed to her call. Ribbons of color encapsulated them until, in one rush, she peaked with him, the colors flooding away.

They spent the evening making love, foregoing food for their bodies. They clung to each other with a desperation that came from the distance that had been forced upon them, and the life riven by the needs and demands of others once again.

IN THE MORNING, a storm blew in, waking them with a deluge of rain. Lightning struck, lighting the early morning darkness and disturbing the horses. Mark ran to them as they neighed and bucked as a strike of lightning hit nearby, setting a tree alight with flames.

"We need to get away from the river and find shelter!" he yelled to Skye.

As he untethered the horses, thunder cracked the sky. The horses pulled quickly, and the wet reins slipped from Mark's grasp.

"No!" Skye called as they galloped off.

"Dammit!"

With the horses gone, they were stranded.

"How far out do you think we are?"

"A few hours by horseback."

The rain continued to fall upon them, only adding to the sullen mood. The raindrops ran down Skye's naked body like sand falling in an hourglass, stirring the desire in him. Setting it aside, he told her to dress while he thought about their options.

"We don't have any options, Mark," she said, ignoring his instructions. "We won't make it on foot. By the time we do, they'll be to Theodore's kingdom. I have to take us."

"No, it's too risky. You said so yourself. We could end up stranded somewhere. What if we end up back in the Shadow Realm?"

"What other choice do we have, Mark? Alex is with them. I can't risk losing him because I was too afraid to try."

He sighed. She was right. Alex was untrained but he was a full mage and all mages had been called to fight. Mark pulled her wet, nakedness to him and brushed the soaked hair from her face.

"I suppose if we're stuck somewhere, at least we'll be stuck together."

"And die together?" she asked.

"If I have to die it will be by your side, protecting you."

She gave him a sad smile. He knew what it had taken for her to get them home before. Her skills were still untapped, her magic in its infancy, and it made her vulnerable.

"Fine, I acquiesce," he said, against his better judgement.

"Make love to me first," she whispered.

"Not satisfied from last night?" he asked, playfully.

She tilted her head to the rain, letting it drift upon her face and said, "No, never."

He licked a raindrop from her skin, tracing it with his tongue. Thoughts of finding shelter slipped away as he made love to her once more, knowing this might be his last moments to do so. He kissed and tasted every inch of her body, memorizing it as he did each time and imprinting the feel of her skin against him, each sigh she made, each quiver of her body. As her climax built, his climbed to meet hers until both were awash with pleasure and nothing else existed.

The rain had stopped and, although Mark wanted to keep her in his arms, to delay the impending unknown, he knew it was time. They pulled their wet clothes on, ignoring the sticky feel of them, Mark's eyes following the moves of her body as she covered it.

"What I wouldn't do for a dryer right about now," Skye mumbled. "Ready?"

"Ready."

Mark watched as she drew from the colors of the rising sun, the droplets of rain that sat upon the tree leaves, the while caps upon the river water. It occurred to him that each time she created a portal, she pulled different colors. This time white and opaque hues licked at the edges of a cream-colored portal. It was distinctly different from other portals she'd created.

"Skye, do the colors you choose effect the destination of the portal?"

She studied it thoughtfully for a moment. "I don't really know. I never thought about it."

An unsettled feeling crossed through Mark, and he had second thoughts about letting her step through.

"There are a lot of light colors to this one. And you usually use the darker hues."

"Maybe I was just in the mood for something different today?"

He looked sharply at her, her words not helping to assuage the sense of foreboding that was nagging at him.

She stretched her hand to his. "It'll be fine, Mark."

Still not convinced and seriously considering what her color choice meant for their destination, he hesitated.

"Mark, we need to go through. You agreed that I needed to take a chance and form a portal. This is it. Wherever it takes us, we need to have faith in my abilities."

She held out her hand, the light of the portal shimmering in her eyes. She was right. He'd agreed that this was the only option. He needed to put aside the worry and trust her.

Taking her hand, he stepped through the portal with her. A blast of cold air raked across Mark's skin as the doorway shut behind them.

"Holy shit, Skye."

"This isn't right, is it?"

He looked around the snowy mountain range, his wet body shivering at the temperature.

"No, it's not. Not even close."

SKYE

Skye stared at the white setting. The falling snow was dropping her body temperature quickly and her teeth began to chatter. Just moments ago, she'd been warm with the aftereffects of making love to Mark. His touch always warmed every corner of her soul.

"What mood were you in to bring us here?" Mark asked her. She heard the distinct edge of fear that layered his words.

"Where is here?" she asked, shivering, the water on her skin turning to ice.

"The Dranth Mountains."

"The mountains beyond Eltander?"

"Yes."

She stared at him with wide eyes.

"I promised you dragons, but this isn't how I pictured the moment. You need to get us out of here, quickly."

"Will they eat us?"

"Who knows? No one has seen them in centuries. We'll likely freeze to death first."

Dragons. The thought was terrifying. She tried drawing her magic, but her body was too cold.

"I can't," she said, her teeth chattering in harmony with the uncontrollable shaking that had overcome her body.

Mark brought his body against hers, trying to warm her arms, but she knew he was just as cold.

"We're going to die up here. Oh my God." As the emotion welled in her, she inadvertently pulled the white hue from where they stood. It circled them, encasing them, a bit of protection from the wind and cold.

The mountain rumbled.

"Uh-oh, did I cause an avalanche?"

Slowly, Mark turned away from her toward the direction of the rumble, putting his body in front of hers.

"Mark?"

His hand reached toward the dagger she'd given him. Only then did she notice he was no longer wearing his wedding ring. She traced the bare wedding finger on her own hand, wondering if he'd removed his when she'd returned hers to him or before.

"Stay very still," he whispered, drawing her attention back and ceasing the emotional reaction the thought had caused.

"How do I do that when my body won't stop shaking?" A rush of warm air broke through her hues and dissipated as warmth spread through her body. "Wow, that was a strange, warm breeze."

"I don't think that was a breeze," Mark said, gripping her hand.

Slowly she looked over her shoulder, her eyes meeting the largest blue eyes she'd ever seen, slits of gold encompassing them.

"M—Mark."

She stood frozen in fear, the blue eyes evaluating her, as if searching for something.

"Don't move, Skye. There's one right ahead of us."

"Ummm, I don't think that one's the issue."

She swallowed as the dragon brought its head closer, its face right before hers. It tilted its head, still studying her, its gaze intense.

She wondered what had drawn the attention of the beasts. Surely not their presence. They were tiny ants compared to this enormous beast. Her magic. It had to have been her magic.

She let go of Mark's hand, and he turned at her move.

"Oh, shit!" He started to push her behind him, but the dragon's eyes narrowed.

"Mark, stop. I don't think it wants to hurt me, but it may hurt you if you don't stop."

"Are you crazy? It's right in front of us."

"I know, but putting me behind you will do nothing to protect me. It will eat us both at once."

"Good point."

"I think it's drawn to me."

"What?"

"Watch." She called the hues from her pants. Pants that were now dry due to the warm breath of the dragons. The idea that dragon breath could dry clothing was one that would have had her excited if she weren't currently praying she wouldn't be an appetizer for the one currently eyeing her. The hues she'd drawn swirled around her, and she let them drift in the air before them.

The dragon relaxed, sitting on its enormous haunches, and watched the colors. Moments went by and she questioned if she'd read the situation wrong. Nerves were bounding through her, causing a shake that made its way from her toes to her hands. Finally, the dragon brought its eyes to Skye before expanding its massive wings—wings that matched the ice blue of its skin but with patterns of black upon it.

Skye stepped back in fear, bumping into Mark, who wrapped his hand around her waist. She stared in awe as it tipped its head and a fury of white and blue flames exited its mouth, lighting the clouds above. They shimmered a glittering blue.

Within moments, dragons surrounded them—white, blue, and pearl. The beautiful mammoth beasts took her breath away.

Mage Warrior, a voice echoed around them, causing snow to shift precariously under their feet.

The blue dragon tipped its head back and stood on all four legs, towering over Skye and Mark. It had to be fifteen feet tall.

She has come, another voice said.

"Mark, what's happening?" Skye whispered. She was a mix of fear and amazement, not knowing which emotion should be greater. Dragons surrounded them. Things of legend, of stories and movies, not reality. Yet, here they were.

"I don't know, but they're talking. Dragon's talk?" Mark mused before saying, "They're talking about you."

Voices erupted around them like a chaotic storm of whispers until a deafening roar overpowered them all, and an avalanche of snow barreled toward them. With the sweep of a wing, a dragon redirected the flurry of snow. The top of the mountain moved and a blue eye opened, the same shade as the others. The dragon uncoiled itself from what Skye thought had been the mountain-top. It was larger than the others, the dark blue of its scales almost black. The other dragons moved to the side as it made its way to them.

Mark held her protectively, and she felt the pounding of his heart. Something about the dragon drew Skye away from him. She left his side, taking small, slow steps toward it as it walked to meet her.

"Skye?" Mark said after her, but she ignored him.

The dragon unwrapped its wings, spreading them so wide they shadowed the others. Skye drew a breath as it lowered its head to her.

Daughter, one of my blood, it said in a female voice, *returned to claim her rightful place in this world. We've waited a very long time for you.*

"Daughter?" Skye asked.

The dragon's eyes smiled then in a flurry of wind and snow that stung Skye's skin, the dragon changed to a breathtaking woman with eyes that matched Skye's, hair the same dark auburn shade as Skye's but with streaks of blue through it matching her dragon hide. An ephemeral dress of silver coated her body.

"Good gods, it's Eliana," Mark said.

Skye turned to look at him, hoping this wasn't some old girlfriend. She could compete with Crimson, but this woman was supernatural. Mark dropped to his knees, his head bowed. Supernatural, her mind repeated.

The woman smiled at Skye, a smile that warmed her heart.

"Rise Markhem of Strantril. You, Daughter, have found your way here at just the right time."

"Who are you?" Skye asked.

"She's Eliana, goddess of the Shadow Realm, sister to Carzent and Derrant, the Mistress of Death," Mark said. "And she's been lost to us for thousands of years."

Eliana's eyes darkened to a rich navy. "Derrant is the reason for my exile here." Her expression softened. "And now, he hunts you, unaware of who you truly are but drawn to you because of it."

"I don't understand," Skye said.

"You are a daughter to the daughters and sons who came from my love—the first of the Mage Warriors. Ancestor to the son I bore with the mortal I loved. I gave up everything for them. I fled so that they could live and left Derrant's hand so that they could have life, so that you could one day be born. You are my salvation and the one who will lead the way to my return and my brother's undoing."

Skye didn't know what to say, and was thankful when Mark asked, "The Mage Warriors are your descendants?"

She gave him a warm smile. "Come, I will warm you and answer your questions."

"Pardon my inconsideration, but we don't have time for talk," he said.

Eliana began walking back toward the cap of the mountain where a large flat, uncovered surface had appeared after she'd woken.

"I know," she said as she continued to walk.

Skye looked at Mark, who shrugged and took her hand.

Together they followed the path of the goddess, where the snow had melted with each step she'd taken.

"The Elite march toward Theodore, who plans to cut them down. Fool, he and Crimson were never satisfied with their own blessings."

She sat upon a throne of rocks that rose from the snow. Two seats formed for Mark and Skye as well.

"Then you know why we must move with haste," Mark said as they sat.

Skye had expected a seat of rock to be hard and uncomfortable but was surprised to find it was soft.

"I do." Eliana rested her chin upon her hand and sat pensively. "It is Crimson's greed and Theodore's shortcomings that got you into this mess. Crimson's line has always been tarnished, they had potential but became warped. Pity, she of all of them could have done great things, but her father traded her to Derrant for power. Lot of good it did him. He's dead, and the power ruined her. Their line was never meant to carry magic. My son had two children, you see, and the magic carried through to both of them because I was hidden away, unable to stop the passage to the second child."

"Two children?" Mark asked. "Mage Warriors only ever have one child. There has never been a second."

There was a moment where Eliana appeared melancholy, but the moment passed quickly before she continued. "It is that way now, as it should always have been, but there were two born that day. The eldest child, Trezi, ruled Kantenda, the other, Vazil, married into Crimson's line and ruled Apendia. My brother, Carzent, drained the power in her line when he discovered she held it. Vazil's husband's line favored Derrant, and as a reward, Derrant struck a bargain with the kingdom of Digremile to protect Vazil's daughter from Carzent, but it was not to be. The entire kingdom of Digremile was cursed for their failure, and Crimson's line was stripped of magic, left as nothing but empty vessels. Vazil's daughter was raped by a usurper, bearing the child who's birth brought about the souring of her line. Kantenda was left as the only ones to hold my magic from that moment on."

She paused, her eyes staring off, seeing something neither Skye nor Mark could see. "Crimson is a result of her family's violent past and her father's greed for power. She is a vessel for magic that she should not possess, damaged by her father and my brother. And what came of it? A woman who manipulates, uses, and misunderstands her potential. And now she suffers Derrant's punishment."

"Wait, are you saying Crimson is a mage?" Mark asked.

"No, she is something else. When Carzent took the magic from her line, he did not remove the potential for it. Derrant taught her how to access that potential when she was very young, younger than she should have been. Desperate for the attention of a man, she turned to a god who used her just as much as her father did. She is no mage. Regardless of what she is, she hails from the original Mage Warrior line."

"So that makes us ..." Skye started.

"Yes, you and Crimson are kin, very far removed, mind you, but kin nonetheless. Both of you are my daughters."

Skye sat back as Mark looked at her, the memories of his betrayal sweeping back before she averted her eyes.

"Ah, you blame him. Crimson's power takes many forms. She does not have magic like a mage, she is merely a temporary receptacle for it. She can borrow magic for a short time and use it to her will, but that is all. Her own power lies in deception, manipulation, and seduction. She was created from a violent affront to the magic within her mother and it clung to her in the womb. Her father was cruel, forcing her mother into marriage, then raping her repeatedly. Crimson is a product of that violation. There is no denying her, and if you do, she uses your emotions, feeding from it, owning it until there is no other than her." Eliana looked at Mark. "You were strong, but even the strongest fall to her. She has more of my brother in her than me. Derrant's claim on her has tainted her blood, but she is no longer a threat to you. My brother, however, is. He hunts you, Skye, and he will stop at nothing to have you. Even now he bangs at the gates that hold him prisoner in the Shadow Realm."

"He wants her power," Mark said. Skye turned to him swiftly, surprised by his words. "He thinks he can use it to escape and overthrow the Upper Realm."

"Yes. He hates Carzent, our brother. But it is not only the power he wants. He wants her. You are much like me, Skye, and you remind him of me."

Skye looked questioningly at her.

"So, the myth is true?" Mark asked.

"Yes," Eliana replied, the sadness in her eyes palpable.

"What myth?" Skye asked. She was already overwhelmed by all that she'd learned and didn't know how there could possibly be more.

"Derrant desired Eliana and chased her until Carzent hid her from him. That's why she hasn't been seen since," Mark answered.

"How abbreviated the story has become," Eliana said. "When this world was created. Derrant was given the Shadow Realm. Carzent sent me with him to balance him. Derrant would claim the scarred and wicked souls, punish them, then obliterate them so there was no chance of returning. I would guide the worthy souls to their resting place in the Upper Realm. The Shadow Realm was a balance of the two of us." She paused, looking beyond them. "I loved my brother, and he loved me, but life trapped in another realm can lead to unexpected things. We became more than brother and sister. We always were."

"You fell in love with him," Skye stated, her stomach turning.

"You have to understand that we only call each other brothers and sisters. All of us came from one source at the dawn of time, but it is only a bond that makes us family, providing a kinship that forms as we grow. We are not truly related because we are not of a woman's body. We are formed from a spark. Some of us form within that same spark, and so the bond begins.

"Derrant was different then, but he became obsessed with his power. Slowly, the souls became part of his collection. Some became his shadow gods and others became the demons that now roam his realm. We were fighting, and it was at that time that I saw *him*. You see, I would shepherd the souls, and as I did, there was always a glimmer of this realm as the soul crossed over. I saw him as he grieved his mother, for she was the one I guided." Eliana paused, her eyes drifting with the memory. "He was lovely and my heart beat for him. I snuck from the Shadow Realm, and I fell in love again."

"With the king of Kantenda? Skye's ancestor?" Mark asked.

"Yes. Derrant was furious, but I loved him. When I found out I was with child, I went to Carzent. I had planned to give up my immortality for a life with him, a mortal life. Carzent agreed, but Derrant found out after the child was born. I was forced to make a choice. Leaving the child with my lover, I fled to Carzent. I begged him to help me, to protect my child from Derrant, to hide me from his wrath."

She looked away, staring at the clouds, a deep sadness in her eyes.

"He made you into this?" Skye asked.

Eliana nodded. "Yes, but not before Derrant reached me and forced himself on me in his anger before I could flee. I was hiding, awaiting Carzent's decision, knowing that what I'd asked of him would cause a rift between him and Derrant, further dividing their realms. He found me...and raped me there in the forests of Eltander. He dragged me back to the Shadow Realm, thinking he could keep me there with him and that I would return to who I'd been before I'd left him.

"Carzent found me as I escaped Derrant for the last time, and in his pity for me and rage at what Derrant had done to me, he changed me. I fled to the mountains, where he hid me from Derrant's eyes. I gave birth to the first two dragons sometime later, our children. It is only in this realm that I am fertile. It's a curse and a blessing. Derrant has hated our brother ever since, vowing to destroy him for hiding me, and to bring me back. That is why he covets you and your magic, Skye. You remind him of me, your hair, your eyes, and the power you hold is distinctly mine, and in you it is tenfold what it was in any Mage Warrior before you. It is enough for him to control and destroy the prison that holds him forever. With you, he can overthrow Carzent."

Skye's mind was reeling. She'd heard too much history to comprehend. All she could do was stare at Eliana, wondering how she'd remained so strong after the brutality Derrant had wrought upon her.

"How do I protect her?" Mark asked.

"You don't, not this time."

"So I just let Derrant find her and take her?"

"No, you must first stop the impending war. Crimson will not escape my brother's grasp. Her punishment is eternal, her throne empty. Theodore must not be allowed to seize it. There is a young boy, the heir of her father's half-sister. Ensure the throne goes to him."

Eliana stood and extended her hand to Skye. "My brother will escape. The binds to the Shadow Realm weaken with each attempt he makes to break free. It will not be long. When you see him, give him this." She brushed Skye's hair back and before Skye knew what was happening, Eliana gave her a long, passionate kiss on the mouth. Afraid to pull away from the kiss, Skye remained in place, her eyes wide in shock.

As she drew away, Eliana said. "That will be what he needs."

"Wait, you just kissed my wife and now you want her to kiss the Death God?"

She laughed. "Check your jealousy, Markhem. It is something she has already done, and it holds no meaning to her. My brother is a beautiful, seductive man. No woman can resist his touch, but then Crimson is so very like him. The claim he made on her soul twisted her to his own likeness." Eliana rested a hand on his. "Trust your wife, for her heart and soul are yours, and yours alone. It is not the body you want to own, it is her heart."

She walked away, and Skye met Mark's eyes. He was studying her, and, in that moment, she felt their love as if it were a physical part of her skin, of her body, layering her like a protective blanket.

Smiling, she took his hand, and he moved to kiss her.

"Eh, eh. Do not kiss her until after she delivers my message."

The blue dragon had appeared as well as a pearl one. "Now take my sons and go stop this war. Derrant's escape is imminent, and you do not want him to find you in the middle of a battle."

"If he does?" Skye asked, uncertain she wanted the answer.

"He will kill everyone, give your lover a slow death as you watch, then steal you again with no chance of escape."

MARK

Mark's heart hammered as he climbed onto the white dragon. Eliana's words echoed through his mind, and he prayed they would make it in time.

Hanging on for dear life as they flew, he thought about what he'd learned. Skye had the blood of a goddess in her. It was evident her magic was formidable. There were rumors that the Mage Warrior line had spawned from one of the gods, but neither Mark nor any of the others had ever imagined the rumor to be true. And to find out that the same blood ran through Crimson, that she and Skye were related, that they were related to the dragons, was surreal.

He glanced over at Skye. Perched comfortably on the blue dragon she was glorious. The wind blew her hair back, and the sleeve of her shirt slipped from her shoulder, exposing the flesh of her left breast. Her eyes were a vibrant blue, alive with electric currents flashing through them. She looked in her element, a queen, a goddess of her own right.

Desire whispered to him, but as his dragon dipped, he clung tighter, the desire fleeing with his fear. As they descended, he saw the armies below. They had yet to meet, but it looked tense. Elite stood in position, flanking the mages. Theodore's army was spread far in the opposite direction. Three horses with riders stood between the armies. They looked up, and he recognized Petrian, Revina, and Theodore. Theodore yelled something to his army, and they began backing away from the incoming dragons. The Elite were too well trained to break rank and held their position. Revina's troops followed their lead.

The dragons landed, their wings stirring the air. The force unsteadied the horses who bucked in an attempt to run from the massive beasts.

Skye dismounted before Mark could and as he landed on the ground, attempting not to vomit, she approached Theodore. She didn't even seem fazed by the heart pounding, tumultuous ride.

"You will withdraw your forces and return to your kingdom!" she commanded Theodore with a fierceness that impressed Mark.

Petrian looked relieved to see them but stayed quiet.

"Your army is on my land."

"Yes, trying to find us," she replied.

"That is not my concern."

Skye lifted her head, drawing the brown of the horse's hide. It reared back, throwing Theodore to the ground. She released the hues as Mark grabbed Theodore by the collar and lifted him. Theodore's troops looked ready to attack, but Mark's dragon stepped between them, emitting a massive roar.

"Get your hands off me! You have no right!"

The punch landed squarely, and Mark heard the satisfying break of cartilage.

"Now, you will shut up and listen. I have every desire to feed you to that dragon right now, so hold your tongue, Theodore," he growled.

Blood gushed from Theodore's nose, but Mark's anger didn't simmer. Instead, it was boiling over. He could feel Skye's eyes on him. The desire to pull his weapon and send Theodore's soul to the Shadow Realm was strong. Mark wanted him to suffer the same fate as Crimson, both rotting with the demons for what they'd done to him and Skye.

He knew what Skye was thinking. Her eyes evaluated him, likely seeing how Crimson had manipulated him. How she'd used his anger that had been spurred by Skye and his emotions for her. He'd had to keep his anger in check for so long, bowing to Elspeth's decisions, her lead, while they were in the other world, letting it simmer as he'd watched the life he'd wanted with Skye play out with another man. The effort to hold it back for so long had faltered and now it engulfed him, overtaking his senses, dictating his actions even to the point that he'd let it dictate his beliefs in Skye's fidelity. It had almost cost him everything...or perhaps it had. He carried the guilt of his infidelity as openly as he carried his anger, not knowing if it would ever fade. But then again, he didn't know if her hurt would ever fade. Both were scars they were now meant to carry.

He pulled his focus back to Theodore, the anger seething within himself. The same anger that had propelled him to the unforgivable act with Crimson was threatening to murder the man in his hands.

"I should kill you for standing by while Crimson killed Mechon, took me prisoner, and handed Skye to the Death God."

Revina let out a cry when she heard Mechon's fate. She hadn't known. None of them had known any of their fates. All of them were likely waiting for word on the fate of the three, and with no answer, had blindly rushed in to save or bury them.

Revina's anguish cooled Mark's ire, and he loosened his grip on Theodore slightly.

"Where is Crimson?" Theodore asked.

"The Death God has her," Mark answered through gritted teeth. "She'll be keeping his demons company for a very long time."

Theodore paled.

"Now, take your men and retreat behind your walls while we decide your fate. The Death God hunts my wife as we speak. If your men are here, they will all suffer his wrath. Their lives are the only reason I will allow you to walk away, but if he so much as touches her again, you will suffer my wrath for all you have done."

Mark shoved Theodore, who stumbled back then tried to recover himself, his face still ashen and blood soaked. Mark stared him down, knowing his gaze was lethal. Theodore glared at him before backing away. There had been a moment when Mark worried the man would do something foolish, but he didn't. Instead, he ordered his men to retreat on the grounds of false pretense, something they readily accepted, moving quickly from the dragons.

Skye's magic touched Mark's skin—gently, seductively—his fury calling to something within her, the fire that fueled her sex drive. He glanced over at her, seeing the quick flush of her cheeks, and the heave of her chest at whatever thoughts had just been in her mind, and gave her a sly grin. If impending doom wasn't barreling down on them, he would have taken her there, regardless of whom they offended. The need within him was spurred by the heavy look of lust in her navy eyes.

"Thank the gods you're alive," Petrian said, interrupting his dirty thought and embracing him. He pulled back, his hands on Mark's shoulders, and gave a quick glance to the pressing growth in his pants. Lifting his brow, he shook his head. "I see you're as happy to see me as I am you. I hope that's not for your wife when you're surrounded by troops and, astonishingly enough, dragons."

"I'll choose not to answer that, Uncle," Mark said.

"Mom!" Alex cried, rushing to Skye, her parents behind him.

"Gods, we thought you were dead. We tried to reach you over and over. Sent emissaries, countless messages, all with no response. We feared the worst," Elspeth said, pulling Skye in for a hug.

"It was the worst. None of us came out unscathed," she answered, meeting Mark's eyes, the weight of her words like a knife to his chest. "Some of us did not survive."

Mark felt Petrian's eyes on him as the others looked question-

ingly between him and Skye. She drew her eyes from his and
glanced over at Revina, Mark following her move. Revina had put
on a brave face, but the paleness of her skin belied the pain below.
Skye excused herself from them and made her way to Revina, and
Mark used the moment to do the same, fleeing the awkward questions that lay before him. He preferred not to tell Alex that he'd
cheated on his mother, or that she'd spent too many days in the
Death God's bed, some of which were not due to any spell cast
upon her.

"I'm so sorry." He heard her tell Revina as he joined her side.
"It happened so fast, none of us saw it coming."

"Who did it? Did the whore do it herself? Did she draw the
blade bravely?" Revina asked.

"No," Mark replied. "She was cowardly and had her guard do
it. It was a quick death."

She nodded. "Quicker and luckier, I suppose, than what the
two of you went through."

"You've no idea," Mark muttered.

"We're not out of it yet," Skye said, ignoring the comment.
"You need to turn your troops back and get to the safety of your
kingdom. Grieve with your people."

"Do you not need our help?"

"With the Death God? I would never ask that of anyone,"
Skye said. "Mechon's death was enough. Take your troops
home."

"I need to avenge my husband's death. I will not turn back."

"His death has been avenged. Crimson is with the Death God
now. Her punishment will not be light."

She eyed them both. "How do you know this?"

"Because I caused her punishment," Mark answered, avoiding
Skye's eyes. "And I watched him send her to the pit of souls to
await her sentencing. She will bother none of us again."

"She is manipulative—"

"But even she can't escape his wrath this time," Mark said.

Revina remained quiet for a moment, and Mark worried

about the time that they were wasting with explanations and reunions. There was little time and too much at stake.

"Very well, I will accept that she has paid her debt and we will turn back. I will carry the news to my people and our daughter. The kingdom will pass to her when she reaches age."

Skye embraced her, and Revina clasped tightly to her. As she drew back, she gave Mark a nod before walking to her horse.

They returned to the others, who were watching them intently. They wanted answers he could not provide, some he wasn't ready to give them. The pain was still raw, the wounds too fresh, the emotions between him and Skye still too fragile. He wasn't sure that they would ever share all the details. Looking at Alex, he hoped they wouldn't. The hurt in Skye's eyes had been punishment enough. To see it in Alex's would be like a knife in the still festering wound.

"Alex, you and your grandparents need to accompany Revina in case she runs into trouble on the way back," Mark commanded.

"Really?" he said, and Mark could see the excitement in his eyes.

"Mark, no, he's too young," Skye argued.

"He was about to ride into battle with an army. I think he's old enough, Skye."

"We'll keep an eye on him. Maybe you can convince Mark to let him bring the girl with us," Elspeth said.

"Girl?" he asked.

"The girl from school, Clover. All mages, young and experienced, were called to duty."

Skye smiled, and it lit his heart. "What do you say, Mark?"

"Fine by me."

Mark watched as they said quick goodbyes and began moving away with Revina's troops, Alex running into the Elite and mage forces to find his girl.

"It seems too calm," Mark noted.

"Do you want to tell me what's happened?" Petrian asked.

"It's a long story, but one for another time. Joahem, Ryland!"

His fourth and fifth in command came running up.

"Markhem, good to see you both safe," Joahem said.

"We're not safe yet. Ryland, I need you to accompany Petrian to Crimson's kingdom. She won't be returning, and an heir needs to be chosen. Noah is there somewhere. Find him."

"He's alive?"

"I believe so. Crimson had him taken somewhere. Trust me, he's either completely scarred or his poor wife will be giving him a lashing."

"I don't want to know, do I?" Petrian said.

"No," Skye answered sourly.

"How do we find an heir to the throne?"

Mark wasn't entirely certain, but then Skye looked toward the two dragons, who had curled up and were intently watching them.

"Take the blue dragon. He'll know."

"Ride a dragon? You can't be serious," Petrian said, and Mark could see the nervous shake of his hands.

"Yes, I am. The dragons know who it is. Take this one, he'll lead you straight to the heir and be your protection," Mark said.

"This just keeps getting stranger and stranger," Petrian mumbled, shaking his head.

"That's an understatement," Mark said. "Joahem instruct the men to turn back. Skye and I need to move before the Death God finds us."

"I thought he couldn't move between our realms?" Joahem asked.

"He's been trying to change that."

At that moment, the ground rumbled. The two dragons rose, their eyes deadly as they looked for the cause. Mark's nerves rose with them, tension mounting as the rumble grew.

"Skye, can you get us out of here?" he asked, desperate to have her far away from wherever Derrant emerged.

"I don't think we have time."

The dragons roared as the sky filled with ebony and gray clouds.

"Go, take the dragon and...take Skye," Mark commanded to Petrian.

"No! You can't fight the Death God by yourself!" she yelled.

"No, but I can buy you time."

"This is my fight. Petrian, Ryland, take the dragon and go," she said, anger flickering in her eyes.

"Damn, you're a stubborn woman," Mark grumbled as the wind picked up. "Get the troops out now, Joahem. No proud march, they run."

Mark looked around. Theodore's troops were pulling away, but they were still too close, as were Revina's. If a showdown with the Death God were here, there would be casualties unless Skye and he could hold Derrant's attention.

"Alex," Skye said, the worry heavy in her eyes.

Petrian and Ryland had mounted the blue dragon and were taking off. The wind was fierce, thunder shattering the air, and the dragon's wings beat hard against the oncoming storm.

"The Upper God is not happy," Skye said quietly to the other dragon. "Protect my son and Revina."

It lowered its head to her palm, then raised its wings and flew to where the others were, landing with a hard thud that shook the already trembling ground. There was screaming as it spread its wings protectively, standing guard before them.

"So much for getting them all to safety. We led Derrant straight to them," Mark said, pulling her next to him as a swirl of clouds formed before them. Black lightning laced clouds moved chaotically then shattered outward, pelting them like shards of glass. Skye drew a shield around them, and the shards dropped at his feet. To Mark's relief, the dragon breathed its ice blue flame, disintegrating the remaining shards before they reached their people. Theodore's men were not so lucky and there were cries as some of his troops were cut down before Skye was able to shield them.

Skye glanced up and met Mark's eyes. He wanted to take the fear from her eyes, to protect her, but he knew he couldn't. He wasn't strong enough to take on a god. But she was. She'd done it once before.

"What if he takes me again?" she said.

"Then I'll find you again or die trying."

Derrant stepped from the ebony clouds in his god form, terrifying and dark. Black swirled around him as his angry eyes settled on Skye.

"Maybe he needs to take us," she said, her voice coming out shaky.

"Are you insane? He'll kill me and enslave you."

"But all of these people are at risk."

She was right. Derrant had already stolen the souls from the wounded men. Mark had seen their bodies fall as Derrant had stepped through. His eyes fell on Skye, menacing and angry. Mark's heart pounded, fear clawing its way through it. How was he to protect her from the Death God? He couldn't, just like Eliana had said. There was no way to fight Derrant, and he would lose her again.

"No one escapes me!" Derrant bellowed. "And no one tricks me twice!"

An invisible force yanked Skye from Mark's arms. He tried to grab her, but he fell back. An invisible hand of magic kept him at bay, no matter how he struggled to move toward her.

"You missed our wedding, Skye," Derrant hissed. "I gave you the easy way. Now you get the hard way."

She screamed, a black mist coating her, the scream slicing Mark's heart in two.

"Stop!" he yelled in desperation.

Derrant's eyes fell upon him, and Skye's scream stopped, her body slumping slightly in the invisible grip in which he held her.

"A mortal assumes he can command me?"

Mark stood tall. "Kill me if you must, but you won't touch her again!"

Derrant let out a laugh that shook the land. "I guarantee she enjoyed my touch. She may not this time, however. Your wife is mine, whether she comes to me willingly or not. You are but a mere mortal, a nuisance that will now be dealt with as I should have dealt with you when that fool Crimson dared bring you to my realm."

Something gripped Mark's insides, and he couldn't breathe. It felt like a part of him was being ripped from him. His soul. Derrant was taking his soul. This was it. He'd lost it all and with his loss, Skye would be enslaved to a life with the Death God. He'd failed her, failed as her protector, as her lover, as her husband.

"No!" Skye screamed. From his haze, Mark saw the colors scatter with the force of it, but she was fading from his sight, the darkness taking him.

SKYE

Skye watched Derrant draw a light, wispy hue from Mark's body, knowing immediately what it was. He was taking his soul, killing Mark, slowly and painfully. The agony that had wracked her body moments before was still pulsating through her but the terror of losing Mark overcame it.

"No!" The scream tore from her. Magic coursed through her body, and she claimed the depths of power that had yet to be accessed. A connection took hold, not only to the hues that now sparkled before her, but to the glimmer from Mark's receding soul. She drew back from its essence, knowing if she called to it, she would bleed it completely, inadvertently handing his soul to Derrant.

The striking blue eyes of the dragon met hers, and she sensed her link to it, the tie to the blood that ran through it. Eliana's blood. In that moment, Skye remembered the kiss. A light feeling befell her, accompanied by the sense of something reaching up and possessing her body.

"Derrant!" she yelled, feeling the shake of the land below her feet, the calm of the storm as even it stopped to listen.

Derrant turned to her as the mist flowed back to Mark, his

body falling. She heard the deep intake of Mark's breath and saw his head lifting as those beautiful hazel eyes sought her out.

"No, Skye," he croaked weakly.

"It's me you want. Take me. I am yours," Skye said.

Derrant walked toward her. "Lies. You claimed to be mine before. Shared my bed, came to my touch."

Skye cringed inwardly, wishing they weren't surrounded and that his voice wasn't so loud. She really didn't need the entire world knowing she'd slept with the Death God. Or perhaps it wasn't a bad thing. There was power in having that kind of control, of having brought a god to his weakest moments.

"If you let him live—"

"No, I will have no more talk from you. You are mine, willingly or unwillingly."

"So you can steal my power and use it to overthrow your brother?"

He looked taken aback, and the sky boomed above them.

"The Shadow Realm is yours, Derrant. It always has been. Once it was more, there was balance and beauty to it."

"Eliana," he growled. "Do not dare bring my sister into this."

"That is why you want me, Derrant. Her blood flows strongly through me, so strongly that I look like her. It flows so strongly that I feel and taste like her."

Thunder rocked the sky, and lightning tore through the clouds. Skye wasn't sure where she was going with this. It was dangerous, but something compelled her.

"You loved her once."

He roared, stirring the wind and blowing everyone, including the dragons, back. Skye risked a peek at Mark, who was struggling against it. Summoning her magic, she drew the hues from the ground around him, using them to support Mark, rooting him in place, knowing she needed him close. If she didn't have him there, Derrant would win.

When the roar stopped, only Mark remained in proximity,

watching with worried eyes. A tingle of shadow magic lingered in the air. The Death God had separated the three of them. She had no doubt he was protecting his reputation, not wanting the mortals to witness anything but the version of the Death God they feared. Eliana was a myth, Death's Mistress and the story behind her disappearance was layered with mistruths and lore. For mortals to know the truth, to know that Derrant had loved her, that her love for another man had broken him, would make him weak.

Mark and she were now the only ones in this battle, and Skye prayed they both survived it.

"And Eliana loved you," she braved, hoping to engage Derrant.

"She chose a mortal over me. She never loved me."

"Love is a tricky thing, Derrant. You have to earn it and hold it firmly, but with a gentleness. You held her too tightly. You hurt her. You fell, and the deeper you fell, the more you hurt her."

Skye saw it now, as if she'd lived it. He'd abused Eliana, the shadows corrupting him, pushing her to Skye's ancestor. "You drove her away. You broke her love for you."

For just a moment, she saw the man below the monster, the one he'd given her insight to see those weeks she'd been with him. Then it was gone, the rage returning.

"How dare you! You will come with me, sit by my side, lie beneath me, satisfy me, and stay silent for the rest of eternity," Derrant said.

Pain barraged her again as he aimed his power to where the portal had been. She met Mark's eyes, the fear in them palpable. She'd lost, and she didn't know how to turn the tide in her favor again.

His eyes hurt her, the hope in them dimming. She knew he was trying to determine how he could stop a god. But then his expression changed, a resolve overcoming the fear. She couldn't drag her eyes from his, even as the pain continued to shred her.

Derrant raised his hand to call the doorway.

"Fine!" Mark yelled.

Derrant turned to him.

"You want her that bad? Take her. She's yours," Mark said. Derrant dropped his hold on Skye, and she caught her breath, confusion and hurt berating her mind.

"I'm serious."

"Mark, what are you doing?" she asked.

"Come on, Skye. You know you've got a thing for him. Who fucks a god, then looks at a man the same way? You haven't been the same since you returned."

Why was he saying all this? He knew how she felt. They'd just made peace with what had happened during their time apart, put it behind them.

"You want him so badly? Then go with him and stop pretending you want me."

Derrant eyed him but didn't move. Was Mark serious? She felt her heart breaking with his every word.

Mark pulled something from his pocket. She squinted, seeing their wedding bands. "I was waiting until this was over, hoping we could start anew, but the hell with it now." He dropped the bands to the ground, and with their soft landing, her heart severed. "Go with him, Skye. In fact, fuck him right here where we can all see what the big deal is. Kiss him. Kiss him now and show me."

The kiss. He was giving her the opportunity, an opening. He hadn't meant any of it. It was a chance for her to give Derrant Eliana's kiss.

Derrant laughed, a deep throaty sound that shook the air.

"You win, Derrant."

"So quick to give me up, Mark?" she said, playing along.

"I should have done it the minute I found you."

"Maybe you should have. Maybe you should never have come looking for me," she spat. "You had pleasure enough in Crimson's bed." It hurt her to say the words, and she saw the look of hurt in his eyes, knowing it wasn't false. Crimson had left a stain on them that would be hard to remove. Regardless, she continued, "You're right. Why would I think taking you back after sitting at the throne of a god, after sharing his bed, would even come close? You are nothing compared to him."

Derrant raised a brow. "You want me? I'm yours. Just like I said. You will rule the Shadow Realm by my side."

Knowing Derrant would want proof and that he liked a show, Skye pulled the string of her tunic so that he could see the cleavage, the swell of her breast as the sleeve fell. She ignored the repulsion in her head at his current form, pulled him forward, and kissed him.

MARK

Skye had understood and played her part well...too well, but Mark knew it needed to be done. It had killed him to throw the rings. He'd been planning to propose to her again when they were through this, to marry her again and start over. The comment about Crimson had stung, but he'd deserved it and his reaction had been true.

Mark watched as she loosened her tunic, Derrant's eyes cravingly eyeing her. He was still in his beast form. Mark hoped the god had been in his blonde, strikingly perfect form the times he'd had sex with Skye—this version of the Death God was horrifying.

She stepped to Derrant and brought his head down for a kiss, his towering stature eclipsing her. Jealousy tore through Mark, but he kept it in check, knowing she was pretending. The kiss went long, too long. As Derrant's form morphed, his arms pulling Skye closer, Mark's doubt crept in. Maybe she hadn't been playing. This version of the god was beautiful, built to perfection. He was a god—powerful, eternal, and offering a throne that no other could match. She'd be foolish not to choose him. Mark's mind reeled with the thought.

As the kiss lingered, he heard the dragon beat its wings from somewhere behind him. He drew his eyes to the sky that was

filling with other dragons. Dropping his sight back to Skye he saw
Derrant pull away, a look of surprise on his face.

"Eliana?" Derrant said.

Skye was glowing, her hair lengthening, her eyes a rich blue
like the color of the night sky.

"Derrant," she said, touching his cheek.

Derrant grabbed her wrist, causing a flash of pain in her eyes
before he slapped her. Power cascaded around her and as much as
Mark wanted to interfere, he knew this was no longer Skye. Her
shape grew until she was the same height as Derrant, her eyes
dangerous. Sparks of color licked the ground around her.

"You pushed me away, Derrant."

"You left me for a mortal, Eliana. Or does your memory fail
you?"

"My memory serves me well, Derrant. You deserve to be free
of your burden, as do I. Set the past aside and return to the man
you were."

"I am the god you made me and nothing more."

Her eyes held pity. "I have always loved you, Derrant."

"Always?"

She brought her hand to his chest. "Always. Free me and
promise to love me as you once did. We will rule the Shadow
Realm together once more."

"And our brother?" he asked with a raise of his brow.

"Will accept what is inevitable. But if you hurt me again, I
make no promises."

There was a streak of lightning.

"I do enjoy pissing him off."

"Take me home, Derrant."

"And the Mage Warrior?"

"Is no longer your concern. You have me. Leave my daughter
be."

His eyes furrowed before he reached his hand out and tore
into her body, emerging with Skye in his hand. He flung her

toward Mark, who ran to her, taking her weakened body into his arms.

"Did you dare trick me again?" he asked Mark.

"Perhaps."

"I should kill you—"

"No, you will leave them be," Eliana said.

"She is your spawn with that mortal?" Derrant asked, his expression growing darker as he figured it out. Mark held Skye tightly, pulling her further away from the gods.

"She is. It is what draws you to her, and I will protect her. Do not push me away again."

Derrant shoved Eliana back, the air around him stirring. A black haze covered him as he morphed back into his monstrous shape.

"Shit," Mark said. "Skye, can you get us out of here?"

"No," she said weakly. "Too tired."

Fear plunged through him, and he pulled her against him, helping her stand and looking for any way to escape with her. He could feel the magic from Eliana still connected to her, Eliana using her as a conduit even after Derrant had separated them.

A dragon landed behind them. The magic of the barrier Derrant had encased them in shimmered but still held. Those beyond were still unable to see the nightmare that was now before them.

"You were a whore then, and you remain a whore. Your spawn will suffer my wrath as I bleed her magic and her soul. Then she will sit upon your throne, subservient to me as you should have remained. Go back to your hiding place, Sister, you are but a shade of the woman you were."

"Derrant," she cried.

Ignoring her, he turned as Mark tried lifting Skye to the dragon. The dragon shrieked, rising on his hind legs and throwing them backward. Mark held fast to Skye; the dragon continued to shriek until its soul departed and its body collapsed.

"No!" Eliana screamed, flinging herself at Derrant, but he shoved her away.

"You are nothing to me!" he spat at her as a doorway formed.

Skye was torn from Mark's arms, landing in Derrant's. She struggled, but Mark knew the exhaustion from channeling Eliana had been too great. He ran toward her, but a heaviness pushed him to his knees.

"I should take your soul, but I believe knowing that her screams will be for me and not you is better punishment. I'll leave you to think of how she's begging me to fuck her instead of torturing her for the remainder of your life, mortal," Derrant said.

He walked through the doorway, lightning and thunder crashing around them as it disappeared. The invisible grip released Mark, but he didn't move. He met the goddess's eyes before she faded, seeing nothing but sadness and acceptance in them. The dragons returned to their home. The one Derrant had killed shimmered as its essence floated away on the wind, taking with it the fragments of Mark's shattered heart.

MARK

Every muscle in Mark's body was frozen with the pain that tore through his heart. His eyes lingered on the space where Skye had been only moments ago. Everything he'd given up to find her, to bring her back had been for nothing. Derrant had her once again and there was no way to reach her this time. He had lost her, again.

Voices permeated the air as the spell broke after Eliana faded. He heard footsteps running to him but still he didn't rise from his knees. His eyes remained fixed on the space where she'd been. His heart was too pained for him to do anything more.

"Mark!" He heard Alex's voice, but he couldn't force himself to turn to him. "Mark, where did she go?"

The fear in Alex's voice finally broke through to him.

Get up, Mark. You are a commander's son. The Elite will one day be yours, he remembered his father telling him when he'd been bested by another child in training. *No matter how your pride is hurt, your heart wounded, your body aches, you rise and fight. Commanders never bend, nor do we break.*

We never break, he told himself. But he felt broken. Skye should have been safe in his arms as they curled in their bed with no scars from others to mar their bliss. *But we aren't. The memories, the events are ours to bear. Get up, Mark.*

He dropped his eyes, knowing Alex was standing next to him. Knowing everyone was looking at him, waiting for an explanation. None of them had seen the interaction. They'd somehow been pushed away, their sight blocked to all that was occurring. Revina's troops had stilled their retreat, and the Elite had readied to protect their queen and commander, but none had seen Derrant take her away. Now that the spell had broken, they awaited his confirmation that the gods had interfered again, that the Death God had found favor in their queen and taken her.

Gathering himself, Mark lifted his head and rose, wiping his hands down his shirt, smoothing the material that had been wet with the rain he'd made love to Skye in earlier that morning. He pulled himself together and stood tall, knowing they needed him as much as he desperately needed Skye.

He turned to Alex whose eyes were brimming with concern. There were tears dammed behind them, waiting to break through. Elspeth stood beside him, as well as Trent, and Clover came quietly to his side, taking his hand.

"She's gone. The Death God has stolen her again."

Alex's face fell, Elspeth's hand going to her heart.

"She was in his clutches this entire time and now he's stolen her back." He glanced over to the place where she'd been, the memory of her in Derrant's hands slicing through his chest. Forcing the emotions aside, he looked back to them, his feelings shoved beneath his duty like he'd done so many times in his past. "We need to ensure Theodore's troops continue their retreat. That they do not know we are weak or that our queen is in Derrant's hands."

"But Mark, they can only assume she is—" Trent started.

"Find something to tell them," he commanded, hearing the edge in his voice and having no way to call it back. "Alex, I want you and Elspeth to continue your retreat with Revina. Assure her we have things under control and that this is only a minor setback. Return to Kantenda when she and her army are safe behind their walls. Petrian is on his way to Apendia to find the heir to the throne."

"I need to stay with you," Alex said.

"No, Alex. I need to find your mother, and she won't want you mixed in with any of this. The Death God does not play games and the Shadow Realm is deadly. Go with your grandmother. I want you as far away from our kingdom as you can be until your mother is safe and home again."

Alex looked hurt, but Mark knew it was for the best. If anything else turned or if Derrant decided to punish Mark for his trickery and kill him in order to finally claim Skye, Alex would be in danger. Skye would want him far away as far away as possible.

"He's right, Alex. Mark knows what to do and your mother would want you safe. Until this is undone, you are safer in Kantenda," Elspeth said. "Clover, you and Alex should go. Tell Revina to continue the course for home. I will catch up shortly."

Alex's eyes searched Mark's as Mark reached out, wrapping his hand around the back of his head and pulling him in for a tight hug. "I will bring her home. I promise you."

He lingering there momentarily before drawing away and nodding, making his way back to Revina with Clover by his side.

"Mark, what can we do?" Trent asked.

"We look for a way into the Shadow Realm. Anything we can find. I need you to portal us to Kantenda so we can begin to search for any way to access that realm. Camin is there. If anyone knows a way in, he will." As he said it, he realized the truth in his words. Camin was in Kantenda. He had traversed the Shadow Realm. He had to know a way in. Perhaps his magic had even returned. Although Eliana had told them Derrant was the only one who could return it, there was a glimmer of hope in Mark's heart. And a glimmer was enough to get him through.

He took that hope and let it course through him, knowing if

he didn't hold on to it, he might break, even if that was something a commander never did. And if he broke, there was no chance of bringing Skye home. So, he let the hope bolster him as he stepped through the portal with Trent. He was determined to do everything in his power to free her.

SKYE

S kye's body hit the marble of the throne room, knocking the wind from her. She was weakened already from Eliana having used her body to project herself, and the force at which he'd thrown her only worsened the effect.

"I should feed your soul to my pets!" Derrant roared as she lifted her head, pushing her body up.

Her shirt remained untied at the top, and it slipped from her shoulder, exposing her breasts. She saw the reaction, the glint of desire in his eyes.

"You'll pay, but I will keep you alive until you beg for me to fuck you again and this time I won't be gentle."

"That was gentle?" she retorted, pulling herself to her feet but leaving her shirt.

"You haven't seen rough."

"Show me," she said, fearing the alternative, the dungeons she'd passed to free Camin.

Her energy slowly returning, she drew closer to him.

"Show me your true self."

He morphed into his beautiful form, and she pressed her body against his.

"Please don't send me to the dungeons. I'll share your bed, I'll serve your every need, I'll be yours." She hated saying the words, but her fear of the dungeons was driving her.

He grabbed her hair, pulling her head back, pain flaring through her scalp. "Lies you spout as your heart yearns for another."

"You don't need my heart, only my body."

"And your magic," he replied, his hand grasping her breast, his touch sending shivers through her. But it wasn't Mark's touch, it never would be, and the part of her that was broken inside from being torn from him again broke through the façade.

"I think not," he said as a deadly look eclipsed his eyes. He pulled her face to his and kissed her greedily, ripping her shirt off and grabbing her roughly. She wanted to resist, to fight him but she feared the alternative, feared what he would do to her if she dared deny him. She kissed him instead, unsure if he would hurt her or if he was tricking her, but knowing better than to question. He forced her hands back when she brought them to his chest, holding her wrists so tightly it hurt.

She tried to bite back the cry, but it slipped from her lips.

"That's the way I like it," he said, pushing her hands down to the bulge in his pants. Kissing her firmly again, he freed her hands, and brought his fingers into her hair. Her scalp burned as he grabbed a handful of it, yanking her head back with the force. The move brought her breasts forward and his mouth ravaged them painfully. Knowing if she fought him, it would only worsen her punishment, she undid his pants, grasping him before firmly stroking him. His bite to her breast was so hard that she cried out in pain.

"Your cries do nothing but hasten my need for you," he said against her skin. She felt a trickle of blood from the fresh wound and winced as his tongue caught it. "Should I bleed you more?"

"No," she whimpered, and he jerked her back.

His eyes held no compassion, only terror and she saw now that she'd been oblivious to his true power. Under his spell, she'd never given it much attention. When the spell had lifted, she'd been in his good graces, participating willingly in satisfying his needs. There had been no fear as she'd plotted her escape while his touches had brought her to climax.

The man who glared at her now, whose power flickered around him, was a god who invoked fear in mortals like herself for good reason. His punishments were lethal, his only goal in his immortal life to break souls like hers.

She whimpered and he pushed her so that her knees buckled, so that she had no question to his intent. There would be reciprocal pleasing of her this time, not that she ever wanted anyone to please her again but Mark. She brought him to her mouth, and he pushed her further, eliciting a gag.

Laughing, he forced her head against his thrusting pelvis, controlling the situation, owning her, and leaving no doubt he was the one who ruled her now. The idea terrified her. She needed to reclaim control, needed to gain the upper hand again. She fought back, shoving against his hand. Before he could punish her, she plunged her mouth down, taking him as far as she could against the urge to gag again. The moan from him vibrated through the room and she felt him relax.

She stroked him with her tongue and grasped him firmly, calming as his hands gave her control. If this was what it took to stay alive, to stay unharmed then she would do it. She'd done it to gain her chance at escape before and she could do it again. What she didn't want was to be forced, to have him think he was controlling her. That would never help her out of this situation.

Closing her eyes, she let her mind drift to Mark, imagining it was him. Derrant's groan was deep as she brought him closer to climax. His hands threaded in her hair as she tormented and teased him, feeling him grow harder with his need until he was on the cusp. She increased her movements as his body shook and his moan echoed through the room, his seed filling her mouth. It continued to stream in long spurts, and she didn't dare stop taking it. When his last thrusts were through, she licked the remaining droplets, peering up at him.

"You are the best with your mouth, on par with that whore Crimson. I do miss her mouth but yours will do." He shoved her, sending her sprawling across the stone floor.

Tucking himself away, he said, "Now you suffer until I'm ready for more."

"But I'll give you more," she said, her fear rising. "Whatever you want of me."

He walked to her and grabbed her chin. "You had your chance. You had my bed, my crown, and you deceived me, again. Until you have my trust, you will bear my wrath."

The doors to the throne room opened. "Take her," he commanded, turning his back on her and walking away.

"Derrant, please!"

"Save your begging," he said. "It didn't help my sister; it didn't help Crimson; it won't help you."

Arms lifted her, dragging her away, her screams reverberating through the now empty throne room.

MARK

The setting sun cast long shadows across the room, but Mark gave them no heed. He sat, head in his hands, going through every option again, the same as he'd been doing for weeks. Several long, tortuous weeks had passed, ones where the days seemed to have no end. Through each day, he'd tried everything. Every mage in the kingdom had been called, but all were unable to portal to the Shadow Realm. None had even come close to the power Skye held. With Camin's help, they'd poured through each book in their possession and Revina's. Mark had even sifted through Crimson's castle in search of anything that would lead him to Skye.

Theodore had retreated to his kingdom with threat of a visit from the dragons if he dared to turn against them again. Mark had no way of calling or even reaching them, but Theodore didn't know that. Petrian had found the heir to the throne of Apendia and had stayed to help stabilize the kingdom. All others in their circle worked relentlessly to find a way to reach Skye, to bring her back from Derrant's grasp.

Alex had put on a brave face, but Mark knew he was as heart wrenched as Mark. With Clover by his side, he'd set off to Apendia to help Petrian, acting as an emissary for his mother.

Frightened to death that Skye was no longer alive, Mark had continued his ruthless search for a way to reach her. Even if she'd slept with the Death God ten times a day or if her hues escaped each time, it wouldn't matter. He only wanted to know that she lived, to know she was safe. It was the not knowing that was killing him.

"I've told you repeatedly that you will not find her with your head in your hands," he heard Camin say.

He looked up to see Camin standing in the doorway, his arms crossed. He'd become a steady companion in the past few weeks, and Mark had grown fond of him. Even without his magic, he was calculating, deliberate, and knowledgeable, putting him on a level with Elspeth and Trent.

"When was the last time you slept, Markhem?"

"A month ago," he said, knowing it was close to the truth.

"Lack of sleep won't help."

"Have you found anything?" he asked, ignoring the comment.

"No. The others have all gathered and are waiting for you. They've been working since sunrise. They need a break."

"No breaks until she's found."

Camin raised a brow. "Well, I hate to tell you, but all of us have disobeyed that command. In fact, I just spent an hour in the arms of that fine woman Jane and feel quite refreshed."

Mark shot him a look. He was happy for Camin, who had taken a liking to Skye's neighbor, and Jane seemed to have given up her solitary, cat-mom life for the favor of Camin. Somehow, it worked. She was good for Camin, who was still struggling to fit in to his new life. With his powers still stripped from him, his adjustment had been even more difficult.

"For a woman who talks nothing about books and those things she calls cats, she is a wicked thing in the bedroom."

Mark stood and stretched. "That's entirely too much information, Camin. Keep your bedroom antics to yourself." He slapped Camin on the back.

He was glad Camin had settled in. Skye would have been

happy. At the thought of Skye, his mood dropped. They walked together in silence.

Upon entering the planning room, Mark found his loyal band of thinkers, including Noah, who had been released and returned, albeit scarred from his time in Crimson's hands. His wife hadn't been too pleased to find that his time in captivity had been spent feeding Crimson's desires, even after having the situation explained. She'd finally accepted that she was lucky Crimson had favored Noah, otherwise his corpse would have been returned. Elspeth had stayed with Revina to help her, but the wizard, Bridget, along with Camin's father, Tomen, had answered Mark's summons. Trent, loyal to a fault, had taken lead of the group.

They nodded to Mark when he entered.

"Where do we stand?" he asked, noticing Jane rise. She'd been chatting with Bridget when he'd entered. He put a hand up. "You can stay, Jane, as long as Camin can focus."

"Are you sure?" she asked, her voice rich with empathy.

"Yes."

He moved to the table and took a seat.

"Nothing different." Noah answered Mark's initial question. The gravity of his voice carried through the room.

Mark wiped his hands over his face.

"We finished the last of the books," Camin said. "There is no mention of anyone but a Mage Warrior ever gaining access to the Shadow Realm, aside from me, and we know where that stands now."

"No luck getting your magic back?"

Camin shook his head. "Nothing but a small spark of useless power, a far cry from what's needed to be of any help."

"Skye is the only one with the ability to traverse the realms," Trent said.

"And she would have returned by now if she could."

They sat quietly, no one with anything left to say.

"What about the goddess? That dragon woman?" Jane asked innocently.

"There's no way to reach her without a portal and none of our mages can even get close to the mountains," he answered. He'd tried running through every full mage in the kingdom. Their abilities enabled them to move anywhere in their world but the Dranth mountains.

"There's no way to get us there. It's blocked to our magic," Trent said, confirming Mark's words.

"Blocked to the magic," Mark repeated.

"Yes, that's what I said. Skye's tie to the goddess was the only way."

"But..." he started as a thought formed, "what if it's only hidden to magic, so that Derrant could never find her? What if it's not blocked by foot?"

"Foot?"

"Yes," Mark replied. "We can climb the mountain to reach her."

"You've gone mad," Noah said. "Those mountains are massive. Even if we could climb them, we'd freeze to death before we reached her."

"Not if we take a mage who can keep us warm," he said, looking at Trent.

"No, no, no. I have a deathly fear of heights."

"Are you kidding me? You travelled to another world to find Skye and you won't brave a mountain?" Mark asked.

"A freezing, blistering mountain that climbs further than we can see," Trent replied.

"Fine, then I'll go myself. Noah, have the stables ready my horse. Jane, please tell the kitchen to pack rations."

He stormed from the room, ignoring the rising cacophony of voices behind him. He was going to find Skye and bring her home. Eliana knew the way to the Shadow Realm. She could get him there or he would die trying to convince her.

～

When Mark reached the stables, his bag thrown across his shoulder, he found the others waiting for him.

"Don't try to talk me out of this."

"We're not. We're going with you," Noah said.

"I will take you by portal as far as our magic can reach, to Eltander. The others will accompany you the rest of the way," Trent said.

Mark looked at them—Noah, Trent, Camin, Jane, and the two wizards, Bridget and Tomen. They were an odd bunch, one he was certain no one had ever remotely envisioned standing side by side, now all fighting to find the queen who had united them.

"Are you certain?" he asked.

They nodded together.

"Thank you," he returned, his heart brimming with the stand of solidarity.

"Can't let you go wandering up there alone. Who knows what kind of trouble you'll make," Noah said.

"Noah, you just returned. Your wife—"

"Understands. My queen comes first. Now let's go before I change my mind."

Bridget and Tomen brought the horses as Trent called a portal. Once they'd stepped through, Trent took his leave, Mark putting him in charge in his absence.

It took two days to reach the furthest edge of Revina's kingdom. The wall shadowed their moves as they traveled. He marveled at the sheer magnitude of the structure to encompass the breadth of an entire kingdom. When they reached the north-west border of Eltander, an open plain sat before them, leading to the base of the white peaked mountains in the distance.

This was untouched territory, protected by Eltander since history was first recorded. Mark wondered if they knew what they guarded. If they knew the mountain hid the fleeing goddess.

"Since Markhem is too lost in thought to steady his pace, this seems like a good place to camp for the night," Tomen stated.

"No, I'm fine to continue," he argued.

"You are, but the horses are not, and I need to stretch my sore backside," Bridget said.

Begrudgingly, Mark agreed. If it were up to him, he'd run his horse to the ground to get there. It would have been a stupid thing to do, but love made people do stupid things.

As they settled around a campfire, having fed and watered the weary horses, his mind wandered to Skye and the last time they had traveled together. He hadn't been able to get his fill of her as they'd tried to move past the weeks prior and his moment of indiscretion. Now she was back with Derrant, and Mark knew whatever she was doing was for survival.

A giggle came from where Camin and Jane had snuck off.

"Must they?" he asked.

"That's nothing compared to having to listen to you and Skye go at it all night. You two never stop, do you? The only one who comes close is Crimson," Noah said.

Mark shivered at the name and the memories of her repeated need. It was never more than he and Skye would do, but it was demanding and relentless.

"I could not keep up with that woman."

"I could," Mark muttered.

"Show off. It was likely because of your comfortable surroundings. Hard to get off in a dungeon cell."

"I thought the point was to not get off."

"Tell me how many times that worked for you."

Mark laughed.

"Relentless," Noah repeated. "And gods, what she could do with her mouth."

"Keep your reminiscing to yourself, Noah," he said. "Some of us don't care to think on it."

"And some of us don't care to hear it," Bridget said.

"I don't mind," Tomen added.

Bridget threw something at him, and Mark heard the plunk as it struck. Camin and Jane wandered back, Jane's hair messy and Camin's clothes in disarray. They sat and grabbed some of the rabbit that was on the fire.

Mark wanted his mind off Crimson and even Skye, so he asked, "Why is that land unsettled?'

"It is said to be cursed land," Bridget answered. "Those who've ventured this far bring back claims of hearing the screams of lost souls and roars of beasts in the distance."

"The dragons."

"Perhaps, although there was a time when people did venture to the mountains. It was a time when the dragons roamed free, when they were worshipped. But with time, the land around the mountains changed. It happened after Kantenda's fall, when the mages were enslaved and stolen from their home. The land changed, the beauty and the peacefulness of it faded until it became what it is today. No one knows if there was a connection to Kantenda, but whatever the reason, no one ventures this far." She looked around cautiously. "I'll be surprised if any of us get any sleep from this point forward."

They settled in as the flames from the fire dwindled. Weariness took Mark faster than he would have imagined.

He woke sometime later, the others still sleeping.

There was only the light of the moon as he rose to empty his bladder. Buttoning his pants back up, he heard a sound he couldn't quite make out. He turned quickly, seeing nothing, and brushed it off as he made his way back. A soft cry touched his ears, then a faint scream. He looked around swiftly, not seeing anything.

Bridget's story came to mind. Were there truly spirits that haunted these plains? It wouldn't surprise him, the place looked like something out of a horror movie at night. Despite the thought, he walked past the others toward where he'd heard the crying, drawn to it as other pained wails echoed around him.

The moon passed behind dark clouds, plunging him into

darkness, and that's when he saw it—shadows of spirits, like ghosts, littered the land. Some in positions that looked uncomfortable, others hunched over or with their hands clasped together, screaming.

One image was distinct, not translucent like the others, more solid as if it were living flesh. Drawn to it, his ears attuned to the cries, he walked closer. As he approached, the figure looked up, and Mark's heart leapt.

"Skye!"

She looked around as if she'd heard him.

"Mark?" He heard faintly, her voice like a soft muffled echo.

Then it dawned on him—this wasn't a haunted graveyard. This land connected to the Shadow Realm, to the punished souls. Somehow, the realm had infected this land, or perhaps it had something to do with Eliana and her tie to the Shadow Realm reaching to call her back.

"Dammit, he's punishing you," he said, his heart breaking at her image and the thought.

"Mark, where are you?"

She rose and whipped around, as if trying to see him, her eyes wild with hope.

"I'm not there, Skye."

She stopped and looked at him, the shadows, white and spirit-like, contouring her beautiful face. A glimmer of a spirit. He reached his hand out to touch her, but it slipped through her form.

"I will find you, Skye. I'm on my way."

"You can't reach me, Mark. No one can. Soon he will claim me. I can't take much more of this torment. He will break me," she said, the sadness in her voice enough to gut him.

"He can't break you because you have my love. My strength is yours, Skye, my heart."

He saw the glint of the tears that fell from her eyes.

"I love you, Mark, no matter what." Her eyes grew wide with fear as she looked up.

"Skye?"

Something behind her moved, a dark shadow slinking above her. She turned quickly.

"Skye, run!"

"I can't," she whispered. "They're always here to break me, to haunt me."

The blackness jumped, her image fading as her scream cut through the night.

"No!" he screamed, the clouds releasing their grasp on the moon.

"Mark!" Noah yelled, running to him frantically, followed by the others.

Furry swept through him, fueled by the fear he had for her. He turned and stormed back to the camp. "We ride now," he commanded.

"But Mark."

"We ride now, Noah."

"What did you see, Mark?" Bridget asked.

"The dungeons of the Death God. He has her there. His demons are tormenting her."

"No," Camin said, paling in the light of the moon. Mark heard the fear in his voice. "What did you see, Mark?" he asked, repeating Bridget's words.

"She's in what looks like a prison, with souls all around in pain and torment. There was something with her. It crawled above her, dark and foul."

"Gods, he has her in the prisons of the tortured souls where the demons feed."

The fear gripped him tighter.

"He'll drive her mad. I spent part of my imprisonment in that place. It's home to the vilest souls for a reason. It's a feeding ground for his pets. That thing, it stalks and when it strikes, you're plunged into a living nightmare until it's done feeding on your fear. We need to reach her before there's no fight left in her."

"She might already be lost," Tomen said.

"Why would you say that?"

"Because time in the Death God's hold runs different. That image may have happened days, even weeks ago, in her time."

"Damn, he's right, Mark," Camin said. "Time there doesn't align with ours."

"How would you know that?" he asked Tomen.

"It's knowledge that is taught when wizards are young. We cast in the shadows. We draw our magic from the hues closest to the Shadow Realm. We must know all aspects of it and that is something always taught. It is why our magic burns quicker than the other mages; it is tied to the realm."

"If that was days ago, then—" Mark didn't want to say the words. "We need to reach her now. We ride."

He gave them no option, rushing to the horses. He prayed he could reach her in time, that Derrant didn't break her mind before he broke her spirit. Against his own pain, he prayed that Derrant took her back in his bed, that she was in the god's arms safe instead of in the nightmare that he'd just seen. He didn't care that it meant Derrant was touching her. Nothing mattered but her safety now, regardless of his jealousy, regardless of everything else he thought had once mattered.

SKYE

The darkness gave Skye comfort, for it meant she could no longer see the nightmares that slipped into her cell. At first, not being able to see them had terrified her. Now she preferred not to—preferred to simply feel them as they slipped into her body, feeding on the precious living soul that Derrant had provided them.

He would leave her there in the dark for too long to count. Days were meaningless. No sun rose or fell to track the time. Eventually, he would remove her, have her cleansed and fed, treat her like a queen, the ecstasy erasing the nightmares. She would beg him to let her stay, to return her to his bed and not the dungeons, but each time, when he'd had his fill of her, he would send her back.

Each time hurt worse; the demons coming quicker to feed. At some point, she'd dreamt of Mark, that he'd been there with her, talking to her, telling her he was coming for her, but it had only been a dream, the nightmares eating away at her hope.

As she lay clenched in a tight ball, awaiting the next attack, she thought of Mark. She missed him painfully, his touch, his kisses, the safety of his arms. A tear fell, but she stopped herself, holding her breath, praying the tear didn't call the nightmare demon. The most frightening of the demons was the black shape that scuttled in the corner, feeding on her tears, plunging her into nightmares she couldn't escape.

She felt its presence and shuttered, squeezing further in a ball, waiting for it to strike. In the silence, she heard steps.

"Well, well, the living soul," she heard a woman's voice say. "Away with you, you've fed enough. Now it's our turn."

Feeling the heaviness lift from her, she peeked up as a low light lit her cell.

"Oh my, you are going to be tasty. I've waited a long time for the master to give us a taste of you."

The demon entered the cell, followed by a male demon, his naked body enhancing his growing erection. The female leaned down to Skye. "Do you know me? My sister died at your hands, now you will suffer at mine."

Skye tried to back away, but the demon grabbed her arm.

"Oh, don't worry, you won't notice. In fact, you'll be begging for more. We'll have a little fun first, then bleed your soul dry."

The male grabbed the female's breast and her head tilted back as he kissed her.

"We can't bleed her dry. Master will kill us."

"We can come close," she said.

Skye watched as her tail wrapped around the male's length, caressing it.

"Isn't there a private place you two can take that?"

"And leave you to your nightmares?"

Her tail whipped around, close to Skye, as the male turned the female demon and mounted her. The female groaned, her head dipping back.

The tail. She remembered Mark saying something about the tail and their breasts. She moved away from it as the two continued to go at it, but it struck, slipping over her breasts seductively, then down to what was left of the dress Derrant had given her during her last round of freedom. Its sharp end protruded, cutting her dress open. The woman lowered her head, taking Skye's breasts in her mouth.

"No," Skye protested, but the female moved quickly as the male kept thrusting behind her. Something dripped from her breast as Skye complained, landing deep in her mouth, flavor bursting through it. Skye licked her lips as more drops fell, then pulled the demon closer, taking her breast in her mouth and drinking. The nightmares disappeared—the past weeks of hell erased with the pleasure that exploded in her body. She wanted more, but the female drew away.

"No!" she cried, reaching for her.

"Shhh, you'll have more."

"From both of us," the male said, coming toward her as she felt fingers enter her, plunging into the wetness that had grown.

She moaned, reaching for the man who brought her to a sitting position. A long, forked tongue forced her mouth open as his hands kneaded her breasts.

"I want to play," he said, shoving the female from Skye.

She growled at him. "I want her first."

"You'll have her when I'm finished with her. Feed her while I take her first. I want to fill her and hear her beg me for more when I'm done."

"But I want you to fill me, too," she said, her mouth taking in his full girth. The male arched, a grunt escaping as Skye watched her mouth move over him. Her body was on fire, arousal flooding her senses. She wanted them to stop playing with each other and take her instead, to ease the need burning in her. Her hands groped at the female's breasts, taking the liquid that dripped from them with her fingers and licking them clean.

The male pawed at Skye's breasts. She tried reaching up to him, wanting more from him, but he forced her hands back. "Feed her and let me have her," he told the female.

She grumbled, then brought her breast to Skye, who happily took it, savoring the nectar on her tongue as it dripped upon her face. The female licked Skye's breasts, sucking on her nipples, pleasure exploding through her as the male penetrated her.

She cried out, lurching forward from the impact. Her hands continued grabbing at the female as he plunged harder.

"She's so warm and living," he said hoarsely.

"Let me play some now."

"Not until I come. No wonder Derrant keeps her to himself. Let's steal her." He gripped her hips and pulled her so that he went deeper, Skye crying out again.

"We're not even supposed to touch her. We risk his wrath now. Her body is off limits, remember, only her mind."

His thrusts hastened and Skye kept drinking, the need to orgasm burning through her, an unmet need that kept her wanting more. A massive yell shook the cell, and the male released her. His body sailed through the air, landing against the wall with a thud. The female scrambled to the corner. Skye should have been frightened but she only wanted them back. The longing to have more nectar, to have the feel of the man inside of her again was enough to send her into madness.

"Come back!" Skye cried as she crawled to the female. "I need more!"

"I commanded you not to touch!" a voice boomed.

"We meant no harm, my lord, no—" the female's words were cut off as the black nightmare in the corner of the cell descended upon her. Black arms broke through the cell door, holding the female still, her scream horrifying to Skye's ears. The male tried to run but the floor opened and swallowed him.

The female's screams stopped, the mass pulling away to its corner. Only a dark imprint of the woman remained, her body stolen by the ground below, her life by the nightmare.

Skye crawled to the remains. "No, no, no. I need more," she cried.

Hands grabbed her and threw her over a shoulder. "You need cleansing to remove her hold."

"Put me down," she whined as the prison disappeared in a haze of strangling blackness.

The man dropped her on a bed but she took no heed, desire firing through her, the need to climax like a need for survival.

"Damn succubus can't mind orders or resist the flesh," the man mumbled.

Skye looked at the beautiful man, knowing she should recognize him, but the cloud of desire and lust in her mind kept the knowledge from her.

"Take me," she said, climbing to her knees and grabbing at his open shirt. "Please."

"The spell needs to be removed, get back, Skye," he commanded, but she pressed her body to his, forcing a kiss—one he eagerly took.

"Take me, please. I need release so badly, it hurts."

"You will find no release under her drug, you must be cleansed of it," he said, trying to push her away again.

She pulled at his pants, kissing his chest as her hand found his hardness. He grumbled, and she freed him. His hands cupped her breasts, letting his thumb drift along her nipple. The sensation only fed her need as she continued to stroke him.

"This won't give you release, Skye," he grumbled against her lips.

"I don't care, just fuck me."

His groan was loud, and her body reacted, pushing against him as her insatiable yearning grew. She craved this man like she had no other, wanted him to calm the storm that threatened to break her. He lifted her, meeting her lips with a ravenous fury, one she matched as he drove into her. Her lips slipped from his in a sigh of contentment when he brought her to the bed, plunging into her with an increasing power that set her body on fire. She clasped her legs around him, clawing at him to go deeper, her need for him only rising in ecstasy.

Throwing her head back with a scream as he took her breast into his mouth, pulling and biting, Skye could feel her climax rising but never ebbing. The need to crumble was coursing through her like a tsunami just beyond the coast. No matter how the ecstasy burned through her, it remained out of reach. As she raked his back with her nails, his moves grew frenzied until she felt him fill her with his climax. His grunts only urged on the desperation for her own release, one that never came to fruition.

The man tried to lift himself from her, but she brought him back, kissing him ardently.

"Again. Take me again." She moved her hips, feeling his reaction as he grew within her, seeing the craving in his eyes.

"No amount of times will satisfy you," he said.

"You will."

He kissed her, his hand moving through her hair, then to her breasts, touching her gently before tugging at her nipples. The sensation sent waves through her as he matched her body's rhythm. She tilted her head back in ecstasy but to her disappointment, he stopped, dropping his hand. He forced her face to look at him and glared at her.

"No, the spell must be lifted."

Before she could protest, his hand hovered over her, the yearning diminishing with its movement, and she recognized him, the memories of it all coming back. Part of her wished they hadn't, the images of the demons fresh and horrifying in an erotic way. Now she understood why Mark had been unable to fight their spell.

She looked to Derrant, searching his eyes, stunned that he'd removed the spell and given up the ability to have her in that state again. "Why?"

"Why what?"

"Why lift the spell? You could have had me all night."

"I have had you all night on many occasions. You please me whenever I take you."

"But not so unrestricted."

He brushed a strand of her hair back, and there was a glimmer of something in his eyes.

"Her..."

"Don't," he said, rising, but she drew him back.

"I remind you of her too much now."

There was a softness to him, one she'd never seen, and he kissed her deeply, sensually. There was something powerful yet vulnerable to it and she accepted it. Knowing he wasn't seeing her but seeing Eliana. He'd been protecting her because it was Eliana he needed to protect.

His hands gently caressed her as he slipped back into her. This time, there was a longing, a need for her to be someone else—the woman he truly loved. Something had broken within him, something in her prior actions, or something else, she wasn't certain. She gave him his moment, letting her mind drift to Mark, imagining his hands, his body, his kisses, just as Derrant was imagining Eliana, lost somewhere in memory.

She met his kisses with the passion she had for Mark, letting her body respond willingly. When he whispered Eliana's name as his climax crested, she let her own join his, knowing it was for the man she loved and not him. Crying Mark's name in her head as he held her tight with the crashing waves, she heard Eliana's name escape again in his passion.

He held her as their bodies stilled, his head dropping to her neck before he rose from her. She watched as he dressed, his eyes not meeting hers.

"You still love her," she whispered, seeing a different side of the Death God.

"No, I don't."

"I've made love often enough to know the difference."

His eyes met hers. "You look too much like her. I should have killed you when I first stole you."

"But you didn't and now that I know the story, I see it differently."

"You know nothing."

She sat up, ignoring her nudity. He'd seen her often enough to no longer care. "You love her, and she still loves you."

"She left me!"

"When you pushed her away, finding favor in your demons and the shadows of this realm."

"I've always lived in the shadows."

"No, you haven't."

He came closer, his eyes sharp with anger, but she pressed. "She only left you when she could no longer reach you."

"She left me for a mortal."

"Yes, but—"

"She fell in love with a mortal, planned to run away to live with him, to give up her immortality for him! She bore him a child!"

"And you hunted her down. What did you do to her when you found her? Did you tell her how much you loved her? That you would change your ways?"

He pushed her down and pinned her arms.

"No, you beat and raped her in your blind rage, pushing her away forever." He continued to glare at her. "I know what love feels like, Derrant, and what you just did was make love—you to her and me to Mark. They weren't here, but they were both on our minds. I will never be her, but you don't want my love. You want hers. That's why you kept me alive, why you wanted to make me your queen. Because I am part of her, that's what drew you to me."

His eyes softened, and he released her arms.

"I see her every time I look at you. And after seeing her that day, it's as if she lingers in you." He touched her lip, tracing it. "Perhaps you will never be her, but I will keep you."

Fear crashed through her. "Please don't send me back to the dungeons. I'll do anything. I will be her if that's what you desire, but please don't let it get into my mind again."

"The Nivrol has been slipping into your mind?"

She shuddered.

"It's one of my favorite pets."

"Good to know," she said, terrorized by the thought that he

considered that nightmare a pet. A shiver ran through her at the thought of it, the memories of how it had eclipsed her mind in darkness and horror.

"You will never be her."

"And you will never be Mark."

"Yet here we are," he said.

"At your doing, mind you. You could send me home."

For a moment, hope surfaced at the possibility.

But his expression dropped. "No, you are right. You hold a piece of her in you. If I cannot have her, you will suffice. You will love me as she did."

"No," she murmured. "I will only ever love him, but if seeing me as her helps—"

He kissed her with all the need of a man who hadn't kissed his love in centuries. He wanted her to be Eliana, and she felt the change in him again. He was waiting for her move, waiting for the stiff actions of a woman he was taking in exchange for freedom from her cell, or the woman he'd just made love to. It didn't matter that she'd been mentally lost in thoughts of Mark. Derrant wanted her to be Eliana.

Could she buy her freedom or at least her sanity by letting herself enjoy this god's touch, pretending he was Mark? Could she do it again?

She relaxed in his arms, her mind going to Mark again as Derrant made love to her. Their moves became one, both lost in the fantasy of another until the passion was too great. Eliana's name escaped his lips again as he climaxed. The sound of her name on his lips was one Skye knew only came from a love that spanned time.

When his body finally calmed, he picked his head up, brushing her hair back gently and kissing her forehead. She knew then that he'd accepted the façade, that she was now Eliana incarnate in his eyes. It might buy her freedom from the dungeons, but it may have cost her any possibility of freedom from the Shadow Realm.

He dressed, his eyes never leaving hers as he did. "Bathe and dress. I'll have food sent to you."

He turned, a tub appearing with hot water.

"You're not sending me back to the cell?"

"No," he said, his hand on the doorknob. "You stay with me now. The demons will no longer prey on you. I am the only one who touches you from now on."

With those final words, he was gone, leaving her to wonder what she'd done and if she could ever undo it.

MARK

It was another day's ride to the bottom of the mountain. Each day seemed to drag for Mark, knowing Derrant had Skye in his clutches. He didn't know how long it had been for her, now that he knew time in the Shadow Realm had no definition. His days could have been months for her. There was no way of knowing if she was still in the dungeons being tormented by Derrant's minions. He prayed that Derrant had pulled her from their clutches and forgiven her for running from him. If she was now under Derrant's protection, Mark worried what she'd traded to escape, to save her sanity.

He'd taken himself through every possible scenario. No matter what she'd had to give up to Derrant, it didn't matter. The end result was always the same in Mark's mind—she was safe. As long as she was with Derrant, she was out of the dungeons. The only thing that would truly devastate him was if she'd fallen in love with the god or had become pregnant.

He didn't think the latter would happen. Derrant was too smart for that. Skye was mortal. The gods in Greek mythology may have seduced mortals and impregnated women, but the gods in this world did not. Or at least that's what he'd always been told.

Now he knew that had been a mistruth, Eliana and Derrant disproving it. He wondered if the Upper God had ever done so and if Crimson and Skye had been the first mortal flesh for Derrant or if he'd taken other mortals before them. Crimson and Skye were both unique, and Skye bore a strikingly similar appearance to Eliana so it stood to reason they had been his first.

It wasn't likely that Skye would end up pregnant anyway. Women's bodies worked differently here, usually not capable of conceiving until well into a few centuries of their lives. Skye hadn't had a cycle since they'd arrived, much to both her excitement and his. Mark just prayed it remained that way in the Shadow Realm. He remembered Eliana saying she was only fertile in the mortal world, a strange concept, but one that gave him hope that the Shadow Realm provided an extra layer of protection. The thought of Skye carrying Derrant's child was disturbing on many levels, too many for Mark to contemplate without going mad.

"Will staring at the mountain help us get to the top faster?" Bridget asked, jarring him from his thoughts.

"No," he answered, taking in the enormous mountain layered in snow and ice before them.

"And how do you suppose we get to the top?" Noah asked.

"We climb," he answered.

"Climb?"

He ignored the response. "Let's go."

"Hold on," Tomen said. "I might have a way to make this less daunting."

He walked closer to the base and put his hand out, the snow melting in a patch to reveal a path.

"Bridget and I can clear it, but it will be a slow process. We'll need to switch off and on."

"How did you know that was there?" he asked.

"As Bridget explained, long ago, our people worshiped the dragons. They would travel to bring offerings to the dragons when they roamed freely and before they took permanent refuge in the mountains. The mountains have always been their home, but back then they were seen in the sky above our kingdom and Eltander. I suppose from your story of Eliana, they chose to stay close to their mother. All that time and none ever knew what secret these mountains truly held."

"Why did they become reclusive? I remember my mother telling me stories of them when I was young, but they never offered the answer to that question," Mark said.

"Ah, the greed of the kingdoms cost us their presence. When our kingdom fell, the dragons stopped venturing past the range. They were visible in the sky above the mountains, but would go no further. Some said it was an omen that even the dragons disapproved of the greed of the non-casters. Others said that the dragons were in some way tied to our kingdom and the destruction of it bound their flight from the mountains. I suppose now that we know Eliana's fate, it makes sense that they became reclusive. One line of her children had been enslaved. Who would risk their remaining children to that same fate? In time, as our history faded, so did the answers until the days of the dragons became a story told to our children."

Mark stared up at the massive mountain range, the home of Eliana and the dragons. Had she looked down at the destruction of Kantenda, unable to save them, her imprisonment in the mountain holding her as witness to it all? He thought of her and all she had suffered. Perhaps she had not. Perhaps she had turned her back and closed her eyes to it, knowing she could do nothing without risking being discovered by Derrant.

The thought settled uncomfortably in Mark, to think she would choose to let her people fall, but then again, she was a god. The gods did not interfere with mortal life. They remained uninvolved, never dictating the course of their people. This was not a world where prophecy defined the course of events. What happened simply happened. At least that was how it had been in the past. Now Derrant had changed things. His obsession with Skye was steering the course of their world. If she fell, if they could not free her, Kantenda would fall again, no matter the allies in Eltander and now in Apendia. Crimson's kingdom was weakened with her own fall, and the new ruler was young. He had not clearly established his authority to rule yet and his hold on the kingdom would be tenuous until he did so.

Theodore would surely discover that the dragons were not a threat as Mark had stated and, in time, would wage war on Kantenda if its queen did not return. Revina would not step in, she and her kingdom grieving the loss of their king. Mark doubted they would ever step foot beyond their walls again after losing Mechon.

Derrant's move threatened to undo everything Skye had done, interfering in a way that would be irreparable if Mark could not bring her home soon.

He looked to Tomen, all of them watching him, awaiting his decision on how they would proceed.

"If you're going to clear the path, then you might as well get started," he said, pushing thoughts of the past from his mind and focusing on his objective.

Slowly they worked their way up the mountain, the lack of speed killing Mark with every minute that passed. The higher they climbed, the more energy the two wizards expended on keeping them all warm, which meant the slower they cleared the way.

It took two more days to climb the mountain and finally see the peak. Mark began looking for any sign of the dragons. He didn't have Skye with him this time, and he wondered if they would show themselves to him without her presence.

They came upon the peak and still nothing.

"Eliana!" he called against the freezing wind. "Eliana! Show yourself!"

Still nothing, not even movement of the snow beneath their feet.

"Was this a fool's errand, Markhem?" Tomen asked.

"No," he said, pushing him aside. "Eliana! I know you're here and that your children are here. Show yourself please! Your daughter needs you. He's taken her again and punishes her. Please."

Silence greeted him, and his hope plummeted.

"She has to be here," Mark said, hearing the desperation in his voice.

The snow seemed to still, the air warming as the tip of the mountain shifted.

"Eliana," he whispered.

The others stared in wonder, mouths agape as the beautiful blue dragon unfurled itself, her deep blue eyes looking at Mark.

Your journey has been for naught. Her voice echoed around them. *Leave me in mourning.*

The other dragon Derrant had killed—she still mourned it. He'd forgotten about its demise in his own sorrow. The loss of a child was a burden no one should bear, and Mark wasn't certain he could convince her to put her mourning aside to help Skye. She turned her back on him and began to settle once more. The snow began its descent from the sky again; the stillness disappearing.

"Derrant has Skye. If you don't help me, she is lost as well."

She is already lost. He replaced me with her, unknowingly at first, but now she has become me in his eyes. You have lost her.

Mark's heart sank as if she'd tossed it off the mountain.

"But she doesn't love him."

No, she bides her time with your image. Her love for you is still strong but each day that passes she replaces me in his eyes.

"How do you know this?"

She set her navy eyes on him.

I asked my brother to release me from my place of hiding. He obliged, and so, I slipped into the shadows, determined to make Derrant pay, to punish him for taking my son.

"But you didn't. Why?"

To risk his wrath against me is to risk it against her now. We are one and the same to him. Leave her. She will be cared for, protected, loved.

"Leave her? Have you gone mad?"

She reared back, her eyes growing darker like Skye's did when she was angry. He should have been terrified, but his fear of losing Skye forever was stronger.

"That is my wife he has, and I want her back!"

Then you will die failing. Her words echoed around them.

She left him speechless, returning to her resting place. She'd been his last hope and as the reality slipped through him that he had indeed lost Skye forever, that nothing he could say would change the goddess' mind, Jane's voice broke the silence.

"Your dragoness." Her voice was soft and hushed as if she feared using it.

Camin tried to tug her back, but she disregarded him. There was a determination in her eyes although the shake of her hands belied her nerves.

"Please."

Eliana looked to her, and for a moment Mark worried she would eat the woman and be done with the conversation.

"I don't know much about you other than what they've told me, but I do know a lot about love. I devoured every romance novel, watched every one of those small town love story movies that I could find—"

"Jane," Mark said in warning.

"No, please, Mark. Skye is my friend, and as much as I know you miss her, we all miss her. I want to help, so please let me say this."

Say it quickly, mortal, or I may be tempted to feed you all to my children. Even the one who carries my blood in him. I smell a Mage Warrior upon you, yet your magic is not present, she said to Camin.

"Courtesy of your brother."

Her cold eyes evaluated Camin, but she said nothing more.

"So, before you feed me to anything," Jane continued, "I know what a broken heart looks like and what it sounds like. If Derrant is pretending Skye is you, it's because he still loves you. Perhaps he has an odd way of showing it, but he does. Don't leave Skye to live a life pretending to be someone else. Don't leave her to be you. Take the chance to heal your broken heart, whatever he's done—"

I was ready to forgive him, but he pushed me away and killed my son! The snow stirred, sliding under their feet at the rage in her voice.

"Oh," Jane said, stopping her plea.

They were doomed. There was no way to make her see past that act.

"Derrant didn't know the dragons are your children," Mark said suddenly, seeing what she'd missed. "He didn't know there was a connection. That they're his children, too. You didn't come to him in dragon form, you came to him through Skye. No one has ever known they are yours, especially not Derrant, who bides his time in the Shadow Realm. If your other brother knew, there's no way he would have told him. It would have revealed your location, and I imagine the two don't do much talking. He didn't know Eliana. Is he so heartless that he would have killed his own child?"

It was the Death God they were talking about, so there was a chance. She morphed to her true form, the others all letting their surprise show. She looked so much like Skye that it hurt. He saw it now. Even the blue streaks her hair had held the first time he'd seen her had changed to the rich auburn that Skye's hair held.

"If you won't get us there, can you at least restore Camin's magic so he can take us?"

"And what will you do when you are there if you even make it through the shadows, past the demons, his minions? I saw what has become of our realm, what he has done to it."

"Maybe it's that way because he's mourned your absence for so long," Jane said.

"He pushed me away, into the arms of another man, a man I loved, and then he punished me for it."

Mark couldn't help but think of Sam and how he'd forced Skye to fall in love with him, to marry him, resenting her for it.

"Sometimes love makes us do unexpected things," he said. "Things we don't want to do. Sometimes it hurts us as we do them, but we move forward anyway, too far onto the path to turn back."

Eliana walked to Mark and traced her fingers along his face. "When I was forced to leave my child, I blessed the guard closest to the king, creating your line. He had two sons. One was the father of your distinct line, the other carried the spark that called remaining Elite. Both lines were meant to protect my child and his heirs, but only one was meant to love him. With every generation, that love continued to cling to one Elite, holding all the love I had for Derrant—unrelenting, unbreakable, everlasting. Until now it has come to you. She loves you and with every day that passes, her love does not wane."

"Neither does yours. Help me bring her home and return you to your rightful place by his side, as queen of the Shadow Realm, as you are meant to be." Her eyes were sad, tears prominent behind them. "Jane's right. If he sees Skye as you, he still loves you."

She turned away, and he heard her sigh. "He will not take me back, and he wants her for more than her body."

Mark cringed, having to put thoughts of Derrant having sex with Skye out of his mind. The images were painful.

"He covets her hues, her magic. Right now, he holds them, bound within her. He's too smart to give her power. I'm guessing that's how she escaped last time?"

"Yes."

"He wants control over the hues, the light of the living realm and the Upper Realm, regardless of anything else that may be going on. His intent is and has always been to escape his realm and take our brother's rule of the upper kingdoms and crush him."

"Why?" Mark asked, but as the question left his mouth, he saw the answer.

"Greed," Camin answered.

"No," Mark said. "He didn't always want that, did he?"

She stopped and turned to him. "No," she muttered. "Not when I ruled by his side."

"Vengeance for hiding you, for helping you escape. If you return to him, he has no need for vengeance, no need for my wife."

Her eyes grew sad again. "I cannot."

"Then at least return my power, so I can take us there and be done with this cold and nonsense," Camin said.

She turned swiftly to him, her blue eyes hard, evaluating him.

"I cannot. Derrant has taken your magic. He must be the one to restore it."

She transformed and returned to her perch at the mountain top; the snow taking her away.

"Dammit," Mark groused.

"Well, that was fun and useless. Looks like we'll be finding a new queen. I know a few pretty women who have a thing for Elites," Tomen said, starting down the mountain.

"Shut up, Tomen," Bridget said.

They all started down after Tomen, Noah slapping Mark on the shoulder. "Sorry Mark. We'll keep trying."

"That was my last hope."

He gave one glance back to where Eliana was now hidden from view. He wanted to go to her and scream for her to do something, to shake off her fear, to help him bring Skye home. But he knew it was futile. She had made her decision.

As he began his descent, the snow shifted to his left, and the head of the smaller blue dragon popped up from below. It tilted its head at Mark.

"Hi, buddy," he said quietly.

It looked at him, its eyes turning sad, and he wondered if it was for his brother or for Mark. It spread its wings and in a flurry of snow disappeared into the clouds above. Mark turned his eyes from the sky and continued his downward trek, his mind running through any possible options, none of which were within his grasp.

They continued their trek down in silence, stopping for the night, the haste Mark had before now gone. Barely anyone spoke. Mark was too heartbroken, and the others were too heartbroken for him. When they reached the base, they found their horses and began the journey home.

About a mile out from the mountains, a sharp crack cut the air. The horses reared as Mark turned back to the mountain. The massive structure now had a huge crack running through it from the base upward as far as they could see. Mark's horse bucked and strained until he finally found himself on the ground with the others, the horses running off as dark shadows engulfed the sky.

The dragons landed, the mountain collapsing before them, a plume of snow hurtling toward them. The goddess appeared before them, the snow snaking around her body as if she were a shield from it. Behind her, the mountain reformed, perched once again in the range where it had been hiding her all this time.

They stared at her. No one moved.

"You are a persuasive bunch, especially that one." She pointed to Jane. "He makes love to Skye, believing it is me. Perhaps he still loves me."

"Makes love?" Mark asked, the term holding more than he wanted to think upon.

"Her only thought is always you, believe me. I can still feel her connection within me. Her heart, her mind, her soul—they all cry out for you."

"I suppose that makes it better," he mumbled, not entirely sure it did. He brought himself from the ground, dusting the snow from his pants.

"Are you ready to journey to the Shadow Realm?" Eliana asked.

"Not really," Bridget admitted.

"Good, because only these two can go." She grabbed Mark and Camin with her magic, and the world became a blur of magic, blackness, and shadows.

SKYE

kye walked down the hall from the bedroom toward the kitchens. The farther Derrant had lost himself in the idea that she was Eliana, the more freedom she had gained. She'd lost count of how many weeks it had been since she'd been taken from Mark. She'd tried asking Derrant, but all she'd received was a gruff, "Time is irrelevant here." When he'd freed her from the cells, lifting her punishment, she'd tried keeping count, but with no sun to track, it was pointless. Her days and nights blended together in a chaotic mix of frenzied sex and loneliness.

Derrant took her every night as he had the first time she'd been imprisoned here but now he'd become gentle, making love to the woman he thought she was. To survive, she filled her mind with Mark, pretending it was his touch night after night, day after day. Of course, she had no idea if it was day or night. Her internal clock was a mess.

They'd settled into a routine of sorts, and some might even say a friendship, when they were outside of the bed. He'd taken to showing her his castle, steering clear of the dungeons to her relief, and sharing pieces of a past that spanned longer than her mind could fathom.

As the time or lack thereof progressed, she'd noticed small

changes—a lighter shade of gray to the black of the walls, bits of white peeking from blankets of artwork. Even the demons that walked the halls no longer seemed as frightening. They were changes from her last stay, but she'd been under Derrant's spell then and things between them had been different. It seemed that with each step he took to believing she was Eliana, the further he fell back in love and the less frightening he and everything around him was.

Lost in thought, Skye realized she'd walked past the turn to her destination and down a hall she hadn't remembered seeing before. The further she walked, the lighter the walls became, delicate patterns appearing upon them. The feel to the space was light and airy compared to the rest of the castle. A room stood at the end of the hall and upon reaching it, she opened the door.

Before her, a grand room appeared, the walls covered with whimsical drawings of ponds, meadows, and butterflies, all things from the living world. A pale green sat below the drawings, and dandelion fuzz floated on an unseen breeze. A massive bed sat in the middle of the room, its canopy attached to the high ceiling, the light fabric falling gently around the bed that was covered in pale shades of pink and blue.

She ran her hand along the banister as she spied a vanity with baubles and jewels atop it, scattered as if someone had been deciding which to wear earlier in the day. A delicate crown of silver and pink balanced on the mirror's corner. On the other side of the room stood a wardrobe, white and bright, its doors open to reveal gowns of silk and taffeta with crinoline that puffed. Tired of the black clothes Derrant kept her in, Skye couldn't help being drawn to it. She pulled out a rich mauve dress with light, wispy material and exchanged her dress for it.

It was soft on her skin, the loose material around her legs caressing each step she took toward the small vanity. Studying herself, she admired how the blue of her eyes seemed to pop against the color, and the tones in her rich auburn hair were brought out by the shade. She'd not seen herself since Derrant had stolen her away, and she slowly brought her hand to the corner of her eye.

There was no physical change from when she'd arrived, but her eyes carried the weight of her burden, the lie she lived to appease the Death God, the pain her heart held with all that had occurred since the first day she and Mark had been torn apart, the scars Crimson had left, and the guilt her time with Derrant had wrought.

She looked away, rising to explore more of the enormous room, wanting to be far away from the haunted eyes that were hers to own for a possible eternity.

Windows lined the wall, and she made her way to them, looking out at a scene that was magically displayed against them. It gave the effect that she wasn't locked away in the dark, sunless Shadow Realm and she was in the mortal realm once again. Rain danced against the windows, the sun shining behind it, forming a rainbow, and giving the illusion that life was not so dark.

She curled up on a light pink velvet couch that sat across from the bed and near the windows, closing her eyes for just a moment.

SKYE WOKE to find the moment had encompassed more time than she'd expected. The patter of the rain against the window scene had ceased, and she looked to see the sun had faded, replaced by a moonlit backdrop of tranquility.

Yawning with a large stretch, she wondered why Derrant hadn't come to her by now. Perhaps he was handling affairs still. She'd been surprised how running a land of souls and demons was so similar to running her own kingdom, although she didn't hold the possibility of eternal bliss and eternal damnation in her hands.

Rising, the grumble of her stomach cut the silence, and she decided it was time to find food, having forgotten her hunger until now. She made her way from the serenity of her new space back to the dark, dank halls of the castle. The moment her foot hit the familiar space, Derrant appeared, anger filling his face.

He grabbed her arms roughly. "Where have you been?"

His behavior annoyed her. "I was in the wing you made for me."

"Wing?" His temper simmered as he took in her dress, picking it up and staring strangely at it. "Where did you get that?"

"In the wardrobe."

"What wardrobe?"

"Don't be silly. The one with the beautiful dresses. The ones you left for me. And that space is glorious. I'm surprised you want me to move from your bed but—"

"I don't. Show me what you found."

She gave him a questioning look.

"Now!" he demanded.

Perplexed but not wanting to stir his ire, she turned and walked back down the hall, toward the end that lightened with each step, glancing back at him in confusion before she opened the door to her retreat.

He pushed past her. "No...it can't be."

Slowly, he moved through the room, fingering the material on the bed, letting his hands drape across the colorful dresses. He seemed lost in memory before he said, "This was Eliana's wing, her sanctuary."

Her eyes saw it differently then. The retreat from the darkness of the realm had been more than a retreat. It had been a reflection of Eliana and her spirit, the light she brought to balance this world.

He sat on the edge of the bed, turning his eyes to hers, as if searching for Eliana in her. "You are not her. You look like her, taste like her, move like her, but this...this is Eliana."

"Why did you open this wing to me?"

"I didn't. I haven't been here since the day she escaped. I blocked it from existence, no longer wanting to be reminded of her, hiding it away the day my brother stole her from me."

She saw it then, the true reason he despised his brother. He had taken Eliana from him, hidden her.

"Maybe it's opening because you're ready to forgive her."

His hands clenched, and the lightness of the room grew heavy.

"I don't forgive her for loving another man."

She thought about Sam, about Mark pushing her to him. "Sometimes we love another when we can't love who we want. We try to replace that love even temporarily because the alternative hurts too much."

"What alternative?"

"Thinking the other person loves us less than we want them to, less than how we feel. She only fell in love with him when you lost yourself to the shadows."

He met her eyes, and below the terrifying god, she saw the man he was.

"It's time to leave the past behind you. It's something we all need to do."

"I can never forgive her," he whispered.

Her heart fell. "So, what then? You'll live a lifetime pretending I'm her? What will you do when I die? You can't live like this, pretending I'm Eliana, and I can't pretend to be her for the rest of my life."

He rose from the bed quickly and grabbed her by the neck, pulling her close. His eyes were angry, his power seeping from him. "You will, or you will return to the dungeons."

Fear clawed at her as he moved his hand and the black form took shape in the corner the room, drifting hungrily toward her.

She felt its essence prod her mind, and she shivered in response.

"Please, Derrant, no."

He put his hand up. The creature hanging just above her, ready to pounce, to drag her into some nightmare, stopped.

"Show me how desperately you want your freedom."

She didn't hesitate, kissing him, drawing him closer, wanting terribly for the creature to leave. She pushed him to the bed. Climbing atop him, she lifting her skirts, and brought his hands to her breasts, trying to forget the creature was there. Replacing his touches with Mark in her mind, Skye dropped to her knees, noting the desperate way Derrant's hand clung to her hair as her mouth surrounded him. She lost herself to thoughts of Mark, his taste, his touch as she pleasured Derrant, hearing his groans until his climax mounted and he released into her mouth.

Knowing he wasn't content, she removed her dress and climbed back to him. She tried to relax, to experience enjoyment in the act like she had been, but the shadow still lingered in the corner. Its presence hung like a threatening cloud, marring any attempt to pretend it was Mark's hands squeezing her breasts and pinching at her nipples. There was no softness to Derrant's touches. This was a reminder of her place, that she was his now, and that she had dared to question him. Dared to present him with a reality he didn't want to see.

She increased the desperation in her moves, stroking him again until he rose with need, and she enveloped him. He pulled her down, kissing her with a fervor, determined to believe that she was Eliana, for the façade they'd built to continue now that his mind had made the differentiation.

She shoved the presence of the creature away, knowing it was the only way to give Derrant what he wanted. Letting thoughts of Mark flood her mind as she moved against him, she lost herself to the motion, her body responding as Derrant's hands wrapped around her hips, urging her pace. The intensity of his need matched hers. Arousal rose in her, only to diminish when he turned her and forced her to her knees. Taking her roughly from behind, he pushed her head down. With each thrust he forced her further into the bed as if her face needed to be hidden. His moves were harsher, returning to what they had been before their unspoken arrangement of pretending she was his goddess.

The harder he pushed, the deeper he went and the louder her

muffled cries. Grabbing her hips firmly, he drove his thrusts at a faster pace. Her body was a blend of pain and rapture overshadowed by the fear of the nightmare that hung over her. As he climaxed, his body tensed, and Skye's moan joined his grunts. When the small quakes of his body diminished, he let go of her hips, falling to the bed beside her.

She dropped her sore body, her eyes avoiding the dark shadow in the corner. She moved closer to him, seeking protection from the same man who threatened her sanity with the nightmare.

"The last time I was in this room, I raped her," he said after a few minutes of silence.

She swallowed, having felt the anger in his moves.

"I didn't mean to. I wanted her to tell me she hadn't run from me to live with a mortal and bear him a child. When I found her, I dragged her back, forcing the child from her breast. I almost killed it. I should have, but it had her eyes. It was a piece of her."

He was quiet for a moment. "She escaped my grasp, but I hunted her down, taking her there, forcing her as I held her down in the forest where she'd hidden. Then I carried her back here, determined that I would never lose her again...but I'd already lost her. I see that now. I locked her away for a long time, too angry to even look at her. Her powers had faded from being with the mortal that long, and they were only slowly returning. She couldn't protect herself from me. I brought her back here expecting her to plead for forgiveness, to beg me to take her back, but she didn't, so I took her again right where we are. She fought me the whole time. I only wanted her to remember what we had, to tell me she'd made a mistake."

"By raping her?"

"I thought she'd warm up to me again, but the more she resisted, the angrier and more forceful I became until I took her, against her will. Each time looking past her fight and thinking she would love me again. The last time was the harshest. I hit her, hurting her as I forced her below me. Angry that she hadn't begged me for forgiveness, begged me to take her back, my rage blinding me to reality. Then she ran from me." He paused in thought and her heart ached for Eliana.

She couldn't understand how Eliana could still love this man. A man who had treated her so callously and hurt her without seeing what he was doing. Yet she did. Skye had felt it in the kiss she'd shared that day Eliana had possessed her body. The love was pure, endless, forgiving. Eliana had forgiven him, but he had yet to forgive himself, yet to forgive her for loving another.

Skye couldn't help but think of Mark and his act with Crimson. It would hurt her for eternity if she let it. But she didn't have to. She could move past it because her love for him was strong enough. Eliana and Derrant had eons of history, marred by this one act of violence, an unforgivable act, yet she had forgiven him.

"Do you see what you did wrong, Derrant?" she asked quietly.

He remained silent for a few moments before speaking. "Yes. I saw it then, and I continue to see it. My anger drove me, and in my anger, I pushed her away for good, into my brother's arms. And I hated him for it. I still do."

"Even though he was protecting her?"

Derrant sighed. "He took advantage of her weak state—"

"No, you did that. He protected her, gave her sanctuary, and hid her from you to keep her safe. You raped and beat her because you couldn't see past your selfish need for her to love you...and she loved you. She always has. She never stopped."

He turned his head toward her, his gaze moving from the ceiling to her, his blue eyes bright with sadness. "She no longer loves me, Skye. She never will again. I have taken many souls against their will, but this was different."

His comment derailed her train of thought, the idea horrifying her. "Wait, you have sex with souls? Forcefully?"

"I'm a Death God, *the* Death God, Skye. I'm not a nice man, no matter what kindness I show you. You bring it out in me as she did. She balanced me, made me the god I needed to be, the one below the surface."

Her mind was still on him forcibly having sex with the souls
he tortured, not sure she understood how hell worked in this
world and vowing to remain a good person, so she never had to
find out.

"Ah, so you want to be shepherded to my brother's realm
when you die? You are a child of the shadows." He brought his
hand to her neck and pushed back her hair, running his finger
along her birthmark. "You have already been claimed, so you will
never know the Upper Realm."

The thought was terrifying, but she kept her expression blank.
His hand traced her neck, then down her back as he kissed her
shoulder, her eyes noting his growing erection. There would be
no more talk of Eliana, no more visiting the past. He was done.
His melancholy disappeared, replaced with his need to bury it
once more.

"Feed me again," he demanded.

"Is that thing gone?"

He laughed. "It is now."

He pushed her over and forced her legs open, prodding her
with his fingers. They slipped along her clit, as his mouth took her
breast, his tongue flicking across her nipple. Shivers ran through
her before she could bring Mark to her thoughts. A moan left her,
and now that he knew she was ready for him, he entered her,
groaning as he slid easily into her, her body filled with his earlier
orgasm and the new arousal he'd brought on.

She welcomed him, moving with his moves, letting him touch
her, and experiencing the increase in her desire as his movements
grew in force. Each touch brought her closer to release, her body
coming alive. Her climax washed over her, his own accompanying
hers. She kept memories of Mark in her mind, refusing to admit
how her body enjoyed the feel of Derrant as he came, the way his
muscles clenched in intensity. Fearful that if she let Mark's image
go, she would accept her place as Derrant's possession. Her fate
was in his arms now, locked away in the Shadow Realm. Her body
was owned by the Death God for eternity.

MARK

The mountain disappeared in a strange blur, and Mark found himself standing in an enormous room of light and airy colors.

"Hmm, something has changed," Eliana said, walking through. "Someone has entered this room."

Mark's eyes fell to the tussled bedsheets, the suspicious stain upon them, jealousy tearing through him. He watched as she walked toward it, picking up the mauve dress that lie rumpled on the floor.

"It doesn't mean anything, Mark," Camin said.

Mark raised a brow. "It means the Death God is enjoying my wife's body again and I'm getting tired of sharing her."

Eliana dropped the dress on the floor, then walked by them.

His eyes glanced at the bed again. "Is it you I pray to that we don't find him on top of Skye when we do find him?" he asked Eliana.

"I no longer answer prayers, and they likely won't reach the Upper Realm from here. You'd be wise to pray that she is not atop him. My brother can be quite seductive and demanding."

"That makes me feel better. Just what I want to walk in on—my wife riding another man. That's great."

"It's you she sees."

"Doesn't help," he quipped.

They walked in silence, Mark trying to erase the image of Skye in another man's arms, until Eliana stopped suddenly.

"What's wrong?" Camin asked.

"I don't think I can do this." She started backing up, but Mark grabbed her.

"You will do this. My wife is being held prisoner by your demented brother. I want her back."

"Leave them, Markhem. Derrant is content," she said, her voice small and shaking. A stark contrast to the powerful goddess she was.

"But are you? Is Skye?"

"Markhem is right. You need to fix this, or Derrant will keep Skye here forever and at some point, he will turn back to his obsession with her magic and break free from this realm for good. The world will be in chaos," Camin said.

She pulled free from Mark's hold. "If you ever touch me like that again, I will show you why this realm was my home."

"Yes, ma'am," Mark said, holding his hands up, relieved that she'd found her fight again. He was willing to risk her wrath if it meant he had Skye back in his arms.

They continued their walk through the hallways silently, and Mark wondered why Derrant hadn't noticed their presence.

"I know how to hide from him," Eliana said, as if hearing his thoughts.

Upon entering the throne room, Mark's eyes went directly to the two figures on the throne. The woman's dark hair moved with her body as she slowly rose and fell on the naked man below her. Mark's heart ripped from his chest at the sight and the sound of their moans that filled the room. Her movement hastened, his hands grasping her hips tightly, both crying out.

The three of them stared unmoving as they watched the descent of the couple's climax, relief only settling over Mark when the man tossed the woman from him. Her brown eyes met

Mark's, her form morphing slightly to a demon's, then back to that of a woman. She licked her lips and crawled back to the man, taking his softening erection into her mouth.

"Care to continue watching," the man said, a subtle shift of his form to a succubus as he tipped his head back in satisfaction.

They were both thrown from the throne, their naked bodies tumbling. Derrant had entered the room.

"What have I told you about fornicating on my throne!" he bellowed as their forms shifted to the strange blend of demon and human.

"Your highness, we meant—" the man's words were silenced, his head ripped from his shoulders. The woman screamed until her body turned a fiery red, invisible flames licking her skin as she writhed in pain. She landed on the floor convulsing until the tremors slowed.

Their bodies disappeared and Derrant met his sister's eyes, seeing her there for the first time.

"Why have you left the room, Skye?" he asked, not noticing Mark and Camin, his eyes focused only on Eliana.

"What has become of you, Derrant?" she asked, her voice sad.

His eyes narrowed, a sense of realization reflected in them.

"Eliana," he hissed. "Why have you come here and what have you brought me?" His gaze fell on Mark, now noticing his presence, the fire in the stare enough to burn him.

"She hasn't brought you anything," Mark said, moving forward. Eliana put her hand out to hold him back.

"Mark?" He heard Skye's voice before he saw her.

She didn't hesitate, running toward him, but Derrant yelled, "No! She is mine!"

Her body went stiff as his power seized her, dragging her back to him.

"Do not do anything foolish, Markhem," Eliana whispered.

"Leave here. Does our brother know you've escaped his sanctuary?"

"Yes, Derrant. I requested that he free me."

"Why would you do that? It changes nothing."

He had Skye in his hands. His magic had released her, but his physical grip remained firm. Her eyes pleaded with Mark, but he was helpless. Her freedom rested on Eliana now.

"You've changed, Derrant, and you are changing again. I know what it is you do. I saw you. You make love to her, but you really make love to me."

Mark cringed at the words, seeing the guilt in Skye's eyes but remembering her in the cells, knowing she'd done what she had to do, just as he had done with Crimson after his initial fall.

"She is not me, Derrant. She belongs to another."

"She is mine, and she will stay with me for eternity, Eliana."

"Please, Derrant, let's talk."

"I don't want to talk! You left me for that mortal, loved a mortal, and birthed his son rather than mine!"

"But I—"

"No, be gone, Eliana. I will keep these two for their insolence."

Mark heard Skye's scream, but the room disappeared, and he found himself standing in a cell, Camin beside him.

"This is not good," Camin said.

Mark recognized the cell. It was similar to the one he'd seen Skye in. He saw the dark mass in the corner as it slowly grew.

"No, it most certainly is not."

SKYE

Skye screamed as Mark disappeared with Camin. Derrant smacked her and squeezed her arm, sending a jolt of pain along it.

"Shut up!" he cried.

"Derrant, stop hurting her. It's me you want to hurt," Eliana said.

"I want you gone, Eliana."

Skye rubbed her cheek as she listened to the two gods argue.

"You are not here. I have all I need."

The throne room disappeared, and she found herself in his room. She slipped, slightly disoriented, but he caught her, kissing her roughly.

"Stop," she said, pushing against him.

"Make love to me," he demanded, ripping at her dress.

"No, not this time. Eliana is here."

"I have you." He pushed her to the bed and held her down.

"Derrant, you've used me enough. Tell her how you feel, tell her you make love to her through me each night."

"I already know," she heard Eliana's voice say.

Derrant's eyes turned feral and he whipped around to Eliana.

"Let her be. This is between us. You cannot continue to

pretend she's me." Skye could see the pity her eyes held, a sadness they carried that was almost palpable.

"You left me."

"And you hurt me terribly. But that was eons ago."

He lifted himself from Skye, and she scooted across the bed, away from them.

"Let us put the past behind us. I'm lonely, Derrant. Our children want to know their father."

"Children?"

She nodded. "The dragons are ours, spawned from that fatal day."

"The day Carzent hid you?"

"The day you raped me in the forests." A tear slid down her cheek, and Skye's heart broke for her.

He sat, and Skye noticed the drop of his shoulders. The anger had fled his body. "The one I killed?"

"Of our blood."

He sucked in a breath. "No wonder you turned angry."

"You turned first."

"Always a competition with you, Eliana," he said, his voice lighter.

Skye felt as a voyeur, trapped behind them with no way to escape. They seemed to have forgotten her presence.

Eliana dropped the straps of her gown, slipping out of it as it fell. Derrant inhaled sharply as she came forward and straddled him.

"Take me and erase the pain of the past. Let us be one again."

He reached his hand through her hair, the other caressing her breast then running the length of her body as she leaned back and sighed. Skye wanted to run, but she was afraid to break the moment, afraid Derrant would see her and change his mind, so she stayed.

Derrant slipped his hand between Eliana's legs, and she purred. His mouth kissed her neck, then her breasts, and as Skye watched, she felt the warmth flood to her lower body. She knew what Derrant's touches were like, the gentle ones that couldn't be denied.

In one swift move, he undid his pants, lifted Eliana's body, and entered her, both of them crying out with the force. Their movements were fluid and Skye finally pulled her eyes away as her mind imagined their pleasure. Knowing what Eliana was feeling, her own body responded to their moves.

Eliana pushed him down, nuzzling his neck and whispering, "Do you want me or a façade of me?"

"You," he exclaimed. "Only you."

Run, Skye, Eliana's voice whispered in her mind.

The command woke Skye up. She snuck around the bed as Eliana worked her way down Derrant's body, pulling his pants off the rest of the way, then mounting him again. His groan echoed through the hall as Skye closed the door.

She leaned against it, one part of her wanting to go back and join them, her desire sparked by them. The other wanting to find Mark. She squeezed her hand in and out; she was still powerless. If she ran into a demon, she didn't know if they would avoid her as they had in the past. There was a high probability that they'd know she was no longer the Death God's pet, that he'd replaced her.

She'd have to take the chance.

She ran through the castle halls, not truly certain where Mark and Camin were, but guessing the dungeon was a fair starting place. Her bare feet slapped against the stone as she ran, her breast exposed where Derrant had ripped her dress. She didn't slow her pace until she reached the dungeons. Covering her hand over the ripped material, she carefully walked through. A chill crawled up her spine, the nightmares of her days locked away returning with every step. Each cell she passed held some form of nightmare torturing a soul. The souls screaming for help stopped as she passed.

She walked on until she spotted Mark. He was on the ground, the nightmare creature stretched through the cell, feeding on him and Camin. She backed up in terror, unsure how to help. Her own memories of the nightmares the creature had plunged her into reared back at her like claws puncturing her heart. Something grabbed her, pulling her to the cell behind her, her head hitting the iron bars with a thud that resonated through her head. A hand pawed at her body.

"Look what I've found, a living soul, the master's mark no longer on it."

Derrant had lifted his claim on her like she'd suspected. His demons were now free to take her as they pleased. The bars disappeared as the thing walked through them, pushing her forward but still grasping her tight. Struggling in her terror, she fought to escape, but its grip was too strong.

"Let me go," she cried, hating how helpless she sounded. But this was a demon, and against it, she was powerless.

A hand grabbed her breast, and she suddenly became aware of the massive erection against her back.

"God, is this place full of nothing but horny demons?" she complained, still struggling.

It laughed and turned her around, pinning her to the cell. The demon's appearance flickered, the image of the man below appearing, but unlike others she'd seen, there was nothing attractive about this one's mortal form. His dark eyes were still creepy, greasy black hair stark against his pale, emaciated face. The image flickered again, interchanging with the foul demon skin he wore, black and wrinkled. His beady red eyes matched the red horns that protruded from his forehead. This demon was horrifying, and she turned her eyes away from it as she swallowed back the bile it had invoked.

"Oh, I am going to feast on your body first, and then I'll feed on your soul."

"Derrant will find you and punish you."

He laughed. "No, you are free now to be claimed, and I claim you."

"Mark!" she cried. "Mark, wake up, please!"

"That mortal? Another living soul. Those two have been claimed already. But you are mine and you will feed me and my pack before this night is over."

He dragged her away, leaving Mark writhing on the floor, still trapped in his nightmare, unaware she'd even been there.

MARK

The images were relentless. Each was another version of Skye in the Death God's arms—atop him, under him, her cries of ecstasy all around Mark. Each time she crawled from Derrant, turning to Mark and demanding he leave her to the Death God. Her mouth spouting words of hate to him before she would turn to Derrant and wrap her mouth around his huge erection. Derrant pushed his hand into her head as he came, repeatedly. Mark was forced to watch each time his seed spilled into her mouth, dripping down her face, her lips lapping it up as she told him how much she loved him.

Each time Mark screamed for her to stop, but still the nightmare continued. At one point, her voice echoed through the nightmare, calling his name, but it faded, his eyes stuck watching her satisfy Derrant again.

His mind nudged at him, telling him something wasn't right, that no matter what either of them had to do, the love they had for each other would never fade. She loved him. It didn't matter that she'd been gone for weeks. It didn't matter what she'd done with Derrant.

Skye appeared before him, Derrant behind her. His hands pawed at her breasts as he bent her over, glaring at Mark. A wicked laugh fled from Derrant as is hardness penetrated her, and her moan echoed through Mark's mind.

"No," he fought. "You're not real. She's not real." The image changed. This time Crimson stood before him, her fiery red hair laying loose upon her naked breasts.

"Markhem," she said, seductively pressing against him, her hand finding his rising erection, and his body now naked.

"This is definitely a nightmare," he mumbled, backing away but hitting a wall. The room shifted, and he was making love to Skye. Her body moved with his as her legs wrapped around him. He relaxed, taking her like he'd wanted for so many weeks, missing her touch, her kisses, all that she was. As he reached the crest of his orgasm, he heard her voice.

"Mark?"

He opened his eyes to find Crimson atop him, His orgasm exploded as Skye ran screaming from the room, vile words of hate following her departure. Crimson's laughter permeated the room as the images faded and darkness surrounded him.

"Not real," he told himself. "None of this is real."

A blur of Skye's hair rushed past him as she ran to Derrant's arms, clinging to him, his eyes meeting Mark's.

She's mine, echoed around him.

"You're not real!" he screamed back.

He repeated the words over and over like a mantra until his fingers touched the blade of the knife Skye had given him. Wrenching it out, he slashed at the darkness repeatedly until it shrieked, the black cloud pulling away to reveal the cell.

He sat up quickly, gripping his weapon while he watched it slink away. Camin sucked in a deep breath, one that sounded like he'd been holding it the entire time.

"I hate those damned things," Camin complained, wiping at his head as if to free his mind from whatever horror he had experienced.

"You didn't have to hurt my pet," Derrant said.

Images of Mark's nightmares flashed through his mind as he

met the god's eyes. Derrant gave him a knowing look, then said, "You should be worried. She is quite delectable in bed and out of bed."

Mark gripped the bars.

"Calm yourself. You are free to go. Take her with you. Eliana has my ear again, and I will do her this favor. Besides, Skye was good company. Her body kept me satisfied once her punishment was served, but I have no further use for her now."

He opened the cell, and Mark rushed toward him, punching him before Derrant could react. He flung Mark against the cell, restraining him while he rubbed his jaw.

"No mortal has ever laid a hand on me, at least not an unwanted hand. You have favor with Eliana, but do not think that means you are free to do as you please. I can still change my mind. Take Skye and leave before I do."

"Where is she?"

"I thought she was down here," Derrant answered, looking around.

"Well, she's not. Now, where is my wife?"

"Eliana sent her away while we were making up. I'd assumed she'd come to you."

They'd lost her.

"Pardon me, sire," a voice came from the cell across from them. Something slinked through the bars, foul and twisted, its grotesque shape morphing as Mark had seen the others do, from man into demon. Mark couldn't figure out why it was happening, but remembered Eliana saying things were changing.

"She was unclaimed when she came down here," the demon said.

"Unclaimed?" Mark asked.

"My claim was on her. I claimed..." Derrant started.

"What?" Mark asked, his anxiety heightened.

"I released my claim on her when I accepted Eliana back."

"What does that mean?"

"It means she's up for grabs to any demon who wants her.

First come, first feed in the demon world," Camin said. "And something claimed her living soul fast."

Mark's heart was pounding, fear overwhelming him. Skye was out there somewhere with a demon who was devouring her soul and body.

"What has her?" Derrant demanded, transforming to his Death God form. Mark hoped Skye had never slept with him like that willingly, then pushed the thought aside.

Derrant reached out and grabbed the demon by the neck.

"A torrent," the demon answered, his form shifting to the beady eyed monster, then back again. "He has claimed her."

"Are you seeing that?" Mark asked Camin.

"Yes, but you should be more concerned with what he said."

"Why?"

Derrant threw the demon, who landed with a heavy thump and skittered away.

"Because torrents are the foulest of my demons," Derrant answered.

"Really? Because I've seen some serious foulness in this place," Mark said, thinking back to his past experiences—the girls gutting the man as he orgasmed.

"Yes. Most bring a soul to rapture first, then strike. Harvesting a soul for sustenance is a long, grueling existence for a soul, with good reason. It is death for a living soul, but the pleasure buffers the feeding. The torrent strikes fast. There is no pleasure but what they glean from it. Only torment and torture, something that brings them arousal. The more pain, the more exhilarating the experience while they feed."

"You son of a bitch." Mark attacked Derrant again, slamming him against the cell. "Find her now!"

"You risk my wrath each time you dare touch me, mortal."

"I'll risk it if it brings Skye back safely."

"I could have killed her, you know. She deserved it, and I should have."

"But you didn't and now she's out there somewhere suffering again in this blasted place."

Derrant pushed him away.

Another demon marched down the hall, bowing when he came upon Derrant.

"Take them to the throne room."

"No! I'm going with you."

"No."

Derrant disappeared in a cloud of black smoke.

"Dammit!" Anger encompassed Mark, but it couldn't remove the fear that was hammering him.

"Mmm, shame you two are off limits. You look tasty, and you're living," the demon Derrant had summoned said. His forked tongue slipped through his lips, a sparkle of desire shining in his eyes.

Mark gripped his weapon.

"Don't get defensive. The Death God has claimed you both, and no one goes against his claim. My cousin and his mate did, they paid the price. Fools couldn't resist playing. The call of a living soul is very tempting."

The demon turned, and they followed his tall, naked form through the dungeon, his horns disappearing off and on as they walked. Mark knew what he was, a succubus. He remembered his time in their grasp and wondered whose living soul the demon had referred to. He hoped it hadn't been Skye, knowing what that insatiable thirst felt like. Being lost to that never satisfied need to climax and being used by the demons for their sexual indulgences as they fed on his soul had been horrifying. The thought of Skye experiencing that wrenched his heart.

It seemed there was never a time when their bodies were left alone. They were always marred by the stained handprints of others, and Mark didn't know if that would ever change.

Sighing, he continued to follow the demon to the throne room.

"Are you certain you don't want to play for a bit first, boys?

It's allowed as long as you consent." His fingers moved to touch Mark's chest.

"Don't make me break your hand."

"Oh, a tough guy, those are my favorites. I like it rough. I have female friends who can please you from the front while I please you from the back." He winked and walked away. "If you change your mind, you know where to find me."

Mark looked at Camin. "Do I want to know if I ever—"

"No, but most run in couples. Yours was female and male, and most work the same here as they do at home."

He felt relieved until the word *most* settled in his brain.

"Although they invite friends to play sometimes."

"Thanks, Camin, that's reassuring."

Eliana entered the room and with her presence, the air seemed to lighten, the black of the surroundings lifting to reveal gray and red tones.

"You're the reason the demons are changing," he said.

"Yes, and no. Skye is the true reason. By giving Derrant a version of me, she's slowly been returning him to what he once was. There was a time when this world held a balance of beauty and darkness. It was lost when he strayed to the shadows, enticed away from me by the seduction that they hold. As he fell, the darkness and the shadows twisted the realm and the souls in it."

"But I thought the Shadow Realm always held terror, an ever-lasting torment for foul souls," Camin said.

"Yes, it is and was. There are two sides to this world, always in balance. I guided the blessed souls to the upper world while my brother punished the cursed souls. There is no beauty in that. It is vile, and his shadow gods and minions are the wickedest of creatures. As he slipped further into the shadows, so they did, too. The evil slowly transformed to their outward appearances."

"So what they were on the inside matched the outside?" Mark asked.

"Exactly."

"I don't know what's worse, seeing a demon inflict the torture or a mortal," he said.

"Don't let the mortal masks fool you. Just like Derrant, they are vicious and deadly."

"Good to know."

"Although dying at the hands of a beautiful woman is not as bad as dying at the hands of a nasty demon," Camin said.

Mark wasn't sure how to reply to the thought, having seen what beautiful women could do to a man firsthand.

"Why hasn't Derrant returned with her?"

She shook her head. "I don't know. Where did she go? I thought she would have run to you."

"I think she did, but something got to her first."

"A torrent," Camin said.

Eliana's expression reflected the fear too quickly to hide it, and Mark's worry grew once more.

"If that's true, untangling their hold is not so easy."

"Can't he just kill it?"

"No, kill the host, kill the prey."

"Jesus." Mark wiped his hands over his face.

"You may want to pray to my brother in the Upper Realm if he'll heed your prayer from here. If Skye is too far gone even Derrant cannot save her."

SKYE

Pain lacerated her, tearing through every part of Skye's consciousness. She'd thought she would suffer more succubus feeding, but this demon was not a succubus. It fed off her pain. There were several of them, like an orgy getting off on her screams of agony. Her body was being shredded from the inside and within each laceration, a fire burned. She was being gutted, her pain used to feed them until they broke her, then they would take her soul, the last piece of her being.

A particularly foul demon came closer, licking his lips and sniffing her. She tried to shut her eyes but each time, some force pried them open. His hands perused her body, the dress she wore was barely clinging to her. Most of it had been ripped from her as the mob of demons had greedily grabbed at her. Pain seared every part of her, and she cried out. The demon's laugh invaded her ears.

"She's almost ready!" he yelled, another demon coming behind and grabbing his protruding erection. The form of a man flashed in and out as he stroked him. Skye saw the man below the demon, a long gash along his face.

"Do we get to taste her yet?" he purred.

"Not quite."

"Leave her be, Franel! We don't want her to feel anything but pain. Only then will she be ready to reap," another demon commanded.

A female demon approached the one near Skye, pulling him close and kissing him. "Imagine how good it will feel when she is ready."

He pushed the hand of the other male aside and grabbed his own erection, his hand taking over his motion before the female began playing with him instead. A surge of pain tore through Skye, the first demon throwing his head back and grabbing the female by her hair, forcing her to her knees. The other male reached back around and stroked him to orgasm, his essence exploding in her mouth with Skye's scream of anguish. They were climaxing to her pain and there was no escape. The horror of it only intensified her anguish.

She couldn't close her eyes as tears fell with each drop of seed that splashed on the female. The demon behind continued to stroke him until the female took him in her mouth, licking him before she rose. "I'll be back for you. You'll want to be ready again when her soul is ready to harvest." She moved to the other male, her hand taking over his long, fast strokes. He leaned over to lick her clean, a deep groan rumbling through him with each swipe of his tongue. "Come, let me pleasure you," she said. "We can writhe in ecstasy to her death."

"But I can feel her pain. It's bringing me so close," the other male demon growled. "I need release."

"I will bring you release and then we will all come again as her soul feeds us."

She led him away, Skye turning her head as he mounted her from behind, the other male mounting him, a severe burst of agony clawing through her within moments. Her scream was unrestrained, driving them all to cries of ecstasy.

She wanted the pain to go away. With each of her cries, the demons became more aroused, many of them having already succumbed to the ecstasy of her suffering. Nothing eased it. Even thoughts of Mark didn't help. They seemed to worsen it. The thought that she'd never see him again was like a dagger to her heart. Would the nightmares hold him prisoner forever as these demons harvested her soul, then desecrated her body? She heard the gratified cries of one male, the accompanying knives of pain following.

A sudden silence fell upon the space, but her agony didn't cease.

"You dare steal from me!" she heard a familiar voice, but it was distant. Her body was finally succumbing to the internal flames.

"She was unclaimed, master!"

"No one steals from me. Break the bond now or I will kill you all."

"We cannot. She's too far into the harvesting."

Something deep within her unlocked and a rush of warmth flooded from her. Screams permeated the air as the warmth fled, the pain returning, blackness filling her eyes until she felt nothing.

MARK

Mark paced the throne room as Eliana and Camin talked. He couldn't sit or think of anything but Skye. It had been longer than he had expected. He didn't know if Derrant had found her or if he'd been too late. The questions berated him as time dragged on, every imaginable outcome playing through his mind.

He was close to breaking completely when Derrant appeared, Skye in his arms.

"Skye!" he screamed, running to them.

She didn't move, her arms lying limp, her head back, eyes closed. Her skin was so pale.

"You were too late?" Eliana said, rushing to them.

"I don't know. Her soul is still intact, but barely."

"Can't you pull it back? Aren't you the god of the dead?" Mark screamed.

"It doesn't work that way on stolen souls. They go to the Forest of Lost Souls in another realm."

"But her soul isn't lost yet, you said—"

"I said it's not completely lost, but it is fading. The harvesting was almost complete when I arrived. If I'd been moments later, they would have fed on her soul before it fled to the forest. It's only holding to her by a thread."

"Come, let's put her down," Eliana said, her voice laden with concern.

Mark pulled her from Derrant's arms; she felt so fragile, so small and cold.

"We'll take her to my wing," she said.

Mark remembered the rumpled sheets and met Eliana's eyes. "I don't think that's the best place."

"It's better than the alternative," Derrant growled.

Eliana closed her eyes for the fraction of a second, then said, "It's clean now. Come."

"You can clean a room with your mind, yet you can't heal her and save her soul?"

"Healing is our brother's job, and I doubt he hears any prayers from my realm," Derrant grumbled as they followed Eliana to the wing where her room had been.

Mark winced as he placed Skye on the lush pink blanket. She was so pale, her breathing undiscernible. She appeared dead, and the thought tore at him. He brushed her hair from her face, wishing life would come rushing back to her body and that the lush navy eyes he loved so much would open. Derrant's words played through his mind, and he tried to comprehend the vileness of the beasts that had taken her, that had tortured her and left her in this state.

"Those demons would have eaten her soul?"

"Some of my demons feed from the soul's connection to the living world and what remains of their memories and emotions, draining them of their identities. The soul then loses its tie to either the Upper Realm or the Shadow Realm. It takes its place in the Forest of Lost Souls striving for eternity to find a way to the proper realm. Some of my demons feed from the very essence of the soul, stripping it bare, not only of its being but of its very consistency so that there is nothing left of it to flee, nothing left of it to be rebirthed."

He was suddenly thankful Derrant had found her, saved her from that fate, his anger at the god simmering slightly until he remembered it was his fault she was like this in the first place. If he hadn't stolen her again, she'd be safe in Mark's arms in the living world, far away from this mess.

"What do we do?" he asked, hearing the fear and desperation in his voice.

Eliana shook her head as Derrant walked to the other side of Skye and placed a hand on her chest.

Mark went to grab him, but Camin stopped him. "Let him be."

The colors from the room began to pool toward her body, a soft glow forming around her.

"You used her power?" he asked.

"Yes, it's the reason she still lives. It severed the connection to the torrent, but not in time to usher her soul back. Her soul is still tethered to her, but it has fled her body. The magic will hold the tether and keep her living."

"Fled? But you said—"

"I know what I said, but it has moved beyond her body now. The ritual was too far in motion, and I did not make it to her in time. It will flow where the lost souls go."

Mark sat, the weight of Derrant's words too much to bear. "I've lost her?"

"No," Eliana said. "There is a chance. If her soul is still tethered, there remains a chance—"

"A risky chance, Eliana," Derrant told her.

"Not if I accompany him."

"No one frees a soul from the keeper of the forest."

"No one has ever tried. I hold sway over the keeper, just as you do."

"I know that, Eliana. I assigned him."

"Cursed him when you finally met his soul. Instead of letting him cross over, you cursed him."

Their voices were rising, and power was seeping from them,

their eyes locked and filled with anger.

"Sorry to interrupt, but who is the keeper of the lost souls?" Mark asked, not certain he understood what their argument had to do with Skye, or why they were becoming so intense.

"My mortal lover, Skye's ancestor," Eliana said as Derrant's eyes burned with anger.

"Well, that adds a new level to this debacle, doesn't it?" Camin said.

"I will persuade Henry to release her. Markhem will accompany me."

"No, he will never disobey me. He knows the price."

"And what is the price, Derrant?" she asked, fire in her blue eyes. Where before she had always seemed gentle, now Mark could see why she was known as the Mistress of Death. "You have punished him to a life in the shadows, guarding souls that have been barred from resting in either realm or lost their way, listening to their wails, and keeping them locked within their prisons. He has suffered enough for loving me."

"No, Eliana! His suffering will never be enough!"

She bristled and for a moment Mark worried that she would flee, leave Derrant again and leave them in this nightmare. But her eyes softened, and she walked over to him. "Derrant, my love, it is you whom I love. My heart no longer belongs to him, it hasn't in a very long time. It never completely did. My heart has always been tied to yours. Even after all you did to punish me, my heart remained yours. Skye's life hangs in the balance. She is the reason I am in your arms again, the reason there is life in this realm once again, love in your heart. She and Markhem deserve to have what we have. To finally be left to love one another."

Derrant glanced at Mark, his eyes still hard.

"You slept with her enough to at least save her," Mark said with a gruff.

Derrant stared at him, then turned his eyes back to Eliana. "You will not tarry?"

"No, it has been too long that I've been torn from you. No longer do I want distance between us."

"You will accompany her?" he asked Mark.

"If you promise to guard Skye, to keep her safe."

"Of course. She is under my protection, claimed by me again."

"Only until I return and claim her back."

There was a glint in Derrant's eyes. "That should be interesting."

Mark wasn't sure if he was taunting him or being playful. His mind went to the changes in Skye's birthmark the first time she'd encountered one of Derrant's shadow gods. The webs of darkness upon it were a constant reminder that she belonged to the Shadow Realm. He'd never thought about it that way before now, before Derrant had become entangled in their lives. She would never be free of the Shadow Realm, and he worried that Derrant had marked her as a sign that she would one day return to the shadows. The thought was one he didn't want to dwell upon. There were more pressing matters, like saving Skye's soul.

"What do you want me to do?" Camin asked, bringing Mark back to the urgency at hand.

"Derrant, return his power to him," Eliana ordered.

"But, Eliana—"

"Return it, please, and send him home."

"But I—" Camin started.

Derrant raised his hand and Camin glowed as Skye had, but with less intensity. As he lowered his hand, Camin disappeared.

"I was going to leave him here to keep an eye on you," Mark complained.

"He is no longer part of this. This tangled web involves only the four of us now," Eliana said.

"I won't touch her. Besides, I've had my fill of her," Derrant said, that gleam returning to his eyes.

Mark rose to lunge at him, but a force stopped him.

"You are still powerless. Your connection to Skye's magic is through her soul, which is currently fractured," Derrant said menacingly.

Mark stepped back, Derrant's words changing everything he'd understood about the bond between a mated Elite and Mage Warrior.

"Derrant," Eliana scolded.

"Oh, fine. Here, in case you have to defend yourself when Eliana turns her back."

The dagger Skye had given him rose from where he'd stored it at his waist, then lengthened, the gem glowing brightly until it turned into an Elite weapon.

"Quite tricky of her to give you that."

Mark pulled out the wedding rings from his pocket. "It cost us everything to fight the tricks you and Crimson weaved."

"Hmmm, I'd forgotten about her," Eliana mused. "We'll deal with her when I return. For now ..." She pointed a finger at the rings and Mark watched in awe as Skye's ring transformed, the stones bright once again, the silver glimmering next to his.

He slipped his on, then leaned over Skye and placed hers on her finger, kissing her forehead.

"I'm coming for you, again," he whispered.

He caught Derrant's eyes as he rose, sensing no judgement there.

"Ready?" Eliana asked.

"I suppose. Where are we going?"

"To hell."

She grabbed his hand, formed a portal, and dragged him through before he could respond, leaving Derrant and Skye behind.

MARK

The world was a fiery blaze; the heat seared Mark's skin. His lungs struggled to breathe against the burning weight of it.

"Hell?" he yelled over the inferno.

"Hush and stay behind me."

"Eliana!" a voice boomed from every direction.

"Brother," she answered.

Mark stayed quiet as she'd instructed, averting his eyes from the endless fields of flame and lava that surrounded them. The low echo of screams brushed his ear, and he took a step closer to the goddess.

"So, it is true. Carzent has finally freed you. Did you return to Derrant?"

"Yes, I did."

"Pity. He does not deserve or appreciate you." The voice had lowered as if he were standing in front of her. "You would have had a better life with me."

Mark's mind was trying to contemplate the flirting in the voice he knew belonged to the devil. The thought sent a shiver of fear running along his spine and he rubbed his arms against the chill that accompanied it.

"With you? It is too hot down here, and the realm rules forbid it, you know that. We cannot trespass on each other's worlds."

"This would not be trespassing, not if I invited you," the devil's voice returned in a tone that was strangely seductive.

"True, but even invited we cannot stay, you know this," Eliana said. Her voice was sweet and delicate, a stark contrast to the inferno that raged around them.

"Ah, the confounding limits of our own doing, confining ourselves to one world. Why did we do that again?" the devil asked.

"To keep from stealing each other's treasures."

The conversation was startling. Mark had known there were other worlds, other gods presiding over them, but he hadn't realized how interconnected they were. The idea of multiple gods all interacting with one another yet governing their own worlds was mind shattering.

"Perhaps. So why is it you are trespassing in my realm?" A flame curled around Mark's legs, yanking him from behind Eliana. "And with a mortal, no less."

"I need passage with him to the Forest of Lost Souls."

"Mmm, why I ever agreed to let our brother's wanderings suffer in my world. I will never know."

Mark watched as a flame formed, a figure as terrifying as Derrant in his god form emerging from it. Any imaginings he'd had as a child learning his Bible lessons were far from the horror that now stood before him. The devil towered over them—red skin, dark with heat, streaks of black like lightning flashing through it. His eyes were an abyss of black that matched the wicked horns protruding from his head. The cloven hooves of legend were thick and gnarled, angry ebony that ran up his calves then receded to the bolts of black that raced up his thighs.

"You agreed because you fancied me," Eliana said seductively, clearly not bothered by the sight before them. Mark wondered if Eliana had another form, aside from the dragon form and if it was as horrifying as her brother's. If Derrant and the devil were this way, he wasn't certain he wanted to know. Perhaps all gods were this repulsive in their original state.

"And you obliged my fancies," the devil returned in what Mark could only describe as a playful tone. Something that highly disturbed him given his current form.

"It is not often that Derrant shares," she cooed.

Mark listened, fascinated by the interaction, wondering at the history that involved his gods and the devil. The god form shimmered to reveal his man form, and Mark released the breath that had been locked in his chest. He looked nothing like Derrant—thick black curls framed his head, green eyes that glimmered with what looked like small flames licking at his irises. He was a massive presence. Where Derrant was a sinewy type, the devil was broad with muscles that bulged on his shirtless chest.

"I've grown to think I obliged Derrant's request to plant his lost souls in my world, and he got the far better end of the bargain."

"It bought you a few days with me," she responded seductively.

"So it did." His eyes were hungry as they perused her body. "It has been a long time, Eliana. I've missed your touch."

"You have women, Brother."

"But I do not have you. Derrant won you first."

"Yes, he did."

"What is it you seek in my forest? Your lover?" His brow arched with his acidic tone.

It seemed this brother hadn't liked her choice of lover either.

"No, the mortal's wife," said Eliana.

Mark felt a bit slighted by the title but remained quiet, knowing this was not the time.

"A lost soul cannot be claimed. You know that. They must suffer in their limbo."

"I do know that, but this one is already claimed. Her soul is still tethered to her body."

"Ahhh, that one. Yes, I saw her pass through. The remnant of her tether still lingers. Why is she so important?"

"She is his mate."

"That means nothing. Why is she so important to you and Derrant?" He crossed his arms over his broad chest, making him appear even larger.

And for a moment, Mark wondered the same thing. Sure, she was Eliana's daughter, the last of the royal Mage Warrior line and the magic of the mages would die if they lost her, but why was she so important to Derrant? His original needs for her had been satisfied, and Eliana was back. There was no further need to avenge their brother for hiding her, no need to use Skye for her hues. It led him to believe there was more that Derrant and Eliana had not divulged. He thought of Skye's birthmark again, and the tangled webs of the Death God's mark. Something nudged his instinct, giving him reason to think there was more to the mark than they'd originally thought.

"She is of my blood," Eliana responded, stating the surface answer that Mark had expected.

The devil arched his brow again. "And Derrant agreed to this?"

"Yes, she is very important to our world. To us. She is the reason I am free again, the reason we are one again."

"Interesting. So, Derrant needs something from me." His hand came out and touched her face, drifting down her body. "I will let you pass there and back, but I demand a favor in return."

She took his hand and moved against him. "What is it you ask in return?"

"For you. Five nights each year. You will be mine to do as I please."

"I will never be yours."

"No," he replied, letting his hand drift to her breast. "But those nights will satisfy my hunger for you."

"And be just long enough to stir Derrant's ire?"

"Exactly. He barged through here not long ago, unannounced. He owes me."

He drew her to him, kissing her, and Mark wasn't sure where to go or to look. The interaction was fascinating, but he didn't want to watch these two gods have sex.

Breathless, Eliana pulled back. "Fine, five days, but I pick the time each year." She removed his hand from her breast as he grumbled.

"How do I know you'll honor our agreement?"

Her hand traveled to his length, and she grabbed him firmly, stroking him. Mark looked away again, his own pants growing more constricted from the seductive interaction between the two.

"Because you have no choice. My word is good."

"As good as your hand, my dear," he returned, grabbing her ass and drawing her against him.

"And my mouth," she whispered against his lips.

Groaning, he kissed her greedily again before she pushed him away. His eyes were daggers of need and the massive erection that tented in the small amount of cloth that covered it led Mark to wonder if he would insist she please him before allowing them passage.

"That time is not now, however. I need to reach the forests. At the spring equinox, I will come to you," she said quickly.

He rolled his neck and backed away from her, his hands clenched.

"Fine." A portal opened behind him. "Go and don't forget our bargain. You will finish what you've started and satisfy me for five days each year, regardless of what my brother thinks of it."

"I will not forget. Thank you, Brother." She lifted to her toes and gave him one more sensual kiss, then ushered Mark to the portal quickly.

"Oh, Eliana," he said before they stepped through. "Do hurry. Her tether is weak and will soon fracture. Once it has, you will be unable to urge her back."

"Thank you, Brother."

They passed through the portal and into a forest, the portal shutting behind them.

"Do I want to know what that was about?" Mark asked, looking around.

"No, he is hungry like Derrant. The two have rivaled since the dawn of time. It is not your concern."

"Where are we?" He let the previous interaction fade from relevance. Skye was his only concern now.

"The Forest of Lost Souls."

The trees towered over him, black and gnarled on their lower half, then faded to a smooth white surface on the upper half. Their limbs stretched upward as if reaching to heaven. He went to touch one, but Eliana snatched his hand away.

"Don't. You will wake it."

"It?"

"The soul within. Each tree contains a lost soul. Forever reaching toward the Upper Realm but rooted in the Shadow Realm, where their soul was destroyed or too corrupt to pass on."

"But this world has heaven and hell."

"It makes no difference. They do not know that. They believe they are still in our world, that the Upper Realm is within their grasp."

"Why keep them here?"

"Derrant had them in our world, but they can sense the two realms too easily there. Their constant screams plagued the world." She was looking around, searching for something as she spoke. "He begged favor with our brothers in this world to plant them here. Now they stay silent save at night when the world around sleeps. The keeper quiets them during that time, soothing their restlessness. That is his one duty."

"Skye's ancestor?"

"Yes," she said, her eyes dropping. "Derrant's punishment to him for loving me."

"And yet you've returned to Derrant? After all he's done to you, to your lover, and to Skye?"

She gave a sad smile. "Love is a funny thing. I do not think there will ever be a time when I do not love my brother, no matter how horrid he is."

Mark studied her, taking in the goddess before him who looked so painfully like Skye that it hurt him each time he looked upon her. She was breathtaking, the power now visible where he'd never noticed it before, clinging to her like a cerulean aura that made her navy-blue eyes even more startling.

"Let's find Skye," she muttered.

They walked through the forest, an endless grove of what outwardly appeared to be beautiful trees. He knew the truth— that the surface disguised the ugly existence of the tormented souls trapped below.

"How do we find her?"

"We look for the tether line. It will be faint and likely only visible once the sun sets completely. Then we will require the keeper's aid."

The setting sun cast a warm orange glow against the snow that crunched beneath his feet. He didn't want to wait. He wanted to find Skye, to bring her soul home, to hold her again, to feel her touch, and to kiss her. His heart ached with each thought.

They walked in silence as the sun slowly lowered, his anxiety rising with each passing moment.

"There," she said, pointing to a tree ahead of them. It stretched higher than his neck could tip. Its long bare, white limbs seemed to claw at the strip of night that hung above the remaining orange of the sun.

"How do you know?" He couldn't see anything that distinguished it from the others.

"I can see her, straining to hold on. The tether is slipping. She holds on for you, her strength like nothing I've seen."

He glanced at her. "I have," he said. "There is much you two share other than appearance."

"I suppose you are right," she answered with a smile, her eyes still staring at the sky.

"Now what?"

"Now, we wait for the keeper."

As she said it, the sun finished its descent, the night sky overcoming it. There was a flicker of light and a man appeared, his long black robe blending into the darkness.

"Eliana," he said wistfully, dropping his hood. His sandy hair framed a strong face, one that held a weariness only a lifetime of punishment could reflect.

"Henry," she answered.

"It has been many eons, yet you are as alluring as the day I first fell in love with you."

"Oh, Henry. I am so sorry for the burden you've carried because of me."

"It was worth the price, my dear." He eyed Mark, then looked up to where Eliana had been looking. "But you have not come to reminisce, have you?"

"No, I have not."

"We have a strong soul. She clings to our world still; they never succeed."

"This one must."

He looked back at her, his brown eyes searching hers. "It is against your brother's rules." His tone turned acidic. "How does he feel about this request, or does he even know?"

"He is requesting it, as am I."

"Together again, Eliana? You cannot resist the temptation of him, can you?"

"No," she answered quietly. "But, my love, she is of our blood, yours and mine. Your descendant of our child."

"Ours? Our son's heir?"

"Yes, the line continued. The magic in her is formidable, beyond any in your line. She needs to find her way back."

"Ah, Eliana, her grasp is thin. There is no way to force her back."

"The keeper can."

"It has never been done and—"

She moved to him gracefully, her fingers drifting along his face. "Her mate, her husband, stands with me to call her home. You have suffered long enough, my love."

Her hand fell to his chest, and he picked it up, bringing it to his lips. "I would suffer another eternity for you."

"Oh, my love." She kissed him, and Mark could feel the passion in it, the remorse she carried for causing his fate.

Mark turned his eyes to the darkness, searching for what it was they had seen, but he saw nothing. Around them, the low sound of wails had begun, filling the night with pain and suffering.

"You will no longer suffer, Henry. The Death God releases you from your service and I will lead you to the Upper Realm. His hold on you is over, as long as you grant this one last request."

"And in doing so, damn myself to an eternity in the Death God's clutches, enduring his wrath yet again, this time for breaking my code to him."

"No, Derrant will relinquish you to me. I have his word. You will see the upper lands where our brother will accept you."

Mark rubbed his temples in confusion. It had been a long day and he was losing his patience. "What is going on and how do I get Skye back? Every second you two talk is another second I risk losing her!"

Henry moved past Eliana and came closer to Mark, his light brown eyes watery in the darkness.

"You love her?" he asked Mark.

"Yes, with every fiber of my being."

"Are you willing to die for her?"

"Yes." Mark's answer was unwavering.

"Good, because that is what you will do."

"What?"

Without responding, the man grabbed Mark's chest, his eyes lightening to a brilliant gold as electric currents tore through Mark's body. Then everything faded.

MARK

Bright lights invaded the darkness and Mark tried squinting against it with no luck.

"Come," Mark heard Eliana's lover say, the light collapsing to form the shape of him.

Mark followed through the darkness.

"Where are we?" he tried to say, but his voice sounded strange, as if he was speaking through an empty chamber. "Am I dead?"

"Temporarily, yes. We are in between the lost souls, between their prison cells, you might say. They exist within this inter-realm, each within their own cage, which are the trees you see in the forest. Only the keeper and the dead can venture into the prisons."

"Skye is here?" Mark asked, trying not to dwell on the thought of his dead body lying on the ground of the forest. It didn't matter if it saved Skye. He'd give his life up willingly if it meant she was safe and alive.

His ears picked up the wails again, long and heartbreaking, the endless sound of souls crying for escape.

"This is what death means for those souls who were feasted upon by a demon. The demon rips the connection from the realms away, leaving the soul with no resting place," he explained.

"There are a few cursed here by the Death God, sentenced to a torment with no end. The hope of forgiveness lies just beyond their reach until the Death God calls them back for their final punishment. The bulk of the souls, however, fell victim to his demons, those who do not feed upon the final essence of a soul."

It was terrifying to think both he and Skye had almost met this fate. Skye's soul was still hanging in the balance, and the idea of it threatened to overwhelm him. The possibility of saving her was the only reason he was still standing.

"There she is," Henry said, stopping and pointing to a cell.

Mark saw it now, the long, thin, ephemeral white line that led to one of the cages, her tree. It was barely there, thin enough to give at any moment.

"What do I do?"

"You love her. Go to her and guide her home. Only if she truly loves you will she hear your call and find her way back to you."

"And you?" Mark asked, unsure of what the man wanted him to do.

"I am your gateway."

"But how will I know when she's returned?"

"You'll know."

Henry's form shifted, lengthening, then flowing into him. Mark felt the strength, the call to the souls as they reached out to him, the tie of the keeper, the shepherd to his sheep. He was weightless, sensing all the souls before he found Skye. The power of her spirit was like a diamond in the darkness. She was fighting to hold on, but her struggle that was waning.

He reached out to her spirit, feeling as if he were being drawn to her until his essence wrapped around that thin tether, strengthening it, fortifying it as he poured his love into it.

Mark, he sensed her voice, not truly hearing it as it settled in him. It was more of a feeling, a brush across his consciousness. He thought of her. The memories he had of loving her rushed by, from the moment he'd first held her tiny hand, to playing games as children, to watching as she'd blossomed, his love for her deepening with each passing year. Her wedding to Sam, the longing he'd had to be standing across from her speaking those vows, seeing her beauty shine in every way that he saw her, up to the day when he'd finally married her. With each moment, the tether grew stronger, and the prison loosened its grip on her.

A surge of emotion swept over him, her love for him, all the moments that he'd never seen, the thoughts, the wishes, the desire that she'd carried a lifetime. They replenished him, overwhelming him with the knowledge that her heart was his. He took it all in, clinging to it and pulling until there was nothing but brilliant blinding light that faded to darkness as his grasp on her slipped away and he was left alone.

The air entered his lungs, and he sat up, gasping, feeling around for his surroundings as his eyes adjusted and Skye's face came into view.

"Skye," he said, reaching for her.

"No, Markhem. I am not Skye," Eliana said. "Now, hurry, we must return to see if you were successful."

He stood, wondering when he'd landed on the ground.

"You don't know if it worked?"

She shook her head. "Henry is the only one who knows. The tether is gone so I cannot tell whether her soul returned or finished its journey to her prison."

"Where is Henry then?"

"Gone."

"Gone?"

"He awaits me to guide him to the Upper Realm. He knew the sacrifice needed. There is only one way a tethered soul can return and that is through the sacrifice of the keeper."

"Sacrifice?"

"We must go before the souls notice he is gone. A new keeper will need to be chosen."

He pulled his arm back. "Wait, he sacrificed his damnation to return her soul? Why is that a sacrifice?"

"Because the keeper is not meant to return a soul. Only through sacrifice of their own soul can it be done and in doing so, Derrant punishes them for eternity. They serve a lifetime of torture in his cells that makes this torment seem like bliss. I have guaranteed Henry safe passage with Derrant's permission, but I must do so soon or Derrant will revoke that gift. We must hurry so that you can see Skye, I can guide Henry to the Upper Realm, and Derrant can appoint a new keeper."

She dragged him through a portal, the fiery underworld blinding him before his eyes could adjust.

"Remember your promise, Eliana," the devil's voice boomed as they crossed through his realm.

"I will, Brother. I will ensure you are rewarded for your trouble."

"I look forward to it."

Another doorway opened, and Mark found himself in the bedroom again. Skye lay peacefully on the bed, no movement to be seen. He rushed to her as Eliana asked Derrant, "Anything?"

He was standing with his arms crossed, overlooking Skye.

"How did you cross through the underworld?" he asked, his voice distinct with ire.

"You know how. Our brother said you owed him a debt, and I am that payment."

Mark glanced back at them. "Are you really going to do this now? Is her soul back?" he asked them.

Derrant ignored him and stormed over to Eliana, seizing her arms. "What payment did you agree to, Eliana?"

"Nothing more than I've done in the past."

"You can't."

Mark took Skye's hand, feeling how cold it still was, but noticing the subtle rise and fall of her chest. Life had returned to her body.

"I must. It is only five days each year, nothing more."

"Nothing less," Derrant growled.

"He has taken me before. I do not mind."

"No, of course you don't. But I do."

She brought her hand to his cheek. "It is only five days. You can replace me for five days' time."

"There is no replacement for you, Eliana."

"Shhh." She placed a finger on his lips as Mark's mind spun his words through his head, praying he didn't go back to that thought.

"There is payment owed on both sides," Derrant said, ending the kiss Eliana had given him.

Mark held Skye's hand tighter, knowing Derrant had not lost the thought, knowing exactly what he would require.

"If you are his payment, then she is mine. As you pass to him, so shall she return to me each year."

"No!" Mark yelled, standing. "You won't touch her again!" Derrant's power attacked him, knocking the breath from him and drowning him in nightmares. "I don't care what you do to me." He struggled to get the words out.

"Be careful with your words or I will have you in the cells the duration of her stay, or better yet, I will force you to watch as I take her."

"Derrant," Eliana said.

The hold on Mark released.

"Is her soul returned?" she asked.

"Yes, it is settling still. I suppose I have a keeper to replace?"

"And I have a soul to guide?"

"Yes, as promised."

"When she wakes, you are to return to your realm," he instructed Mark. "And I will collect her when Eliana takes her leave."

Mark went to object, but Derrant was gone before he could do so.

"I am sorry," Eliana said. "Everything the Death God does comes with a price."

Her eyes lowered to Skye before she, too, disappeared. He sat back down, dropping his head, unsure of how to feel. He'd brought her back only to have her thrust back into this world for a never-ending debt.

"Gods, Skye, I'm so sorry. Every time I try to protect you, I fail you."

Five days. He would lose her again. Granted, it was only for five days each year, but it would seem a lifetime. He never wanted to be anywhere but by her side again. And she would be in Derrant's bed, forced to sleep with him as she had been all this time.

The cost of her life.

SKYE

S kye fought the void that surrounded her. The pain had subsided, but something had severed. She felt disconnected from her body.

Mark! She searched the darkness for a way out but found nothing but endless night.

There was a pull in her, a light that seemed to draw her attention, and she reached for it. It was a beautiful tree, so tall it appeared endless. The white limbs stretched invitingly until she thought of Mark, the sense of him not in the direction of the tree but behind her. She tried to look back but couldn't, the pull to the tree growing stronger.

No, she thought. *Mark. I need to find Mark.*

She reached back and held fast to that thought, praying he would wake her from this nightmare before her strength gave out, but she was losing her fight. The tree was calling to her, the warmth it offered, the comfort tempting. Her grip behind her, where she knew Mark remained, was slipping. Just as she was about to let go, another warmth enveloped her, a strong, familiar, protective one. She strengthened her grip, sensing that she needed to keep hold no matter what, and she embraced the warmth, letting it surround her. A flood of thoughts and images bombarded her, and she felt the connection to her heart as it leapt at the touch. Mark—his love was embracing her. He was here to save her.

Mark, she tried to call out but had no voice. In the light of his love, the tree no longer looked so comforting, taking on an eerie stature, its branches reaching for her. She drew back, accepting the strength Mark's love was giving her and returning it, letting thoughts of him replenish her. All the time she'd loved him since the first of her memories to the day he'd finally claimed her, emboldened her. Like the rush of the tides flooding in, it pushed her away from the tree.

She turned back, sensing she needed to heed her urge to run from the tree. As she did, it grabbed at her, stretching to ensnare her. She pushed further into her sense of Mark when a brilliant light flooded her world, sending her back. Ripped from the warmth of Mark's presence, she was hurtled through a fiery inferno of flames that licked at her essence. In a sudden rush of force she plunged into her body again.

The re-emergence was shocking, her senses disoriented as she accustomed herself to her body, feeling the internal trauma that had occurred. She seemed to float within her body, unsettled, like she didn't fit right anymore, as if she were changed. She heard voices, Derrant's, Eliana's, then Mark's. As the lush sound of his voice echoed through her mind, she recognized the differences. The deeper level of his love for her, one that she knew beyond any doubt matched her own. An unending love that held no boundaries, timeless, limitless. She accepted it, calming as the voices disappeared and she slipped into the comfort of herself. The magic that had been missing from her for so long brushed across her conscious, and she embraced it. It mingled with the overwhelming feelings of love, healing every part of her.

She sensed Mark's touch on her hand and woke, taking in the breath that had been slowly forced from her lungs as she'd returned to herself.

Her eyes opened to meet his relief filled ones, the weariness lifting from his posture.

"Skye?"

"Mark."

"Thank the gods you're back. You're alive."

He pulled her to him, and she leaned into his embrace, safe in his arms finally. She held him tight, and he drew her even closer as if he never wanted to let go. Finally, he brought his hands to her face and looked at her, simply looked at her as if he were drinking her in, filling an empty well.

"I missed you," she whispered, a tear slipping from her eye. His thumb gently caught it.

"I missed you. Gods, how I missed you."

She reached up and pulled his mouth to hers, kissing him as she'd imagined doing countless times. He dropped his arm, drawing her to him. Their kiss was one of passion, of renewal, of understanding. One that accepted all that had happened and placed it far behind them, not forgotten, but part of who they now were, a part of a history that would define them and their relationship from that moment forward. The good and the bad of it, for all of it had brought them to this moment. The moment they'd discovered that they were unbreakable.

She pulled him down, the sleeve of what remained of her dress falling to expose her breasts. His heart raced against her chest, but he stopped, his lips leaving hers.

"Skye, you just woke, you—"

"Need you. Please Mark. I want to erase the memories."

"Wait, Skye. You need to know what's happened."

She drew back, searching his eyes, his tone concerning. As she listened, he told her what had happened after the demon had taken her, the insight into Derrant and Eliana's past, the price it had cost Eliana, and the price that Derrant had exacted on them. Once he finished, she sat quietly, too shocked for words, too heartbroken at the thought of being separated from him again, of being forced to return to Derrant's bed.

Mark stayed silent, giving her time, and she wondered if he'd been without her for weeks, and she'd been without him for longer, time in the Shadow Realm running different. She couldn't fathom being without him again, not for one day, and certainly not for five.

"Say something, Skye," he said, his eyes sad.

She looked into those hazel eyes, knowing the burden they held, the guilt from Crimson, the pain from her own time with Derrant. They were heavy with the burden of losing her to the Death God and knowing she'd been forced to give herself over willingly in order to survive. And now this. Having to lose her every year for five days. Neither of them could fight it, and she understood that if she fought Derrant, if she resisted his advances, it would cost her greatly, the touch of the nightmare demon still holding a shadow over her mind.

"We'll make it work. We're us, Mark. We've been through more than anyone we know, more than most couples could survive. This is just another bridge for us to cross, another challenge to conquer. I pray that this is the last of it. That the gods, fate, destiny, dumb luck, or whatever you want to call it, leave us alone. If so, then I will gladly accept the debt Derrant commands."

He smiled, his eyes lightening as he reached his hand out to caress her cheek. "I love you, Skye. Nothing will change that, no matter what comes our way. And, you're right, I'd settle for this curse if it means that nothing else will tarnish our happiness."

Leaning into his embrace, she kissed him. She brought herself to her knees and let the shredded dress fall.

"No, Skye, not here."

"Mark, I need to erase the memories."

"We can never do that, Skye."

"Then we leave them behind and start anew. Declaring our love here so that each time he steals me away, I have you here with me."

"In the same bed he took you in? Really, Skye?"

She searched his eyes, seeing the hurt. "We left it behind us. Now let's replace it." She pushed him back, feeling powerful again, her magic having restored her, and knowing it was her turn to leave her imprint. "I claim you, Mark. I claim this space as mine, just as it is my goddess mother's, just as you are mine." She grabbed his shirt and kissed him.

"What has gotten into you?"

"It's been a really long time since I've felt you inside of me, Mark. I don't want to wait. I've imagined it every day that I've been here."

He gave her a sly grin. "Really?"

"Yes," she replied, pushing him down.

"So, you did think of me when he was—"

"Every single time." She nibbled on his lip.

"Well, that does change things a bit, doesn't it?"

Skye leaned over him, holding his arms down. "It wasn't he who made love to me, it was you. It wasn't his touch that made me come, it was yours."

He searched her eyes as he freed his arms. Wrapping his fingers through her hair, he brought her to him, and kissed her deeply, greedily.

She yanked at his shirt, reveling in the strength below it, the power of him as she lifted it from his head. The remains of her dress fell away as his hands tore them from her. He kissed the bruises left from the demons and Derrant, each place until he'd reclaimed all of her. While she fought to remove his pants, he kissed her again, his hands skimming her body. His touches lit the spark that had been simmering in her, setting fire to her soul. She'd never realized how deeply she loved him, how tied they were to each other until now and she wanted nothing more than to be one with him.

"I missed you, Skye," he said against her lips.

She lifted her lips from his, letting them trace their way down his body. Her fingers outlined the contours of his chest as she made her way lower.

"I missed you more than you can ever know, Mark. All of you," she replied, freeing his length and running her tongue along it. His groan was unrestrained, and he bucked against her mouth which took the thickness of him. Between the way his hands caressed her breasts and the feel of him as he moved in her mouth, her body was a raging inferno.

Unable to wait any longer, she lifted herself, enveloping him as her moan met his and broke the silence of the room. He moved so he was above her, taking the control from her, slowing his moves as he took her breast in his mouth, rolling his tongue around her nipple and sucking. Sensation barraged her and a cry escaped as her body lurched. She'd missed his touch, missed how her body fit with his, how even the mere presence of him completed a part of her soul she hadn't known was fractured without him.

His hand swept over her other nipple, and her desire flared, his touch sending currents through her that she welcomed. Her need swelled, her climax building with his until it was tearing from within and begging for fruition. He rose from her breasts, driving into her. Each plunge went deeper until her cries met his groans, the climax hitting her with an intensity the sent her head falling back. The quakes of her body continued as his own trembled through him.

She wanted more, knew once hadn't satisfied her appetite for him. Her body continued to move against him even as the ripples of her climax remained. The need for release rose again, and she came a second time feeling him grow again in reaction.

"Jesus, Skye."

She stopped his words with a kiss, intent on reaching that high again and bringing him with her, knowing Derrant would know what she'd done, know the statement she was making and knowing he would leave them be. He owed her that much.

"OH, THANK THE GODS!" Noah cried, as Skye stepped through the portal with Mark.

The group was there, just as Mark had told her they would be. Camped out at the base of the mountain, waiting for them. They gave their greetings, then sat by the fire, sharing their stories. Night had fallen just as they'd arrived. Skye looked at Mark and smiled. They'd made love countless times, even taking the time to bathe in the filled tub they'd found near the window. She had no doubt Eliana knew she was laying claim to her room and the tub had been a gift of acceptance. Derrant had let them be, no doubt occupied by Eliana.

Mark had bathed her, only managing to arouse her once more, then obliging her with his mouth until she'd succumbed again. When they were finally sated, Mark had sat her down on the soft pink sofa near the window and held her close, taking a few minutes more of peace before they were thrown back into the chaos of their lives.

There they'd stayed until the sound of Eliana's voice had danced through the space.

It is time, she'd said. *Be well, my daughter. I will stay your sentence until the spring equinox when I will be forced to go to the other world. Then Derrant will call for you.*

Now as they sat around the fire, listening to the story of why her friends had stayed at the base of the mountain, of Camin's emergence from the Shadow Realm, his powers finally restored, his new relationship with Jane clearly apparent, she wondered what life had in store for them next. Mark kissed her head as if knowing her thoughts, then brushed his hand along her wedding ring. Seeing it there made her feel whole again. Not having it had been like a part of her had been missing. It was her physical tie to Mark, her soul spiritually tied to him. The ring was the visual sign that no matter what storm they faced, they would weather it as they always had, together.

MARK
TEN YEARS LATER

Mark's fingers traced the curves of Skye's body, lingering on her hips, then circling along her breasts.

"Now who's insatiable?" she teased, nipping at his fingers as he traced her lips.

"Just memorizing you once more," he said as her tongue slid over his finger seductively before she engulfed it with her mouth.

He rolled his eyes back as his erection grew.

"I could go for that one more time to hold me over, then maybe another round of lovemaking and feasting on your body. That might do the trick," he said.

She slid her body down, her mouth taking him in before he had the chance to say any more. It didn't matter how many times she used her mouth or how many times their bodies met, each time was ecstasy, even after ten years.

Ten erotic and fulfilling years save for one week of hell each year, physical for her, emotional for them both. And the time had drawn near again. He pushed the thought aside, losing himself to the sensation of her mouth until she brought him to climax again, his body overcome by the force of it. His fists remained clenched in her hair until the waves settled and he could breathe again. She continued to lick him, her tongue taking each drop, his greedy length rising again to her command.

"Damn, Skye, no rest for the weary," he breathed.

"You did say we could make love again."

"A man needs a minute or two to rest."

She drew her tongue up his shaft, and he groaned.

"Are you getting old on me, Mark?"

"Funny," he said as his length came back to life. "Clearly not."

She worked him until he was firm, and he didn't argue as she brought herself up, ready to mount him. He stopped her, moving his hand between her legs and feeling the wetness that had grown before he flipped her and returned the favor, tasting the mix of their fluids. His need increased upon hearing the sigh his fingers elicited from her when they sank into her. She was wet, her climax close, but he wanted to leave one lasting impression, well, maybe two. He pulled his fingers out, sweeping his tongue deep into her, a moan escaping, her legs drawing back. The sound of her pleasure threatened to take him from his task. There was no sound quite like it.

He lapped her up, bringing his fingers back and plunging them deeper, two, then three, until she was quivering with expectation. He felt her muscles clench as the orgasm hit and her cry escaped. In the throes of her climax, he pulled his fingers out and lifted himself, thrusting into her against her still convulsing muscles. She felt amazing, and he groaned, letting his head drop to hers. Her legs, wrapping around him, still quivered against his skin. She drew her tongue along his lips, then licked her taste from his chin, driving him mad.

Bringing his hand up, she licked his fingers, tasting herself while seductively eyeing him, her blue eyes growing dark with desire.

"Gods, Skye, what you do to me," he grumbled, kissing her breathlessly. He wanted to make love to her for hours and never stop or let her go. But as he moved deeper, her hips rising to meet his, he knew it wasn't meant to be. He picked her legs up, holding them tight and pulled his chest back so that they rested upon it, watching the rise and fall of her body as he came, gripping her intensely with each wave that shook him.

When the waves settled, he stilled, releasing her legs. Lowering himself over her, he searched her eyes, finding only the love she held for him.

Her hands lingered along his neck before she pulled his head down and kissed him.

"It's time," she said, and he dropped his head to her neck.

"At least I wore you out before you go," he said, nibbling her neck then rolling from her.

"Is that what that was? Or were you marking your territory?" she asked, rising from the bed.

"A little of both," he replied, stretching out with his hands behind his head as he watched her body move.

She cleaned up, then dressed, his eyes never leaving her movements.

"Don't clean up too much. I want to make sure he knows where you've been." She shot him a look. "And wear something with a few more ties to make it challenging for the bastard."

"Mark."

"Hey, if I have to put up with losing my wife to a god for five days, then I can gripe about it."

"Yes, you can, but you know I can't get out of it. We tried that the first time."

He remembered. It had been the worst. They'd avoided the summons, prayed it wouldn't happen the day Eliana had warned she would be going away, and Derrant had snatched her from him. No warning, no words, ripping her from him, then tossing her naked and angry ass back out when the days were up. They'd understood the message, and she'd gone voluntarily each subsequent time to far better treatment.

"I still don't see why I have to be fine with you getting five free days to fuck a god, and I can't have someone warming my bed like he does."

She placed her hands on her hips, her eyes dark with ire.

"Just saying."

"And who would you have in *my* bed?" she shot back. He noted the emphasis on the word my.

Just to peeve her, he said. "It wouldn't have to be our bed. I could pay Crimson a visit. I hear she's quite lonely."

A hue of blue snapped from the bed sheets and hissed like a snake before him, ready to strike.

"Bad choice?"

"Bad choice," she growled.

"I'm playing, Skye. I don't want anyone else but you, even if I am stuck sharing you."

He rose and walked to her as she clipped her hair up with the silver pins he'd had made for her on their first anniversary. She'd worn them each time since.

Drawing her closer, he kissed her birthmark, feeling the shiver it elicited in her.

"You'll have me, Mark. You know that. It's you each time, and the magic carries that to you."

"A constant reminder that he gives me a run for my money. Talk about insatiable. I swear he doesn't sleep with Eliana all year and saves it up for you."

She shot him a look.

She'd used her magic to connect them. The sensation had been strange at first, but she drew on the connection whenever Derrant took her. Through it, Mark could feel the way she was thinking of him, sense the magic in her mind. The experience was erotic, and he'd even managed now to respond as if it truly were the two of them. A mental version of sex.

"Just try to pick the right time. Last year you caught me out with the Elite, and I about came in my pants from your dirty mind."

"I have no control over when he gets horny."

He stopped the kiss she was about to give him. "You use that magic each time, right? Not just at certain times."

Her eyes twinkled. "Of course, dear."

"You're a bad liar, Skye. Dammit."

She kissed him then walked away to form the portal. Ten years of practice made the ability effortless now.

"Five days," she said.

"Five days."

"Check on Alex while I'm gone. He's up with the dragons."

"You mean the menacing dragons. Ever since Eliana left, they've become a nuisance."

"They're sweet, and they're family."

"Revina's going to take one out if they burn any more of her precious wall."

"It's like a chew toy for them."

"A fifteen-foot wall as a chew toy," he grumbled.

They fell silent, neither wanting to say goodbye. He walked to her, taking her in his arms and kissed her one last time.

"I love you, Mark," she said, clinging to him.

"I love you, Skye." They kissed again before she walked backward through the portal, her eyes never leaving his until the portal closed, stealing her away again.

"More than you'll ever know."

MARK MADE his way to the training fields. He would immerse himself in practice until Skye returned. Maybe have Camin portal him to the Dranth mountains to check on Alex, who was spending the month studying the dragons with his wife, Clover.

Things had changed in such a short time, it still seemed odd. He wondered if he'd be able to drag Camin away from Jane long enough to steal him. Between Jane and teaching at the magic school, it was hard to get a free moment with him.

Mark hurried out, trying to free his mind from Skye. Derrant must have taken her as soon as she'd entered the realm. He'd felt the tingle of magic, but with no true connection. She wouldn't be climaxing for the Death God any time soon. Mark had made certain between last night and this morning that she was beyond well satisfied. Let the bastard suffer. It was bad enough Mark was forced to share his wife, but knowing another man was arousing her, bringing her body to ecstasy, only wedged the knife in further. It didn't matter that her thoughts were on him; it was still another man touching and tasting her, god or no god.

"Mark!" Noah called from behind him.

"Not a great time, Noah."

"I know. It's that day, but this is urgent."

Mark stopped and looked at Noah, seeing the seriousness on his face.

"What is it?"

"The king of Apendia has fallen ill."

"Crimson's cousin?"

Noah nodded.

Nadin had only been five when they'd found him. Crimson's father, in his insanity, had killed every remaining member of his family before his death to ensure there would be no threats to Crimson's reign. One had been hidden—Nadin.

"The people know and there are already rebel groups rising."

"Damn. If he dies, it will be a civil war with no royal left to claim the throne."

"No chance of Crimson ever returning?" Noah asked.

"No. Keep an eye on the kingdom. Reach out to Revina and to that asshole Theodore."

"Yes, sir. What happened to Crimson, anyway? Do you know yet?"

Mark shook his head, and Noah ran off to follow his orders. It wasn't the first time Noah had asked, nor was it the first time Mark had avoided the truth. He thought of Crimson. Something he rarely did other than to envision her death at his hands or to rile Skye up.

He did know what her fate had been. It had been a harsh one, handed down by the Death God while Mark had made love to

Skye in Eliana's room. He'd never asked, not caring to know. Whatever her punishment, she'd been cruel and wicked. But Skye had asked on one of her visits and reported it back to Mark. Even she had thought the punishment harsh. Perhaps it was, but perhaps it was justified. One can only expect an eternal fate worse than death when crossing the Death God.

Mark had been the one to cross her, payback for trapping him, tormenting him, seducing him, tricking him into fucking her, and taking Skye from him. The list went on. He'd had a nudge of guilt when he'd first heard, but every time he thought of the mess she'd made of their life, the days each year he was forced to hand his wife over to the Death God, the guilt faded.

Let her suffer in agony for eternity, just as he was forced to do each year for the rest of his life. A wave of magic hit him hard, and he gripped his hands tightly, knowing Derrant was at it again. He picked up his weapon with Crimson's head in mind and with one swift move, the head rolled clean off the practice dummy.

CRIMSON

TEN YEARS EARLIER

The torment and eternal darkness faded as a force pulled Crimson from the grips of the tortured souls. She landed with a hard thud on the solid marble, grunting in pain. Was life to only be about pain now? She missed the pleasure.

Derrant towered over her. He was in his mortal form, beautiful and seductive. His eyes were dark, though, and spiteful.

"Derrant, have you come to take me back to your bed?"

She tried standing, but his magic held her down. He didn't move, only crossed his arms over his bare chest and frowned.

"Do you truly think I'd have you in my bed again after you betrayed me?"

"I never betrayed you, Derrant—"

"You do not address a god by his given name!" he boomed, the room shaking.

"My lord," she corrected. She'd have a time getting back in his good graces. Damn Markhem and his trickery, and that bitch Skye.

As Crimson brought herself to her feet, she smoothed what was left of her glorious green gown as Derrant's magic freed her from its hold. She'd chosen the gown purposely for him that day she'd fallen for Markhem's betrayal, knowing it brought out her eyes and the red of her hair. The color should have been a splash of brightness in the dark of the Shadow Realm.

She leaned into him. "That was Markhem's trickery, not mine. He deceived me. Let me back into your bed, and I will show you my loyalty."

He snatched her wrist, roughly removing her hand from his chest. "Skye and Markhem will rule their kingdom in peace. Your kingdom no longer needs your presence, a successor has been found. Your father was faithful, but I never trusted his allegiance to me fully. One heir was hidden."

"My father was always loyal to you. As was I. You said her kingdom would be mine. That she would never leave the Shadow Realm again!"

He smirked. "Well, my dear, things have changed. It was never your father's allegiance I should have doubted. It was yours. You have loyalty only to yourself, Crimson, and to bringing yourself pleasure."

"There's nothing wrong with a little pleasure in life."

He let his hand drape down her body. "Shame, you were quite tasty."

"Then forgive me, and you can have me."

He pushed her away so that she fell to the floor. "I no longer want you."

Turning from her, he climbed the steps to his throne as if he were ready to serve punishment.

"De—my lord?" Fear etched its way in her voice. She didn't understand why he wasn't taking her body. He'd never resisted her charms before. Had always fallen for them. Something had changed. Swallowing her fear, she gripped her hand to the floor and awaited her sentencing.

"Your father gave your soul to me long ago, Crimson. You are mine in life and death and as so, I sentence you to a long, lonely existence. In life you will serve as keeper to the lost souls."

Her dress changed to a midnight black that draped across her as a second skin, loose and constricting at once. The red of her hair deepened, the brightness turning rich and thick.

"My lord?"

"In death, your sentence will continue. For eternity, you will be the keeper of lost souls, silencing their wails, shepherding them to their prisons. For eternity." He leaned over and glared at her. "You chose to betray the Death God, Crimson. Now you will serve him forever."

The floor opened, and power yanked her body through the tormented souls, who moved away from her this time, none daring to touch the keeper of lost souls. Pressure ripped through her before flames engulfed her in a heat so intense she thought she was melting.

Her body froze, hanging in stasis while the burning continued. A disembodied voice boomed through the space.

"So, my brother has chosen his keeper. Pity to waste such a beauty on such a solitary life."

An opening formed before her.

"You may pass," the voice said, and she was pulled through, landing ungracefully, rolling to a stop, the dress tangled around her. She looked up at the night sky, seeing the endless rows of trees that reached toward it. Wails of agony, cries for release that filled the night sky, assaulted her.

She covered her ears, tightening herself into a ball and screamed, her scream blending with the cries as it carried through the endless night.

COMING SOON

The Shattered Shades of Crimson
Summer 2023